GOODNIGHT
MR STONE

To

Sheila

With love

Best Wishes

Denise

Denise Lunt

**Grosvenor House
Publishing Limited**

This book is published by
Grosvenor House Publishing Ltd
Link House
140 The Broadway, Tolworth, Surrey, KT6 7HT.
www.grosvenorhousepublishing.co.uk

A CIP record for this book
is available from the British Library

ISBN 978-1-78623-090-4

This book is dedicated to the phenomenal staff at the Christie Hospital, whose dedication and love, so many people who have battled cancer like myself, owe their lives to.

Chapter 1

Robin Stone

My name is Robin Stone, the only child of Johnathan and Lucinda Stone.

I now stand on the threshold of adulthood, having attained my eighteenth birthday. This is the time, I suppose, when the majority of young men feel the need to have a serious talk with a member of the male fraternity. Being someone who invariably holds their own counsel, I knew that it was not going to be an easy task for a person like myself; to sit and talk about certain personal feelings and emotions which I am now experiencing. The type of thoughts young men generally have at my age are at present disturbing my clear thinking, these emotions have therefore brought me to the conclusion that it is probably now the right time to try having that serious talk with my father.

Unlike a lot of young men, I am extremely lucky in having the caring father that I do have. As a small boy I remember him always being a very patient man. Even today he is still very happy to listen, no matter what it is I may have to say and regardless of how busy he may be. Knowing I am able to approach and talk to him is in itself going to be a huge help.

I have no idea why, maybe it's due to my age, but I will as usual probably talk a great deal of rubbish.

My father will sit patiently with a twinkle in his eye the way he always does, he will have a gentle smile here, or a kind word there, that being part of his understanding nature. He will try his level best to give me the confidence that I require to speak my thoughts.

My father seems to have a special ability of bringing the conversation around to any subject I want to discuss with him, on this occasion a subject which I feel must be aired at this juncture of my life. For the present I still don't know the exact direction my life will eventually take, though I am hoping to succeed in following my parents by becoming a lawyer.

The melange of emotions and thoughts that I am now experiencing are not helping, the burning questions I want to ask him, will I hope become easy to voice. Naturally my friends and I talk about sex and women; it is after all what young men normally do, having active imaginations. Young men are almost always honest with each other, particularly when discussing women, it is in some measure the way we learn about sex, as well as being great fun. Even making silly jokes from time to time, including making assumptions about this or that woman. Choosing a particular time to talk to my father on this subject left me feeling rather unsettled, my conscious thoughts becoming annoying, occupying my mind far too frequently, when I should really be concentrating on my studies. No matter who else I may speak to, in the end it will be my father's advice that I will eventually adhere to. I have no idea as to why I felt it was absolutely necessary or the correct thing for me to do. Being guided by my father's wise counsel has always been important to me; now more than ever.

So many intimate questions I need to ask about loving or desiring a woman that may attract you.

Not wishing or wanting at present to get too deep into a relationship with any woman, I needed to know how a young man goes about choosing a particular special person. On the one hand, trying to distinguish between wanting a woman for the simple desire of just wanting to have what you may call easy sex? On the other hand, how do you know if your feelings are becoming more real, especially when you feel they are starting to run a great deal deeper than normal for a certain person? Each relationship needing to be handled carefully, differently, but how does a young man know how differently that may be?

You hope safe sex is on the agenda at all times, especially when you have been led to believe you are in a long-term relationship. The ability to trust the other person in any relationship is vital, praying they are not playing around behind your back, that one thought I do find disconcerting. If I found someone had betrayed my trust I know full well it would be hard to handle, not just hard to handle, but incredibly difficult for me to believe I had made such a bad judgment about a woman I thought loved me.

When making love, giving full gratification to your feelings, more importantly in turn to each other; is it then I wonder that the realization hits you that something more serious could be developing? Particularly when ones emotions are becoming more deeply involved, how does a man tell it is not just the sexual experience they are enjoying when they are with someone they feel is special? After all I have heard and read there is a fine line between sex and love.

Why did I feel I the need to voice my thoughts out loud as I already knew, I must be incredibly careful about what kind of woman I eventually decided to make my wife? Now I am of an age that, should I wish to, I could marry without my parents' consent; even stupidly think about running away with someone. Neither option would be implemented of course, those thoughts naturally being totally immaterial. No matter how much I may think about going down that path, it is definitely not an undertaking I would participate in. As a member of the Jefferson Stone family, I have to be scrupulously careful about the sort of woman I may become involved with. Every undertaking that I carry out, or responsibility given to me in everyday life; no matter how small it may be, I am expected to carry it out to the very best of my ability.

When it comes to marrying it is doubly so, the ability to choose that perfect person to spend the rest of my life with is not just incredibly difficult, but at the present profoundly daunting; yet I have no idea as to why.

I made my way to my mother's beautiful, though fairly small, sitting room. Most days, if my parents were working from home, I would find both of them there; particularly in the evenings and at the weekends. It was a room my mother had fallen in love with on first entering my father's house. There were quite a number of rooms, all larger compared to this one, all of which were available to her had she wished to have chosen one of them. Apparently the moment she had opened door to this room my mother had fallen instantly in love with it; due I am told, to the light that was still flooding in as the evening sun began to set. Over the years it has become the most favoured room in the house.

It has developed into one of those rare rooms that everyone loves to spend as much free time in as they can. My mother would laugh and say, "Even the walls are made of love". A room that has a wonderful calm atmosphere, where a person can sit and think, if that is all they wished to do. This room had become my parent's sanctuary. Occasionally they work in there, certainly it is a room they loved to relax and dine informally in if they are alone. With both of them having busy lives it is where they gravitated to each evening, and still do when returning home from work. There they will frequently sit and talk about business or read. My mother sometimes will do a little embroidery, my father would bring in his brief case to look over some papers, which perhaps needed his attention fairly urgently, something he still does today. On numerous occasions he will ask my mother for her professional opinion, as she is also a brilliant lawyer.

Some evenings having been out with friends, I will look in to say goodnight. My parents may still be awake which gives us time to chat. Other times I could find them asleep in each other's arms. Maybe having shared some very private moments together. Time permitting there is nothing more I love, than to be with my parents in that magical room. It is never more magical than on Christmas morning, when opening our presents.

When my father brought my mother home after they married, he gave her free rein to have the house redecorated any way she may have wished. It was a momentous decision for him to make, as he hated any kind of change to our home. When my grandfather moved out my father had the house redecorated as it once was, before my grandmother was killed. My mother understood how he felt, so settled for this one room, a room she could call her own to stamp her own personality on and one she filled with great love. As for the rest of the house, she left it the way my father loved it to be, though ensured that it was naturally filled with love.

My mother had the walls in this special room, painted in the palest shade of blue. Giving it a feeling of being cool in summer yet warm in winter. At the windows she hung blinds and drapes matching the carpet, all in the same colour, everything blending so perfectly, generating a warm calm welcome. My mother ensured it became a comfortable room, with two huge settees covered in cream damask, a very large oversize armchair that matched, along with a couple of large footstools. Scattered around the room are various small vases of heavenly smelling flowers, all of which have been grown in our garden. My mother's favourite flowers are of course, roses, with lilies a close second, giving off their wonderful perfume during the evening. There are small yet sturdy coffee tables with beautiful white starched cloths covering them, some trimmed with lace, others my mother had patiently and lovingly embroidered. Each table being placed in a strategic spot, which allowed you to enjoy the smell of the wonderful flowers. Everything about this room reflects my mother's elegant taste.

It was a sacred tradition that afternoon tea be served at three thirty when my mother was home, regardless of whether father or I were, a tradition she has upheld having been brought up in England. This ritual was now accepted in our home as normal practice. Little cucumber sandwiches, which I love, were served alongside delightful dainty cakes, pure magic for a small boy, in many ways it felt like each day we were having a tea party. Even my friends loved coming over at that particular hour as they, like myself enjoyed the goodies. I still love afternoon tea no matter where I may be, if I can manage; it is one English tradition I love and will always try hard to keep part of my life.

On the way to see my father, having decided what it was I wanted to ask him, my thoughts turned to wondering should I ask if he would indulge my curiosity. I wanted him to throw some light on how he and my mother met; we had never previously discussed such personal or intimate matters. I am now wondering if it would be at all possible to do so, daring to hope he too felt the right time had come to have this very personal conversation with me, as I desperately wanted to know how they fell in love.

Another question I wanted to ask, what was it that had brought him to the momentous realization, that my mother was the most perfect person to be his wife? Knowing my grandfather my mother had to be perfect, I doubted my father would have married without my grandfather first giving them his blessing. So many burning questions that I needed answers to. It would mean having some kind of prior knowledge about the huge undertaking, I shall probably one day be expected to make.

My father was indeed where I expected to find him, though surprisingly alone. My mother, I doubted would be no further than the garden, more than likely having a chat with Mr Darby, our gardener on whom my mother totally relied. He always ensured the gardens where kept in perfect condition, the way my father wished them to be. It inevitably pleased my father that my mother tried her level best to keep our home both indoors, as well as outdoors the way it had originally been before my grandmother had been killed in a car accident.

My father loved this house as much as his mother had. It had been his home from the day he had been brought back from the hospital. We own many other houses around the country, but it is to this house he is always eager to return home to after travelling the world.

Entering mother's sitting room, it took my father a moment or two before he looked away from a document he was reading. I'm guessing it must have been fairly important or complex, as he seemed in deep thought with little lines running across his forehead. After a few moments he put his papers very neatly away, then looking up and seeing me standing there, he said, "Hello Robin if you are looking for your mother she is still in the garden with Mr Darby."

"No dad, I would like to talk to you," I replied.

"Nothing serious?" my father asked.

He must have noticed my voice sounding a little more serious than usual. The frown my father had worn while reading his papers, which had disappeared once he put his papers away had suddenly crept back.

"No dad nothing serious," I answered.

His frown once again disappeared just as quickly. On hearing those words his whole posture became more relaxed.

"It is always a pleasure to talk to you Robin. Your mother and I love the fact you feel you can approach us. More importantly you are comfortable in trusting us enough to do so, whatever it is you wish to confide to either of us, no matter how inconsequential you think it may be, we regard that as a privilege."

Listening to my father's loving reply always made me feel at ease, setting me a wonderful example that will endure, should I have children I will try just as hard to be the way he is.

"Thank you dad," I said then continued. "While there is nothing wrong for you to worry over, I do wish to have a serious conversation with you. Do you have some spare time to talk?"

My father replied, "Robin I always have time to talk to you, no matter what I may be doing, besides your mother you are the most important person in my life".

Deciding I was going to be as direct as I could, I looked my father straight in the eye, a habit I had picked up from my grandfather. However I lacked my grandfather's ice-blue eyes, or his stare that terrified most people.

I started my conversation by first approaching the subject of going to Harvard.

"Dad, you know I am so looking forward to going away to Harvard and hoping that while I'm there I will meet a great many lovely women, all of which I hope will enter my life the way men like them to."

My father smiled. He was about to answer but before he could I continued.

"Dad, I do not wish to embarrass either of us, I just feel that I really do need your advice. You know, a man-to-man type of thing, about women."

The words once spoken sounded utterly ridiculous; I looked away for a few moments feeling rather stupid, and then looking back, my father then gave me a gentle encouraging smile. That warm smile in turn enabled me to keep my voice steady, trying hard once again to express to him what it was I wanted to say. Somehow after that it became a simple undertaking to reveal my thoughts.

"Dad you obviously know what I am talking about having been young yourself, not saying your old!" a comment we both laughed at. I found myself telling him of my feelings when ... I suddenly stopped. I was about to say one thing, but instead changed my mind by saying, "to be as direct as I can dad, may I politely ask you a number of personal questions?"

"But first I need to tell you something." I took a deep breath and ploughed on; "Dad there is a certain young woman I have known for a while, this young woman is part of my circle of friends. My feelings for her are pretty strong, though I am not sure how I really feel. Is it love, or could it be nothing more than infatuation? Dad how does a man tell when he is in love with someone, I mean really in love that is? Or could it be purely a case of simply wanting to have sex on a regular basis?"

Before I had finished my sentence, my father looked at me then gave a most unusual but small pleasant chuckle.

"Robin believe it or not, sadly I never managed to have this intimate conversation with your grandfather when I went up to Harvard. It was to Bates who since he joined our home and has looked after us since then, that I have always been able to have this type of deep talk with. This is one of the reasons I am so delighted you feel you can talk to me. Unfortunately I never spoke to your grandfather about personal matters, as sadly I never felt comfortable in his company, just as occasionally I do not today."

"At that time I also had certain feelings emerging from when I first entered the dining hall at Harvard.

Feelings, which I did not of course recognise in any way for quite a long time. It was a great deal later that I came to realise exactly what those feeling were, I had fallen madly in love with a certain young woman.

"Like you I was not sure if it was a case of wanting to simply have sex with her, or had I at long last found someone whom I was falling truly, madly, hopelessly in love with. Once I realised my emotions had become so serious, I did not mention anything to your grandfather until just after I had turned twenty-one. No one in their right mind would want to have a confrontation with him, I definitely wasn't prepared to have one. Well at least not over a woman, particularly not this woman.

"Naturally I did have a very normal, healthy sex life, there were always a bevy of beautiful women for me to choose from who loved to hand over their favours. There were also many different things happening in my life for my emotions to cope with, most of which I could handle. The one emotion I did not understand I experienced after having spotted a strange girl with a magnificent head of blonde tousled hair, in that wonderful Harvard dining room."

I was so pleased my father had said that to me for it seemed to have made the task of asking him the questions I wanted to know the answers to a great deal easier to ask. I tried to sound calm, though my feelings were far from it, my father instinctively sensed this as I went on to relate those most burning of questions.

"Dad there is something else I would very much like to ask you."

Taking the bull by the horns as the saying goes I then asked: "I would very much appreciate it if you would please be kind enough to tell me, though of course it is none of my business, how you and my mother met. How did you come to realise you had fallen in love with her and knew she was that one very special person? Not just because you wanted sex with her, but because you undoubtedly knew she was the woman you wanted to marry. What was that very special quality she had that the men in our family must look for?"

By asking my father these questions I felt it would give me some kind of insight into what I truly wanted to know. By revealing to my father the thoughts and feelings that I genuinely felt were becoming, not just bothersome or oppressive, but were now taxing the enjoyment of allowing me to concentrate on my studies. This as I said was a situation I could not allow to continue.

The combination of enjoying sex for one reason or another, along with thoughts I was now experiencing about marriage, were I guessed just what my father may well have been feeling at my age. My guess turning out to be quite wrong once I heard what he had to relate to me.

In his understanding, gentle voice my father replied: "It will be a pleasure to answer your questions Robin. I have already started my story, though I am not quite sure at this stage if I will go into a great deal of personal detail. Loving your mother the way I do is a far cry from just talking about the normal run of women, the feeling of needing to release sexual urges is normal for young men at your age, let us see how far we go with our conversation".

Inviting me to sit next to him my father asked. "Would you care to join me in having a cup of coffee?" which for the moment I declined opting for a sparkling water. It gave me hope that maybe for the first time he would open up, about his love for my mother, and how deep his emotions for her ran.

From what many people have told me, my father shares many traits with my grandfather, especially when it comes to having had a vast number of affairs, but loving only one woman. He is a very handsome man with dark hair and warm blue-grey eyes. When talking to someone, he appears to look as if he cares greatly about what they are saying. He has an amazing physique having always loved sports; he is a confident, well-spoken charming man with perfect manners. An honours student who became a brilliant lawyer with a mind like a steel trap, he also has a terrific sense of humour, which never fails to amuse me. A man with all his emotions well under control.

As a father and husband he is incredibly loving; allowing absolutely nothing to faze him, always in control in every sense of the word. Now listening to my father's voice, usually very steady, slowly it began to change. For the first time in my life I heard deep emotion creeping into both his words and voice, once he started to unravel his feelings, or a better description would be his deep love for my mother.

Both his words and emotions became more and more pronounced, as he started describing anything that involved her. His eyes seemed to soften, even though she was not in the room, for an odd moment or two he would stop talking. His mind, it seemed, was drifting into a world where they both may have been; a world in which only they belonged. Listening to him, even after such a short space of time, to hear the love my father had for my mother did indeed run as deep as any ocean.

Dad began his story by saying: "When I first went up to Harvard I knew as any new student does, that if I wanted to achieve my ambition there would be many years of hard work ahead. It was vitally important that I understood this, as practising law meant everything to me. I desperately wanted to follow in my father's footsteps, who as you know is indeed a brilliant lawyer, also there was the realisation that I would eventually one day take over the family business, just as I hope Robin one day you will.

"Being born into this family I quickly came to realise how very lucky I was. It provided me with a great many material things, which of course made life incredibly comfortable. The older I grew the more I began to understand what those material things entailed. Living in this beautiful house, which I have always loved and having a number of staff to look after me twenty-four hours a day. My father frequently spent huge amounts of money on travel, enabling both my mother and I to see the world. When we went on holidays, there were always people to protect us. Those holidays were wonderful; sometimes on rare occasions my father joined us if work commitments allowed him to do so.

"It was the realisation that I belonged to a family of brilliant intelligent men, men who earned a living playing with other people's lives, for good or for bad. Men who were responsible for hundreds of other people's jobs, and who were involved in running our numerous businesses.

"I also came to realise how lucky I was in finding my school work reasonably easy. The gift of being academically clever had of course been passed on to me, which certainly as you can imagine was a blessing. The fact you are going up to Harvard means that you have also inherited our predecessor's razor sharp brilliant brains. Many of our predecessors had intellectual horizons second to none, including the ability to learn and speak many foreign languages fluently; often before reaching their eighteenth birthdays and on top of doing normal school work. Your grandfather in particular being one of them.

"Allow me to tell you a little about him. He was a gregarious young man, the leader of the pack you could say. He was also an incredibly handsome man, let's face it he still is even today. If I am being honest, you are growing so like him, but please do not let that go to your head".

Once again my father made me laugh.

"The men in our family Robin are very fortunate to have good genes. We have good health, reasonable good looks and more importantly those excellent brains, on top of having a fantastic business acumen. One thing for sure your grandfather is certainly better looking than me, even if he is not quite as tall." Again my father and I laughed. "I am pleased you have grown taller than both of us."

"Your grandfather was very athletic, and still has a very good physique for a man of his age. When he was young he dazzled either sex, he was a man who knew how to handle women, with the ability to charm the pants off any woman he fancied. Not just having women eating out of his hand as and when he wished, he ensured he commanded the utmost respect from every man he came into contact with. His friends worshiped him following him like puppy dogs, as they still do today.

"Everyone fell under his spell, naturally the opposite sex fell deeper as charm oozed out of every pour, again even as it does today. I have been told, when he looked at a woman he fancied with his large blue eyes half closed, she would simply melted into his arms without question.

"Bates has mentioned, that Mr Godfrey, who was my grandfather's butler, had apparently said: "There had indeed been many beautiful women in his life. Some he brought home from time to time, far too many some thought, before he fell in love and married my mother. After marrying her, he never looked at another woman, being insanely in love with her.

"As far as men were concerned should your grandfather at any time have found them offensive, displeasing or thought them just plain rude he would deal with them in his imperious manner, along with his rapier tongue which is deadly as you know. My father ruled his empire until he handed it over to me; he ruled it with a rod of iron, even as he sometimes does today forgetting I am the boss.

"Have you noticed when he finds someone annoying, his eyes open wide? Then slowly they become the colour of ice! He holds that stare like a snake hypnotizing its prey. His habit of staring directly at the offending person, yet not saying a word, I swear makes a person's blood freeze. On occasions when he does have something to say, his words become as sharp as that rapier I just mentioned. I have had the privilege of learning from him when conducting numerous unpleasant cases in court. My father is certainly a deadly adversary.

"As far as the opposite sex goes, his handsome looks, with his chiselled chin, no woman back then stood a chance. Women found him totally irresistible. I would not mind betting he could still attract any woman he wanted with his charisma and dangerous smile.

"Personally I regard him as the most stylish man I know, he is incredibly flamboyant the way he dresses. Have you taken note of the way he wears his clothes, ensuring he out dresses all other men around him? No other man that I know of can dress, or does dress, the way he does. When your grandfather relaxes he unbuttons his shirt just a couple of inches or so, he then turns up the cuffs of his sleeves, not far yet far enough, which makes him look incredibly provocative. He still dresses that way, making him, I feel, even more enticing to woman than ever. It is as if every inch has been meticulously scrutinised, allowing my father to enjoy feeling not just comfortable, but look perfectly turned out.

"In evening clothes no man should stand next to him, they look ridiculously shabby when doing so. The crease of his trousers you could cut a finger on. Your grandfather is a man who certainly knows how to look good at all times, whether it be at work or relaxing. I must admit I did try from time to time to copy him when trying to impress some girl or other. Somehow it never worked for me so I gave up. The lesson I learnt is everyone must find their own style. When I felt low at one time, your grandfather emphasised to me the need to always remain clean and tidy, particularly in our world of work.

"Your grandfather, being a Harvard man, completed his degree with the highest honours available. He would not have settled for anything else. He always loved, and of course still does love, being the very best at everything he undertakes. The standards he sets both for himself as well as everyone one around him are nothing less than perfection, as that is all that matters to him.

As a lawyer there is no finer. He never seems to take a case on unless he knows he can win it, making his reputation forever deadly. I remember a particular time I sat in court observing him. He was prosecuting a particularly nasty case. It was fascinating watching him, you could even say mesmerising. The way he toyed with the accused, allowing him to think he was on his side, making him feel totally relaxed, even to the point of thinking that he had been wrongly arrested. This is a trick a good lawyer still uses today; my father had it tuned to a fine art. You could say he has a predilection for discovering facts without appearing to do so, one of the reasons he never loses a case.

"Have you ever watched a lioness stalking her pray, slowly, quietly, and deadly? That is my father. His persuasive powers meant the accused felt confident. Confident enough to think he had my father in his pocket. Then the stupid man would begin to open up to him. Once that happened my father was like a Samurai with a sword in his hand who swiftly went in for the kill. He never missed! Just as an assassin's bullet never misses.

"Occasionally I have watched my father talking to someone about something of absolute no importance, still employing the habit of directly looking at them with that icy stare. He would almost convince a person to the point of allowing them the misery of thinking they may have done something appalling. Regardless he knew full well they were completely innocent of any crime. Would I lay money on, that for a few moments their blood would run cold as if they were guilty; you bet I would! Can you imagine Robin, how someone who has committed a crime must feel once his name is mentioned?

"What amuses me, is the strange way my father tilts his head slightly to one side when directly interviewing someone. He appears intense, as if in agreement with everything that is being said. His face will show no emotion, never missing a single word or gesture of a person's body language, when he behaves in that manner he is then at his most deadly. Watching him in action is totally fascinating. There is always something new for young lawyers to learn. You know instinctively you are watching a brilliant lawyer executes his chosen profession to perfection.

"It has, I must admit, always been a pleasure observing him in court. The fact that he is my father makes it doubly so. He leaves me feeling so proud yet strangely apprehensive, with even a constant fear that there is a much deeper level to him than the one I am observing!

"Robin you are already picking up some of your grandfathers habits, which I find most amusing. Especially that direct stare, it will hold you in good stead in the future"

A remark that again made us both laugh. My father then continued.

"One could indeed describe your grandfather as a complex man which he certainly is, please do not ever become like him in general, stare or no stare.

"Your grandfather was, to start with a protective loving husband that any woman could have wished for. As a child I felt safe in the fact he was my father, even if he seemed rather distant most of the time. No two people could have wished for more security in their lives, as I told you before, he employed an army of men to protect us twenty-four hours a day. As a very small boy I did not see a great deal of him, I must have been around six or seven, when first joining him at breakfast. For the life of me I barely remember what we talked about, though I do remember when reaching around ten or so talking at breakfast, or dinner in the evening when my parents at long last allowed me join them, if and when they dined at home. We would talk mostly about school as it was my schoolwork that pleased him the most. I worked damn hard in trying to gain good marks all round. By attaining that standard I hoped I would fulfil his wishes in following him in becoming a lawyer, something that was deeply important to him. You have no idea how hard I actually did work; trying to ensure my schoolwork was kept up to scratch, just to get his approval.

"My father was and still is a man I find very hard to understand, some men have a strange way of showing love to their children, being overly generous in the material things they buy for them. It was my mother's company that he appeared to want or seemed interested in. After finishing my meals as quickly as was polite to do, I then asking to be excused. My father always smiled at me then permission was given. He would be delighted that he had the love of his life to himself once I left the room.

"Bates related to me the love my father had for my mother, not just when they first married but particularly before I was born. He showed it in many ways; dressing her in what were regarded as the finest clothes money could buy, coming from the very top couturier houses. He spent a fortune on the most beautiful jewellery he could find to please her.

"On rare occasions when I was still quite small, I would see my parents going out in the evening. To a small boy my mother resembled a fairy princess, sparkling in her finery. Bates related once that to my father, my mother was his whole world. 'Mr Johnathan your father was hopelessly in love with her, never leaving her out of his sight. When she did go out he ensured she was always well protected.'"

My father continued, "along with a few friends your grandfather had decided to go to France, for a long summer vacation after leaving Harvard, and before joining my grandfather at their Head Office. My father loved everything there was to love about France as well as French history, of course having read a great deal about both. The way of life over there appealed to him, as did the culture and etiquette, which is a must at all times in his life. French manners suited him very well, along with the good food, which he loves. What could be better than French food when prepared and cooked well? There is no food in the world like it.

"Everything that is related to France or its people is still perfect to him. One of the many reasons he frequently goes back on holiday is the fact he speaks French fluently, this enabled him from the start to enjoy the country so much more. Many years later my father told me the thought of seeing France for the first time made him feel very excited. I daresay he was hoping to have the pleasure of enjoying the favours of a beautiful French mademoiselle or two. The first stop of course being Paris, exploring that most beautiful of all cities, wanting to see as all tourists do what she had to offer. *Belle Paris une ville de l'amour*, a city of love.

"The plan was then to drive down to the Côte d'azure, it is a wonderful drive Robin which one day I hope you will consider doing. A drive your mother and I thoroughly enjoyed. When the eye first captures the beauty of the Mediterranean Sea it is breathtaking. Calm as glass shimmering under the summer sun, to me it was the colour of the Madonna's robe. Perfect in every way. At night there is no more romantic sea to swim and make love in.

"Business class had been booked, allowing my father and his friends a great deal more privacy. My grandfather it seems, had decided he was not going to allow my father to take his private plane. Heaven knows he told a close friend, where they may have ended up had he allowed them to do so.

"Years later my father told Bates, that as he and his friends where settling down for the long journey ahead, just a few minutes before take-off, into the cabin walked my mother accompanied by a couple of her friends laughing the way girls do, excited to be going over to Europe. Apparently this was to be their first trip also. From the moment my father saw my mother he fell instantly in love with her.

"On numerous occasions he had confided in Bates by telling him, "If I had to Bates. I would have followed my beautiful wife to the ends of the earth, until she married me. That is of course exactly what my father did. He married my mother the moment they returned home. That burning love stayed with them I have been told, every day until the end of her life.

"Robin to be honest with you, I never had the courage to ask your grandfather personal questions, especially with regard to how he knew my mother was the right person to marry. Talking to Bates about my father's life or things in general connected to him, including my mother, has from being a small boy been a normal thing for me to do.

"Yes I dearly would have loved to have discussed with him, the questions you are now asking me, even talking to him today, unless it is to do with work I find very difficult though he has mellowed a great deal. A father and son conversation, sadly for me was never encouraged. Quite often I have felt as if I was a necessity, ensuring that next generation had been born in order to take over the family business.

"The one time I did decide to speak to him on an extremely personal matter, was just before leaving Harvard. I needed to inform him of the major decision I had every intention of making with regards to my personal life, but more of that later.

"Without Bates I have no idea what I would have done during my early years, or for that matter today. Bates has been with the family since he and my father were young men. My father got on exceedingly well with him, a strange but trusting bond grew between them. Luckily for me, having Bates was like having a second father figure in my life. He is the one person I can talk to on any level, as well as trusting him implicitly; I trusted him as a small boy; as a young man growing up; as well as now. If my father was able to trusts Bates with looking after me when I was young, then that is a good enough reason for me to trust and care about him for the rest of his days. With Bates not having any sons of his own, we do have a wonderful bond of mutual respect. Yes. I dare say in his own way Bates loves me like the son he never had, he is to me as close to the type of father I would love to have had.

"So feeling as you do now Robin, I felt the need to know how my parents met and fell in love, but sadly never got the chance to find out face to face. After my mother was killed in that horrendous car accident, my father's world seemed to have collapsed, it was as if he too had died that day. Even today he does not appear to be the man he once was. He did start to appear a great deal happier, once Meredith entered his life. That relationship being totally different to the one he had with my mother. He has unfortunately never been a man even at the best of times, to show very much emotion to the outside world. So it is hard to judge what he thinks and feels.

"In his defence I will say, he is a good and fair boss to those who have worked or still work for him. As long as they carry out his orders the way that is expected of them, or at least show they are trying their best in all they do. Usually he will then leave people alone to get on with things.

"As a father you could say he was predictable in being kind to me, never raising his voice or showing disapproval. As I told you he was overly generous as far as material things were concerned, still he has left me with the feeling of being cut off from him. The older I became, the greater the distance between us grew. When at last joining him at the office, he still rarely discusses anything with me unless it is to do with business.

"Funnily enough from time to time he does tell me how proud he is of me, so I am happy to settle for that kind of praise. He is also very proud of you, he frequently ask how you are getting along, naturally always interested in your school work, that being the main topic of his conversation ensuring history will be repeating itself. This does mean everything to him. Believe it or not he was very delighted to hear from you on the day when you phoned to inform him you were going to become a

Harvard man. He was truly pleased; you could not have given him a piece of more welcoming news.

"Like everyone who works indirectly for him in our many officers, I often feel the same way they do. He takes everyone and everything for granted, including the fact I would apply for Harvard, which of course doubly pleased him once I had been accepted.

"One, I would be following his footsteps in going to Harvard, and two he would have my mother's undivided attention at home, giving him the opportunity of taking her with him as and when he wished. Having no distractions from me to interfere with his plans, besides his work my mother was now his top priority".

After relating to me a little about my family and a little of how he grew up, it was at this point my father's story began. I sat transfixed, listening intently to every word he had to convey.

Chapter 2

Johnathan Stone

Having been at Harvard for just over nine months, The Deans personal sectary came to see me and request I go to the Dean's office which was unusual. To be called to the Dean's office in such a short time after settling into the university's way of life, could well have meant I had done something stupidly wrong. What that could have been I had no idea.

Knocking on the Dean's door I felt unpleasantly uncomfortable, reminding me of how I felt on the rare occasion when I was summoned and knocked on my father's office door. My father would then tell me we were going on holiday, or that my parents were planning to take me somewhere of interest. Yet I still hated that summons.

On entering the Dean's office I noticed his grave face. For a moment I thought I must indeed be in some sort of serious trouble, to the point of being sent down.

"Please come in Mr Stone," Dean Carter-Baxter requested, indicating to the chair opposite the one he was for the moment standing beside. The tone of his voice, grave and low. The unpleasant task that had directly fallen on his shoulders was to inform me of the horrendous accident that had taken my mother's life. The memory of each painful word is still very clear; therefore I am not going into detail, even after all these years they still hurt. The initial shock was indescribable leaving me to feel totally paralyzed. Time eventually does heal in a strange and remarkable way, which we must be thankful for.

While Dean Carter-Baxter tried his very best to break the tragic news as gently as he could, his words felt like an iron grip around my brain. I could not, or did not wish to take them in. It was not just the shock I felt, but the emptiness that instantly engulfed my person. Those first few days were hellish hard, the loneliness that encompassed my whole being, was the hardest of emotions for me to cope with. No one to put my arms around to enable me to have a hug. At that moment in time all I wanted was human contact, and yes, if someone had offered me sex, that to would have been more than welcome.

While everyone was so kind trying their best by giving me words of comfort, on top of the kindness shown by my friends and from people I did not know. All the thoughtful words spoken were of course very much appreciated. Still I could not find in any one of them anything that remotely gave me the comfort I needed. There are no words in the English language that are capable of doing so, no matter how anyone may try to find them.

Wanting nothing more than to return home as quickly as was humanly possible, I booked the first available flight back to California, wondering most of the time how my father was managing, knowing the one person he loved, had now been taken from him.

Strange though it seemed to be thinking of my father rather than myself, I had no perception of my own grief as I felt totally numb. Living in a void would be the closest to an accurate description in conveying my feelings at that time. To this day I have no Idea why my thoughts went in that direction. The knowledge of having just lost one parent I suppose made me scared, I could so easily have lost both my parents, had my father been in the car with my mother that day. Not even as a small boy had I felt the intensity of being scared in this way. Now with the loss of my mother, so many other emotions started to creep in.

Many thoughts crossed my mind; never seeing my mother's beautiful face or lovely smile again, the sound of her sweet gentle voice when we spoke on the phone, or spending some of our vacations together talking and laughing. It was so much easier to talk to my mother than it was my father. Worse thing of all, never again having the pleasure of my mother's company at Christmas.

There were indeed too many disturbing thoughts running through my mind. Not just thoughts; now I understood like any other unfortunate teenager how it felt when losing a parent they loved. I found myself asking would my mother's demise herald huge changes in both my father's life as well as mine; which for me indeed proved to be the case.

On arriving home terribly tired, decimated at my loss, feeling empty as well as very dirty and wanting nothing more than to have a shower then go to bed, Bates met me at the door with the rest of the staff, he was very kind and understanding. Taking my suitcase while trying to give me words of comfort as gently as he could.

He then went on to tell me; "Your father Mr Johnathan is expecting you in his office the moment you arrive home".

Although I wanted to see my father I dreaded that summons. Feeling drained as well as tired on top of all my other emotions, I thought a night's sleep would help before going to see him. Instead I made my way directly to his office knocking quietly on his door, walking in before he requested me to do so. That was actually the first time I had entered without his permission, I made sure I did not make that same mistake again, though my father never made any comment about it at that time, which surprised me, no way was I prepared to risk his wrath in doing so again.

I came face to face with a man that looked like death itself. His skin ashen, his eyes red and bloodshot, one can assume from crying. Something I doubt he had ever done from being a small boy, even if then. His clothes where badly crumpled, as if he had slept in them, which under the circumstances, would not have surprised me in the least. Yes I was shocked, never having seen his appearance as dishevelled as it was at that moment in time. From being a very young man, he had always been fastidious about how he looked and dressed. I am delighted to say, that was the last time I would see him in that state.

It was a very short painful interview for both of us; as would the following initial few days prove to be. Everyone found it hard living in such close proximity to him. No one person able to judge exactly what was going on in his mind. The atmosphere in the house was unbearably tense, my father showed no further emotion, not even at my mother's funeral.

A few days after the funeral had taken place, once again Bates came to inform me, that my father had requested I go to his office after breakfast. Since the funeral I had neither seen nor spoken to him. Dreading this new summons, I was unsure how he would react towards me, I also was now worried about what plans he had now drawn up about my future, my main concern being would he allow me to continue my studies at Harvard?

The office had become his retreat, a place of safety for him to hide from the world. Had he been an like animal that had been wounded, his office had become his den, which I suppose he felt comfortable and safe in. It enabled him to lick his wounds until he was ready to once again face up to his responsibilities. Since my return home my father had stayed in there the whole time, that damn room became the place he both ate and slept in. Fortunately there is the small bathroom next door. Bates brought in his food, as well as fresh clean clothes daily.

Before I entered this time I waited until my father summoned me to do so, wondering at that particular time what state of mind he may have been in. When I did enter, to all intents and purposes, he appeared to be quite civil, notwithstanding that his voice still lacked any kind of warmth. I had grown accustom to this cold-ness in his voice. It had become the acceptable way in which he spoke to me in general. Maybe that was all he was capable of, often leaving me to think why could his tone of voice not have a little more warmth in it as Bates had in his?

Facially he appeared to still be suffering from his loss, yet his attitude continuing to be without emotion. Quietly he greeted me then said; "Please sit down Jonathan".

Following his request, which sounded more like an order, he pointed to the two armchairs placed either side of the fireplace. Coming from around his desk he make his way join me. This time pointing for me to sit on the opposite chair to the one he had chosen. Once again I looked around the office, having so rarely been invited into it for many years until these last awful few days.

As offices went, in one's own home, it was quite a comfortable medium-size room, very masculine; definitely reflecting my father's personality. Covered in warm wood panelling, the floor to ceiling shelving held some of the finest historical books money could buy. Sharing that shelf space, were various personal objects, which he had acquired over the years, each obviously meaning a great deal to him. On the opposite two walls stood floor to ceiling bookcases. They contained hundreds of wonderful interesting books, along with a fabulous set of books naturally being associated with the law. Understandably another reason why my father was brilliant at his job; the research one could achieve from those books was second to none.

The window blinds were drawn down quite low, making the room fairly dark. In a strange way it was also comforting for someone who wanted to hide from the world, there was still just enough light entering the room, allowing me to see the awful state in which it had now become. Papers were strewn across his desk and a large number of opened books were covering most of the floor. His wastepaper basket was full and overflowing, this was not the normal way in which my father conducted his life, he was a meticulous person with everything needing to be in its place.

Entering a dark room was something my father would never anticipate; he hated even the thought of doing so, never mind sitting in one. What the hell was happening to him? It was not going to be long before I found out. Sitting once again in one of the comfy armchairs offering me the other, almost trying to make the meeting seem less formal than I had expected it to be. To be honest I had fully expected him to request that I sit opposite him at the overpowering desk, which had originally belonged to my grandfather. That huge desk always made me feel very small and very inadequate, which in turn I grew to hate.

Even though my father was making an effort, I still could not help but feel intensely uncomfortable. After looking around the office waiting with bated breath, preparing myself to hear bad news. My father looked at me for a few moments searching my face, though not with that cruel stare he would normally reserve for someone he disliked. With not a sign of emotion in his voice he said; "Johnathan I would like you to return to Harvard as soon as possible. If you go sometime during the weekend, it will enable you to start a fresh week. Anything you feel you may require you know to ask Bates, or phone our main office".

How I never jumped out of my chair with joy on hearing that news, I will never know.

"Furthermore Jonathan," he continued: "I have decided to go away. Where and for how long I have no idea. You can I am sure understand my reasons as to why."

His next words were to totally take the wind out of my sails! Words I would never have expected to hear in a million years!

The tone of his voice was still devoid of any emotion as he continued to say; "Johnathan, if there is anything you would like of your mothers, then please feel free during the next couple of days to go through her personal things. Either take them to your room, or ensure they are packed away safely. You may have all of your mother's jewellery. I am sure one day when you marry your lovely wife, whoever she may be will be more than delighted to wear it. I do not think you need me to tell you; your mother's jewellery is worth a serious amount of money and therefore should for the moment be kept in a bank vault. On returning home Johnathan, I have no wish to see a single stick of furniture which is in the house at present. Anything you would like to keep can be taken and stored at the top of the house or put in storage elsewhere. The rest of our things will be taken and given to charity, or sold.

"Another decision I have made is that once you marry I will vacate this house, if not already having done so. Johnathan I know you love living here and that is why I have already gifted the house to you. I am hoping one day you will bring your lovely new wife home, as well as bring up in this house any grandchildren you deem fit to provide for me to enjoy. I will continue to pay for the upkeep of the house, at least until you leave Harvard and join me at the office. Once all the furniture has been removed, Bates will ensure that the house is once again refurbished, should you wish to return home during vacation time".

Listening to what my father had just divulged, the feelings of becoming confused even angry surged up inside of me. These were emotions I had never experienced before my mother had died. It was difficult to understand the contrast in my father's behaviour. On one hand he was taking care of me, yet on the other being totally ruthless. Systematically he was getting rid of everything that reminded him of my mother, knowing he loved her and that she was his whole world. Could it be he now no longer had the capacity to still enjoy what they had built together? He was obviously still in emotional pain at the emptiness of her loss? Which seemed beyond anyone's imagination, certainly beyond mine. Like everyone else I had no idea at the time how her death was to change our lives forever.

While having divulged to me his plans, there was still not a trace of any feelings showing either in his face or the cold clear words he spoke. It appeared he was totally detached from all human emotion' he was like a man who had not a drop of warm blood flowing through his veins. Deprived, it appeared, of every human feeling. Yet looking closely into his huge cold blue eyes, I swear it was taking a huge effort for him not to shed a tear.

Sitting there staring back at him, I could hear my pathetic meek reply, "Thank you for telling me all this, if those are your wishes sir, so be it". Then going on to thank him for allowing me to keep my mother's personal belongings; my father knowing full well I will always treasure them.

The fact my father was allowing me to keep the house I loved was amazing, obviously knowing it would be a joy to continue living here as well as an honour. The thought of bringing my future bride home seemed at that moment a million years away.

At that point our conversation concluded. My father sat there not moving a muscle or saying another word. Strangely I desperately wanted to give him a hug, yet did not dare do so. Instead I shook his hand, which was unexpectedly soft to the touch, noticing his beautiful manicured nails. Turning to leave after taking the few paces needed to reach the door, it felt I had walked a mile. Just as I was about to turn the handle my father called me back in the same unemotional calm voice. Once again asking me to sit down next to him.

I had no choice but to comply with his wishes. His eyes, cold and empty, where now firmly fixed on my face. He sat there not saying a word for a good minute or two, once again making me feel seriously nervous, until at long last he broke the silence. His voice still devoid of any emotion, he then continued to say, "Johnathan I have decided to give you temporary power of attorney to all of our businesses during the time I am away".

Stunned! Unable to say a word it felt like I had just entered someone else's dream. Unfortunately it was not a dream it was my reality! Now it had also become my nightmare, a nightmare I could not escape from. I swear my father was trying to read my thoughts, yet he said nothing waiting for my reaction.

My father of course had already made up his mind about what he was about to say next, continuing in his unemotional voice he went on to say, "Johnathan I have left you full written instructions. You will find all the necessary documents pertaining to our business should you need them in an emergency, they have already been deposited with the bank. Copies of course will be at our Head Office with the company lawyers. I am hoping that our staff are able to work without the need to contact you. Johnathan I do understand how important your studies are and that you have every wish to become a lawyer. I must ask you however, also to remember as well as being a lawyer you will eventually with my demise, permanently take over the reins of the many companies we own. I have every confidence in your ability in handling everything that needs to be handled. You are a very mature young man for your age, blessed with an abundance of wisdom. You also have the negotiating skills of an experienced diplomat. That will more than hold you in good stead".

My father had never given me that amount of praise in my entire life, now here he was drowning me in it. At least that was how it felt, that kind of praise left me feeling totally perplexed. It was an overwhelming statement for him to make, as well as one for me to hear.

Sitting there like someone who did not understand English, listening to all he was saying. I needed time to think, time which I did not have in trying to take in the enormity of his words. The potential of the power he was asking me to accept or should I say, thrust on my shoulders. Dear Lord! What were his motives, knowing I was way out of my depth? Once more I felt like a small boy being asked to swim the entire length of a pool, yet one who had never been taught to swim.

The enormity of what my father had just divulged to me or expected of me, I could barely believe. My ninetieth birthday was still a couple of months away, yet here he was making me at eighteen totally responsible for a multibillion dollar empire. What had just happened to my life? Before I could answer him my father continued, this time his voice had sharpened to a more commanding tone as he made his thoughts clear: "Do not let me down Johnathan! I need you to do this for me. I have never asked you for anything, now be the man I had hoped one day you would be".

With his next words it felt as if he had read my mind as he went on to say. "Johnathan I appreciate that giving you the responsibility of running our companies is indeed a huge undertaking. It is perhaps a little sooner than I had anticipated. As you are my son you are more than capable of carrying out my wishes regardless of the fact you are still fairly young, yes the responsibility, although temporary, means many people's way of life now depends on you; you will be responsible for them and the firms they work for. Johnathan I need some time away".

Such persuasive words, strangely kind yet I had never once heard them at all through school or college. Now he was allowing me so much power, even if it was for a short space of time. His trust in me was beyond anything I had expected at eighteen. Too much trust, too much power of which I wanted neither.

Thoughts formulated in my mind that he may be having a nervous breakdown. Then I doubted them, dismissing them just as quickly as they had entered my head. Every detail had been calculated to the very last full stop in just a few short days, or had it! Did my father already have contingency plans drawn up, in case anything should have happened to him? Now that seemed a great deal more logical, after all I was James Stone's son.

After leaving my father's office I made my way directly to my own room, on the way there just for a moment or two, the thought that I was going to throw up became very real. Just what the hell was my father thinking? What the hell was I thinking in agreeing to his wishes? Not just feeling nauseous, I now felt dirty to the point of thinking about taking a shower, irrespective of the fact I had already had one that morning. Showering then changing into fresh clothes I went looking for

Bates, needing to talk to him as I always did when troubled, or requiring good advice.

On top of having lost my darling mother, my world was now being further turned upside down by my father's complex wishes. No not wishes, dammed commands. It suddenly dawned on me, had Bates already been informed in advance of my father's wishes. One thing was for sure; I knew I would need a huge amount of help from him before my life retuned to some kind of normality, if it ever could!

Bates was in what we now regard as his personal rooms. As a young man when he first came to work for my father, he had been offered the small suite of rooms on the third floor. They had stood empty for a number of years, which was great for me as they are situated in the left wing of the house.

I loved Bates living in the opposite wing to the nursery. Knowing he was there during the night, especially when there were serious thunderstorms which I hated, was a convenient relief. From time to time when my parents were away, either on holiday or business trips, the knowledge that he was just up the corridor I found greatly comforting. Had I needed him in an emergency he always endeavoured to make me feel safe.

My nanny back then, I rather suspect, may well have also been pleased to have his company. It gave her the opportunity of having an adult to talk to, not just the constant company of a small child. She would I dare say, have asked Bates for his sensible advice, as I do today. Indeed with her being quite young, having taken on the responsibility of looking after James Stone's son must have been daunting, but with Bates on the same floor my father trusted her completely. He may well have been regarded as my father's back up. Bates went on to give her away when she married, I can assume like myself, that nanny probably looked on him as a special figure in her life.

Knocking on Bates sitting room door as I usual did, what should have felt no more than a second or two seemed like an hour before he came to open it. The fact Bates came to open the door himself, rather than shout for me to come in, told me that he either knew of my father's plans, or like myself was expecting bad news.

"Please come in Mr Johnathan," Bates said in his quite calm voice, 'rough interview?"

"That would be putting it mildly," I replied.

"Like a drink Mr Johnathan?" Bates asked.

"Whisky would be deeply appreciated rather than coffee," I requested, then thanked him.

"I think I will join you this time if you do not mind," Bates said with a gentle smile.

Going over to one of the comfortable settees, which I had often sat on when growing up, I sat down. I had spent a great deal of my young life in Bates sitting room, sometimes he would read to me or help with home-work. We played board games, I loved him helping me to do a jigsaw puzzle, or we would just sit and talk, he even taught me to play poker.

When Bates moved in he set about decorating each of the rooms, allowing me to help in any way I could for a small boy. Probably making more mess than he would have liked, yet taking it all in his stride. My father had informed him that he could go to one of the furniture store we used from time to time. Choose what he needed to furnish his rooms, then have the bill added to the household account. That first kind gesture by my father to Bates I feel was the beginning of the bond that grew between them.

Handing over my drink, Bates then sat himself down alongside on the comfy old settee. Once he had made himself comfortable, I then asked him if my father discussed any of the plans, or given him any of the orders he had given to me perhaps passed on his thoughts in regard to my mother's personal belongings including gifting me the house?

Before Bates could answer I went on to say, "Bates I feel so despondent. I want nothing more than to mourn the loss of my beautiful mother rather than starting to make massive decisions about material things, which for the moment I could not care less about. Bates my life is being turned completely upside down, why is my father getting rid of everything that reminds both of us of her? I hate what my father is now doing, as well as what he is asking of me. Knowing I am completely powerless, unable to disobey his damned orders, the feeling of despair is becoming insurmountable".

Knocking back my whiskey I looked at Bates, waiting for him to answers my questions. Once again before he could do so, I interrupted by saying, "Where do I start? Not just in regard to the house and my mother's personal belongings, but with everything else my father is expecting of me?"

Naturally wondering if Bates also knew what plans my father had drawn up for me in regard to the business, during the next few months. When I had finished pouring my heart out Bates gently said. "Mr Johnathan, your father has indeed given me a number of orders; he does not discuss any plans with me, ever!"

"I am sorry Bates you are quite right. Damned orders! Damned commands! Fit the bill very well. Bates rather than either you or I repeating ourselves. May I ask what orders he has actually asked you to carry out?"

"Not a problem, Mr Johnathan," Bates replied.

His voice sounding so kind. One of the things I loved most when talking to him, he always sounded as if he cared about everything I had to say, the same way Robin I care about everything you have to say to me. Bates taught me well on how to achieve that ability.

"Your father, Mr Johnathan," Bates went on to say, "has made it abundantly clear that once you return to Harvard, all the furniture you have no wish to keep will be sent to either charity or sold. Your father has asked me to help you should you wish me to help. Help that is, by putting different coloured stickers on the possessions you would like to have stored at the top of the house, which possessions you would then like kept in storage, the rest of what you choose to go to charity".

Bates repeated practically word for word what my father had clearly stated to me, including saying; "I believe your father has gifted to you all of your mothers personal belongings including her jewellery. Mr Johnathan, I am so sorry that the very last piece of jewellery your father had bought for your mother, you never managed to see. It was returned to the store shortly after the accident, as your father could not stand to look at it. It was a beautiful necklace, the setting was indeed something to admire. The rubies and diamonds used in the setting were I believe the finest quality money could buy. Your mother would have looked very lovely wearing it. Your father bought it to go with the ruby and diamond earrings which originally accompanied the necklace, purchasing them a few months previous".

"Bates I had no idea my father had bought my mother another necklace."

He never mentioned it to me, as was his normal pattern of behaviour. No matter what it was he purchased, jewellery, property, businesses or most other things, he never discussed anything with me just as he does not today. As you know I would only see such lovely pieces of jewellery, which my mother wore, when she was going somewhere special. Sometimes if she went out to dinner with my father, which became infrequent as I grew up. By the time I returned home from Boston, I dare say the necklace may well have been in one of the drawers of his desk. Knowing my father he could of course have already ensured it was put away in his safe.

"May I ask Bates what other orders my father has given to you?"

Bates then went on to say. "Basically Mr Johnathan, your father asked me to try to make things as simple as possible for you. Once you have chosen what it is you wish to keep, I will then ensure a team of packers are brought in followed by a further team, this time of removers. Then I will consult a number of stores ensuring the house will once again be refurbished. Do you have any preferences as to what you would like organised for the house once you return home?"

"No thank you Bates, just buy whatever you think my father will feel comfortable with."

"Bates I would like my mother's clothes to be carefully packed then sent to an auction house. Once sold, I would like the money to go to the cancer charity she supported. My father has as you said, gifted to me all of my mother's jewellery. Advising I ensure it is banked as soon as possible. A job perhaps you and I could carry out tomorrow. If you are free for the next few hours Bates, perhaps you will start helping me with the stickers."

Chapter 3

Where to start I did not have a glue. The thought of looking through my mother's treasured belongings already began to hurt terribly. Having to choose what to keep were thoughts I should not have been thinking about so early in my life. How I wish there had been someone present, who had the ability tell me why the hell my father felt he had to go down this road so soon after my mother's death.

In his gentle voice Bates then said. "I am dreadfully sorry Mr Johnathan, you and I both know as does everyone else who comes into contact with your father, we are given no choices, we just have to respect your father's wishes. I doubt very much anyone will ever know what goes on in your father's thoughts, even at the best of times. He is not a man anyone dares to question, or countermand his orders".

When talking with Bates there was never a problem about being open and honest with him, due I suppose to the easy relationship we had built up over the years. It was a relief being able to share and discuss the sort of things I would never dare to talk to my father about. That particular day I decided to convey to Bates my deepest thoughts, I went on to say.

"Bates I love my father as well as respecting him, you could say I admire him when it comes to being a brilliant lawyer. He has ensured I have had all the material things a boy could have wish for, including a very good education. He is continuing to pick up my fees, enabling me to complete my studies at the university of my choice. You know how much I truly wanted to follow him in going to Harvard. He has though always been a parent from a distance, I suppose being his only son he does care genuinely about me, yet as a father I stand in awe of him. He is someone I have always found difficult to talk to, now as a young man under normal circumstances I should not be afraid of him, unfortunately I still am. When having a conversation with him, no matter how simple the subject may be, I feel my hands starting to become very clammy. Believe it or not, during the last few meetings since my mother's death, my whole body is soaked from perspiration by the time I am dismissed from his company.

"Bates, has my father told you about what is going to happen during the next few months in regard to our business?"

"No Mr Johnathan, the furniture and your mother's personal belongings are all that have been mentioned to me".

"In that case Bates you and I had better have another drink, as I divulge to you a couple of even more radical decisions which my father has put in place for me. Maybe for both of us, as well as all the staff that work at the house".

For one moment Bates looked at me rather strangely, I thought he was about to say no to pouring another drink. Instead he said nothing, he walked over to his drinks tray to replenish our glasses. Once there he turned then looked hard at me asking. "Does your news really require this second drink?"

"I am afraid my news most definitely does merit a second drink. Take it from me the way I feel I could drown myself in that bottle, or any damn bottle for that matter".

Again Bates stood still looking at me for a minute, he then said very quietly, "If you were my son, I would very much appreciate it Mr Johnathan you make this the last time you go for a bottle in this way. No matter what problems the future has in store for you, there are many ways to sort difficult problems out without resorting to drink".

"Yes I know you are right, I stand chastened, turning to the bottle will indeed make my life more difficult. From now on Bates I promise I will digest another piece of your sensible advice; in the meantime please may we at least enjoy another drink. You will need it that I do promise."

Once again Bates joined me on the settee, waiting patiently for me to disclose to him what I regarded were the very worse decisions my father could possibly have decided to implement. Taking a deep breath I then enlightened him by saying: "Unfortunately my errant father has decided he no longer wishes to live in this house, once he returns from wherever it is he has chosen to go. He has, as I mentioned gifted the house to me, though he will continue to maintain it until I start work. That is a fairly minor decision come to think about it, the worse decision of all he has stipulated is that I take temporary control of all of our businesses".

Bates took a gulp of his drink as the colour drained from his face. I swear Robin, if I had not been sitting next to him, you would have thought in that instant he had seen a ghost. Bates looked at me shaking his head in total disbelief, yet knowing full well what I was saying would be the absolute truth.

For the first time since I had known Bates, he disagree out loud with what my father had decided, continuing in a slightly raised voice he went on to say. "What the hell is your father thinking?" Half talking to me yet sounding as if speaking to himself.

"I have known your father to give everyone who comes into contact with him, requests or orders as I would describe them, even demands if the word suits. Whichever word you may like to choose, every order had to be fulfilled instantly, but I have never known him to do anything as out of character as this. To expect you at your age to run his empire having no experience, regardless of the fact it may be a temporary situation, to me is nothing short of utter madness"!

"Bates I agree with you, unfortunately I have no choice. Had it been my father instead of my mother who had been killed, automatically I would have taken on the business permanently. At least I know it is just for a few months, heaven help me. Now more than ever, I am going to rely heavily on you. Your wise council which I have always listened to will be of great necessity. Other than my father I trust no other person in such a way as yourself. Bates, if I am honest it is you who has always been the main stay in my life. You ensured I had a happy childhood, and you have looked after our lives, which you still continue to in the same excellent way, always striving to run everything as smooth as possible. Unfortunately under the circumstances we now find ourselves in, your ability to continue to guide me will be even more vitally important".

"My father has not told me where he is going, or for how long he intends to stay away. On top of now ordering me to return to Harvard very shortly, which I am actually pleased about, how he expects me to devote my mind to my studies is beyond me. Does he honestly think I have all of his capabilities including having no emotions? He forgets there must be some of my mother in me".

"Once again in his quiet calming voice, Bates went on to say: "Truly I am sorry Mr Johnathon, of course I will do my level best to resolve what problems, or worries, you have for the present. I am sincerely honoured for the trust and confidence you have in me. Also I am very humbled that you feel you can talk openly of things you care very deeply about. In many ways I am so sorry you do not have this kind of relationship with your father".

"It is no good me complaining as nothing will ever change in respect of my father, though like you I am sorry he and I do not seem to be able to talk. At least Bates I am lucky, you have always given me your precious time, as well as many happy memories. As far as the businesses are concerned, I am hoping that as we employ the finest lawyers in the country, they will know exactly what is expected of them without giving me too much hassle? With real luck, not even phone me once".

Both Bates and I laughed at that thought, knowing that was never going to happen.

"Bates should I need some down to earth basic advice, I hope you will allow me to call or come to talk to you?"

Bates gave a wide smile then said: "Mr Johnathan, I will be honoured should you wish to take me into your confidence in regard to emotional matters. You know I have always been very happy to listen to what you have to say. In regard to the law or business matters, unfortunately I am afraid I know practically zero about either. As for anything else you may wish to talk about, I will do my level best to try to help you in any way I can, may I suggest Mr Johnathan we make a start as painful as it will be. Perhaps you would like to start with your mothers personal things?"

There was no pity in Bates voice, just gentle encouragement, which I was most grateful for.

"Thank you Bates that is what I will do," I answered, "by the way when you order the new furniture, I would like to make my first request. Would you please consider refurbishing your rooms, the way you and I would like them"?

The look Bates gave me was one of pure joy, even admiration. I had given my first request to brighten the life of someone I highly respected. Maybe in a strange way I loved, as Bates always behaved like a father figure. We exchanged smiles then I left the room, making my way directly to my mother's bedroom.

Entering my mother's bedroom without her being there was indeed hard for me to do. Gently opening her door without first knocking felt awfully strange. It was something I had never done before. I stood in the doorway for a few moments then walked towards a chair that had been placed close to her bed. Sitting down trying to take in everything I saw about her lovely room, the cool cream walls with matching carpet, the matching elegant French reproduction furniture, painted in the same cream as the walls. At the windows, hung warm peach drapes matching her bedding.

Suddenly I spotted my mother's tiny slippers peeping out from under the bed. Everything about this room was so light, charming, very feminine, exceptionally neat and clean with not a thing out of place. A room that was cool yet warm, it had a refinement about it, which mirrored everything my mother originally had been to me.

Her bedroom was not a place I had often been invited into. On the few occasions I had been allowed in, there were certain things that I did remember, the wonderful large crystal vases containing beautiful smelling flowers, now no longer on display. There were matching silver photo frames, which held photos of my parents as well as myself. Again now no longer on her dressing table. Dear lord what else would no longer be where it should. It did not take me long to find out.

While sitting in her chair for the first time, the reality hit me that she would never be part of my life again. Covering my eyes as the tears I had so far not shed, slowly began welling up. With not wearing my watch I did not have a clue how long I sat there, I suppose you could say until my fragmented emotions were spent.

Making my way to my mother's bathroom to wash, I found there were no longer towels hanging where they normally would be for available easy use. That became my breaking point, the thought made me as mad as hell. Going over to the internal phone, and for the first time in my life. I vented my anger as well as my frustration at the voice on the other end. It did not matter to me who it was I spoke to, more importantly I did not care.

Instinctively I knew that I had no right to be cross with the person on the other end. Sadly it just happened to be our housekeeper who like Bates had always been so kind to me. Unfortunately she received the full force of what had become my unbearable pain. Naturally there were more than plenty of towels in the units, it was the fact that none were hanging where they should have been that had hurt so much. On returning to the bathroom pulling some towels out from the unit that housed them, I then washed.

Within minutes Bates walked in with a bundle of towels in his hand. He looked at me then asked calmly, "did I wish to send my apologies to the housekeeper. It was not her fault that my mother's bedroom had not been serviced as normal".

For one moment I felt I was being torn in two. Loyalty to my mother's memory, then quickly trying to understand everything had now changed.

"Yes of course Bates, you are quite right I was completely out of order. Please send down my apologies; perhaps I should have said something in a much quieter tone of voice."

"We all understand Johnathan it is hard for you, we are also trying our best to help in the best way we can," Bates replied, he then turned and left the room leaving me alone. I now had to face what I felt was the worse task of all.

Returning to the bedroom, I decided to start the disconcerting task that lay ahead of me. Gently opening my mother's draw units; I found it contained her exquisite underwear. Closing that draw I then systematically did the same with all of the other draws, each containing items of her beautiful clothing. On opening the middle draw of her large dressing unit, I found it contained her wonderful collection of silk scarves. Lifting one out, the smell of my mother's perfume still lingering on it. For a few moments I held it close to my cheek, I then put it deep into my pocket. That scarf was to stay with me for many years, including taking it with me to

Harvard. I continued to open and close each draw respectively without touching anything".

It was not until I reached my mother's desk that I decided to treat the task a little differently. Having no intentions of reading her various mail, or the large bundle of what, I presumed, may well have been my parents love letters. The letters being tied up in a pretty peach ribbon which matched her room. Sometimes I wished I had taken one or two out to read at a later date. Had I done so it may well have given me some kind of an insight into their romance; or could well have thrown some light onto my father's character. I regarded my mother's letters as very private, and not for me to interfere with. What became of them I have no idea, like everything else I am sure my father would ensure they were disposed of?

Carefully going through the desk drawers, again not knowing exactly what it was I would find until towards the back of one of them, I saw a small black velvet box. I gently opened it, inside lay a gold locket which contained two photos, myself on one side as a little boy, the other I assumed was my mother as a baby girl. Along with the scarf I carefully put the locket into my pocket. After that I never bothered to open any of her wardrobes, making my last unpleasant task my mother's safe. Opening the small safe I found her main jewellery box, including a number of smaller boxes. Removing everything that the safe contained, I then made my way towards the door. Taking one last look around the room I knew that all I saw would not be here next time I returned home. Once again gently closing the door behind me I felt I was saying goodbye to my mother for the final time.

From early morning until evening, the next couple of days were filled carrying out my father's orders. It was so hard choosing which pieces I wished to keep, wanting to keep everything. Which of course was impossible. Having Bates to guide me on particular pieces my mother loved best was a tremendous help.

We left going to the bank until the day before I flew back to Harvard. Just before taking that journey with Bates I decided to speak to my father. Foolishly thinking there may have been something else of my mother's he would like me to have, or something he may wish to deposit in his safety box. Knocking on the office door automatically waiting until told to enter.

"Good morning Johnathan how may I help you", my father asked, his voice cold and devoid of human kindness. I did notice as I stepped into the room it seemed a great deal tidier than my last interview with him. Even the blinds were raised allowing in the light. Apologising for disturbing him, I asked if he needed me to take anything to the bank for him. Looking directly at me with his cold empty eyes he replied, in his inimitable manner.

"Thank you for asking Johnathan, but no there is nothing further I wish to deposit at the bank. As I have told you all the necessary documents you may require are already there. You are I believe now in possession of all of your mothers jewellery. Thank you for coming to ask me I do appreciate it. Bates will ensure both your wishes as well as mine will be carried out in full once we leave. May I ask is there anything else you would like to know while we are having this conversation?"

"No sir," I replied, "It is all I came to ask you".

"My father then surprised me, continuing in his predictable manner as always, his voice still devoid of any warmth whatsoever, he requested, "please sit down," offering me the chair opposite him. His next words went on to astound me once again.

"Your mother Johnathan, has left you a great deal of money in her will. Part of which you may use instantaneously, the rest is in a trust fund. On reaching twenty-five the residue is yours".

"I had no idea sir, though I am exceedingly surprised, perhaps shocked would be more to the point". My brain once again spinning at this fresh news. "May I ask you sir if you would please enlighten me as to how much money my mother has actually left to me?"

"Your mother Johnathan has left you in excess of twenty-five million dollars. Of which you may have full use of three million instantly."

My father's words revealing this prodigious amount of money sent my brain into overdrive. All I could think about was being further burdened by this vast amount of money that was now mine.

My father's voice bringing me back to reality as he went on to say: "Johnathan I am sure you will be most careful how you handle your generous inheritance. I have no intention of interfering on how you handle your personal fortune, unless of course you wish me to do so. I am trusting you implicitly to do the right thing with it, even enjoy having a small spending spree which will not come amiss".

Truly dumfounded at this revelation, I replied: "Thank you sir for telling me. You could say I am a little shocked to say the least, also most grateful that you have decided to tell me all this before either you or I go away".

My father seemed relieved that I had taken this further piece of unexpected yet disturbing news in my stride. He then asked. "When will you be returning to Harvard?"

"I have booked a seat to fly back tomorrow sir," I replied, I hoping that our conversation was drawing to a close.

"Very well, I hope you have a safe journey. Remember Jonathan do not let me down, I am depending on you. Make me proud to know you are my son."

Those were indeed to be his last words to me face to face for nearly a year. He did phone after six months, when he decided to return home to find his empire still intact.

I made my way to Bates sitting room to say my good-byes before catching my plane, already having informed Bates of my newfound wealth.

In turn he told me, "be most careful and please do not reveal to anyone about your inheritance". His concerns were duly noted, which I would of course take on board, as I listened to all he advised.

"We chatted about a few unimportant things enjoying a last cup of coffee together. Normally I hated leaving home, this time I could not wait to get away, though knowing I would miss Bates.

"Will you please drive me to the airport?" I asked him.

"Certainly it will be my sad pleasure to do so," Bates replied. "Mr Johnathan I shall miss you, please keep in touch with me, if you do not mind me asking".

"You should know I never mind you asking anything of me. I will also miss you terribly," I answered.

We eventually made our way downstairs. Bates took my suitcase putting it on the back seat of the car along with a new travel bag I had bought. I stood for a few moments in the hall, hoping my father would have come to say goodbye, yet I was not really surprised there was no sign of him. After saying goodbye to some of the staff, I climbed into the car taking a last look at the home I loved and now legally belonged to me.

As Bates drove to the airport I sat next to him instead of in the back". For no reason I started to feel a little unsure as to how I would cope with the enormous responsibility my father had now placed on my shoulders. Looking at Bates I asked him: "Are you sure you will not mind me phoning should I require your help or advice?"

We had to stop as the lights turned red. Bates was then able to look at me for a few moments, in his steady, calm voice he said.

"You must never be afraid to call me, it is what you have always done from being a small boy. Nothing has changed as far as I am concerned between us. Maybe we now have a better understanding than we have ever had. Even though you are now a man, you are what I still regard as fairly young."

A remark at which we both laughed aloud.

"Thank you so much Bates," I replied, sounding like a child who is grateful for the help that was now being given. Knowing I can talk to Bates my burden is indeed halved.

At last we reached the airport, Bates pulled into a parking spot. He jumped out, opening the back door handing my suitcase over. Once I had taken out my travel bag we shook hands. Bates steadily looked at me then said: "Mr Johnathan, I have no wish to interfere in your life as well you know, that is not my place to do so". Just for a moment he sounded like a father talking to a son.

"Mr Johnathan there is something however I do wish to say just before you go. You know how very proud of you I feel, having been a great part of your life watching you grow up into the fine young man you are today. There is nothing under the sun we cannot discuss with each other. You do understand don't you"? He continued, "Should you have girl trouble at some time in the future, which all young men occasionally do have from time to time." Bates stopped for a moment changing the subject, then went on to say.

"I have never spoken to you of Mrs Bates. Sadly she died when having our baby. There was no one for me after she passed away. One day if you would be interested, I will tell you about my deep love for her. When it comes to pretty girls, I like to think that I understand when ones emotions start to run wild. What I am trying to ask you is something I have not always done, and sadly paid a dear price for. That is that you practice safe sex, now go before I give you a lecture."

Stunned even shocked at what Bates had revealed to me. I was totally taken aback that after all these years, he had never openly told me of his sad secret. Never saying a word now made me wonder if he had mentioned it to my father. The first opportunity I have I will try tactfully to ask him to enlighten me about his lost family.

"Looking at him now as if for the first time. Realising I knew so little of this gentle natured man, a man that I had come to greatly admire. Bates had indeed been a huge part of my life. The way he had always treated me, now made me wonder, was I the son he wanted and lost? What a wonderful father he would have made. Telling him I must go or would miss my plane, and yes

I will take on board the fact about practising safe sex. I did not have the heart to tell him that was something I had already been doing for a good number of years.

Thanking him with all the sincerity I could muster in my voice, I promised him I would keep in regular touch. We shook hands once again, then quickly turning away as I felt the tears pricking my eyes.

Stepping on board my plane, I settled into the more comfortable seat I had purchased having upgraded to first class, due of course to the excessively large, and generous inheritance my mother had left me. It was going to be a long flight back to Boston, which this time I was so grateful for, my emotions were in a whirlwind having endured three weeks of my father's authoritarian behaviour. Everyone tiptoeing around him, terrified to say a wrong word; blast him. He was not the only one feeling the stress, the utter despair each of us feels when losing someone one we have loved. It is hard for those of us left behind, my father should have tried to have been more sensitive to that thought. How foolish of me to even think he was capable of such sensitivity.

Now all I wanted was my structured uncluttered life back, the realization that was not going to happen made me feel not just annoyed but totally exasperated. Thanks to my father's assumptions that I had the ability to run his empire. On top of everything else I felt sick to my stomach, heaven help me should I put a foot wrong.

Not just with my father's decisions, running around in my head. Now I had to deal with the shock of Bates revelation. That certainly was the last thing I expected to hear. How in heavens name had he held that fact from me? He had been married, had a wife and child, and then had lost both in childbirth? What else did

I not know about him? Had there been other women in his life?

Let's face it, he is still a damn good-looking man, even if his hair was now very slowly receding. He would look at me with his big blue-grey gentle eyes, never a cold stare in them. Not even when he was admonishing me, for something I perhaps should not have done.

Feeling totally drained all I wanted to do now was sleep, yet found it impossible to do so. My thoughts drifted towards being back at Harvard. I had loved those first few of months, sharing my room with a couple of friends from my childhood days. Those boys had become like brothers to me. Even after all these years, the three of us were very much on the same wavelength, which allowed us to get on brilliantly well. As I had been an only child, having their company made my life fun.

We would go to the Annenberg, not just to eat or discuss our intellectual horizons, far from it. Sitting there the guys and I had huge amounts of fun observing the gorgeous girls, which seemed to be in abundance, speculating as to how many potential affairs lay ahead. Those thoughts always brought a smile to my face as well as to those of my friends. Let's face it; it is after all every healthy young man's dream, seeing how many women you could notch up under your belt.

Going to classes together became part of our routine, or going over to the magnificent Langdell Hall. Even if you had been granted ten life times, it would not be enough time to read the millions of wonderful books available. I loved the treasured hours I spent in that amazing building, which I could only describe as pure enjoyment. Books are like beautiful women, some of the books being exceptionally delicate, those you handle with the upmost care, and respect. Others are commonly collectable, you pick them up knowing they have been handled frequently, yet still hoping you may learn something new from them, though invariably that rarely happens; once you realise that, you lose interest in them putting them aside very quickly. Then if you are incredibly lucky, you find a very rare one. The rarest you just look at, but do not ever touch.

During the last few miserable weeks I have missed that way of life, now I wanted it back desperately. The thought of going to breakfast each morning and seeing the same faces, usually sitting at their chosen table, made me pine for those times again. Even the strange girl with the blonde tousled hair who would usually sit in the farthest corner, her head always bent in some book or other, strange to be thinking of her, yet she too was now a familiar part of my routine. Dear Lord I needed to get laid, the sooner the better, if for nothing more than the human contact I desperately ached for. At least I could predict there would be enough little whores to help release my feelings, that was for sure guaranteed.

In the end I did manage to drift off after having had something to eat and drink. The next thing I knew one of the airhostess was gently waking me, requesting I fasten my seatbelt as we were preparing for descent having reached the landing approach. Our pilot landed his plane perfectly; it felt good to be back on land as it had been a long flight, even if I had been sitting in first class.

Collecting my suitcase and bag from the baggage carousel, which always seems to take forever, I went to look for a taxi. Seeing my friends once again would be so good, then looking forward to taking a shower and going to bed. I doubted my friends would see things my way, naturally wanting for me to catch up on their news. For an hour or so I guess it would not be too much of a problem, after all that is what having brilliant friends are all about.

As I stepped out of the taxi, it felt wonderful standing there for a few moments taking in the air, this is what I needed, and this is where I needed to be.

Making my way to the rooms that had been allocated to my friends and I as freshmen, I swear there was a spring in my step I had barely noticed before. Opening the door and throwing my bag in while putting my suitcase on the floor, my friends looked up in astonishment at this intrusion. As they jumped up to greet me with huge smiles on their faces, as well as words of welcome, we exchanged handshakes even hugs. I knew then I was home.

Chapter 4

It was a great deal later than I had originally intended when I managed to take my shower and thankfully go to bed. Having been away for three weeks meant there was a huge amount of gossip for the boys and I to catch up on.

My friends offered to help in many respects in showing what written work first required my attention, including books that needed to be read to ensure I became completely up to date with course work. Having a reasonable capacity for studying, it was not going to be too difficult a task for me to carry out. While at home I had managed to browse a couple of law books from my father's amazing collection while trying to take my mind off so many of my other problems.

Holding my own council and trying hard to keep my composure, as if all was well, I did not find too difficult either. The plane journey gave me the time I needed to do a great deal of thinking about a number of issues, starting with the fact Bates was quite right in advising me not to discuss my financial position in regard to my vast inheritance. As far as the emotional pain I had experienced during the last weeks, I certainly had no intention of discussing it with anyone. Thanks to my father's ridiculous decision, I was not prepared to air the situation amongst my peers, which for the present time has brought me to become one of the most powerful young men in the country. When my friends conversation drifted towards the opposite sex that became a perfect way to end the evening.

The following morning my friends, Jeff Adams, and Ethan Phillips, who I share my rooms with, decided to accompany me to breakfast, not a normal practice for them on a Sunday but I was delighted by their company. Having them along always made it pleasant, today in particular, as I once again familiarising myself with the wonderful dining hall, which I had missed so much during the last few weeks. After deciding what to eat we found a table in a discreet corner of the hall. It felt so good to be sitting there with the boys, talking and laughing about the different interests we each had that made our lives pleasant.

Jeff started the conversation by telling us of a girl he thought he may ask out on a date. My eyes subconsciously drifted around the hall thinking to myself, so many lovely women that would give me a great deal of pleasure, but which one would I favour.

"Johnathan are you listening?" Jeff asked.

"Yes of course I am, what was it you said Ethan?"

Jeff and Ethan started to laugh.

"I am sorry Jeff I do apologise, I was just eyeing up a little of the talent for myself."

"Why does that not surprise us," Jeff answered laughing.

Trying to pay attention to the continuing discussion my friends were having, once again my eyes began searching the room. What I was searching for I had no idea, until at last I spotted exactly what it was that I wanted to see. A head of tousled honey-blonde hair bent over a book as it always appeared to be.

Returning to reality I asked my friends what their plans for the rest of the day were. I wanted to discuss with them about joining me at the end of this term. Our family have a house that my great grandfather had bought close to the university. He had purchased it for my grandfather when he became a Harvard man. While on the plane I thought the house may be an interesting project and would, hopefully take my mind off the other issues that were disturbing me. Moving to the house was one decision my mind was fully made up about. The house naturally being an old rather distinguished building, would allow me a perfect base in which to spend the rest of my time at Harvard.

How long we actually stayed in the dining hall I had no idea, it was one of those rare times that none of the the three of us wore a watch, and were not really bothered about the time. As Jeff, Ethan or I were not in any particular hurry to leave, it gave me the perfect opportunity to ask them if they were interested in moving into the house with me. Both were thrilled at the idea, we were more than a little cramped, which was natural under the circumstances. Having more space to spread out seemed perfect.

This was also a good time to tell them I had every intention of buying a new car, another statement that went down very well. Explaining to them I wanted something comfortable, rather than something sporty. Ethan and Jeff ribbed me unmercifully, stating they knew exactly why I wanted a bigger car and could they borrow it from time to time.

The banter between the three of us made life so pleasant and was something I loved. Naturally I was delighted they had both agreed to move into the house, had they disagreed to join me I suspect I would have missed their company, even found myself rather lonely. It was after all an overly large house where one person could well have felt isolated. There were other students I suppose I could have asked, maybe even a couple who were looking for accommodation that I was not as yet acquainted with for the present. On reflection I decided that option was not for me.

Returning to our room I settled down to do some catch up work, poring over my studies industriously for what seemed hours. Breaking off sometime later I asked both Jeff and Ethan if either one wanted to go for something to eat? They both looked at me then Jeff asked, "Why are you thinking about food again as that is not your normal pattern of behaviour?"

"I have no idea why I feel so hungry must be the change of air," came my reply.

"Count me out," Jeff said, explaining he had a definite date with a girl named Trudy Hamilton.

"Lucky son of a gun," Ethan jumped in before I could.

"Pay attention Jeff," Ethan continued to say, "We want to know everything there is to know about her when you return. You could also ask her if she has a friend, or friends that would like to double date with Johnathan and I"

Turning to Ethan I stated: "With all respect Ethan I prefer to find my own lower blanket".

"Wow! Johnathan bit harsh a statement to make about a woman."

"Not at all," I replied, "let's face it, the majority of women are no more than whores. They want sex just as much as we do, yet expect to get well paid for their favours. If I am expected to pay then I want only the very best".

Ethan looked at me but did not say another word.

Ethan and I returned to the dining hall. Browsing along the counters I realised I was not particularly hungry after all, so settling for just a plain sandwich to go with a cup of coffee. Ethan suddenly decided he would after all join me in having a coffee.

"Ethan, looking at the simple fare I had bought then stated, "Thought you were hungry Johnathan".

"I thought I was hungry too maybe I just needed a break," I replied.

Once again I found myself taking a slow look around the dining hall, there was nothing of interest for me to see. At least not what it was I particularly wanted to see.

Ethan and I continued chatting until at last a couple of good-looking girls came in. They had decided to sit at a table close by. Ethan looked at me; I nodded then quietly said, "ok, let's try, why not, I have needed a good lay for ages".

The evening was pleasant enough, as usual nothing special to write home about. We had arranged to meet up later then walk back to our hall.

"Well are you going to see that girl again?" I asked.

Ethan replied, "She was a damn good lay", he said making me laugh as usual then continued. "Not quite sure if I will see her again, I'll wait and see how things go. Anyway what about you Johnathan are you going to see the girl you were with?"

"Not a chance my dear friend, not a chance."

"We reached our room just as Jeff was returning, now it was his turn to be interrogated. We both looked at him waiting to see the broadest of smiles. Sadly there was not a sign of one, not even a flicker of a smile, which unfortunately told us he most definitely had not been granted the charms of his date. Jeff looked at both of us, then in a slow sincere voice I had not heard him use before he said, "Not a word you guys. I MEAN IT... I think I am in love".

Ethan and I stared incredulously at Jeff on hearing his thoughts. I responded to them by saying. "No way! Steady on, that is one big statement to make. How the hell can you possibly be in love with a girl you have just met?"

Ethan then joined in, "what makes you feel you are in love? Are you saying you have already reached first base?"

Jeff's voice sharpened, "Ethan I do not want to hear one single derogatory word come out of your mouth about Trudy, which also applies to you Johnathan as well".

I Looked at Jeff perhaps seeing him for the first time. Having known both Jeff and Ethan since we were children, somehow I had not noticed they, like myself, had now grown into men. Discretion being the better part of valour I made no further comment. Ethan being ever the joker of the three of us, persisted by asking. "Does this young woman have a friend or roommate that may like to go on a double date?"

"No idea Ethan, I did not ask Trudy if she has a friend, or roommate who may consider going on a date with either Johnathan or yourself."

"Please do not include me," I told Jeff. "As I have already told Ethan I will choose my own little whores when I am good and ready." I continued: "Jeff now you have made your feeling perfectly clear about this young woman. Please understand I am not implying in any way the lady who you feel has stolen your heart is of that nature".

Jeff again made his feeling and thoughts clearly known by replying, "I appreciate your word on this matter, and that both of you respect my wishes and my new girlfriend. Strange as it may be to you I am very enamoured of this lovely funny lady. Oh by the way, Trudy does have a roommate, but she does not date or have any interest in men".

"Are you saying she prefers women?" I asked.

"No not at all," Jeff replied, "Her roommate it seems is in mourning, as her parents were killed in an automobile accident just before she started Harvard".

"Oh dear well never mind," Ethan sighed, "it was a nice thought while it lasted, I guess I will have to keep looking". Ethan's remarks leaving Jeff and I to once again laugh at him.

The following day I phoned across to the Deans office, asking if I could please make an appointment to see him. An appointment was made for late afternoon that same day. Considering how busy the Dean normally is I counted myself very fortunate, it had crossed my mind I may have had to wait quite a while longer until he was eventually free. Until the appointed time that had been designated to me, I decided to spend it judiciously by doing a further spell of much needed course work, diligently working through until it was time to keep that inevitable appointment. Pleased with myself as I had managed to clear a fair amount of work which was a huge relief. Closing my books I felt I needed a quick wash and a change of shirt. After which I walked over to the Deans office.

I found his office door open, still I gently knocked then waited for him to call me in. Dean Carter-Baxter looked up giving me a welcoming smile holding his hand out greeting me at the same time.

"Please come in Mr Stone," taking my hand and shaking it firmly while saying: "Nice to see you again".

"Thank you sir, I appreciate your time knowing how busy you normally are."

Dean Carter Baxter went on to ask, "How are you Mr Stone? Please take a seat," indicating this time to the chair opposite his desk. "I hope you are faring a great deal better than under the circumstances when we last spoke."

"Thank you sir," I replied then continued. "It is difficult at present, the loss of my mother will, I suppose take quite a while to adjust to. If I am being honest sir, I am somewhat relieved to be back here. No more than somewhat. Greatly relieved in fact".

Before giving the Dean time to reply, I went on to tell him the reason I had asked for this meeting by saying. "Sir I do apologise," emphasizing once again for taking up his time. "Unfortunately I wanted to have a serious word with you, I have some very important news which I feel needs to be divulge for your interest alone."

"Sir, I have come to the conclusion you should be made fully aware of my present position. For someone of my age it is both awesome and most certainly not welcome. What I am about to tell you Dean, I would greatly appreciate if it is kept within these office walls as I have no wish for the rest of the university to know, if possible, of the dilemma I am in, at the present time."

Dean Carter-Baxter looked at me hearing the serious tone of my voice; he then asked if I would care to join him for a cup of coffee. I suspected he was trying to now make this meeting feel a great deal less fraught an experience. "Thank you sir," I replied, "I would very much appreciate a cup of coffee, it would be most welcome indeed". I then went on to say. "What I am about to divulge to you Dean you may regard as a far-fetched tale, but frankly it is a true account of how my life stands certainly for the next number of months."

Dean Carter-Baxter phoned for a tray of coffee for two. He then decided that we cross to the two arm-chairs which were close to his window; allowing him an open view of the courtyard. In front of the armchairs stood a good size coffee table, taken up mostly by books with just enough room to deposit a tray. Once the coffee tray had been brought in, the Dean's secretary set it down efficiently, sweetly smiling before making her way out, closing the door quietly behind her. Dean Carter-Baxter handed me the cup of welcome coffee. After taking a couple of sips I started to relate my news.

I revealed the content of my news to the Dean, which I knew he would find hard to believe. Sitting there patiently waiting to see the changes in his face, actually feeling quite sorry for him, as I felt for myself. Unbeknown to him, until the moment until I divulged the full extent of what I needed to tell him, he had no idea he had been put in the position of possibly coming to an eighteen year old youth should he wish to purchase anything of real value for the university?

Taking a deep breath I related to him that I now owned my father's empire. I owned so much it was terri-fying. It included the Jefferson Stone hospital, which was the main hospital in the district. I was now one of the universities biggest financial contributors and it was then

I told him, it was to me he must come and not my father; should the university require anything special. Also I now owned many of the housing blocks around the university that house a great number of the students.

On top of all that I was responsible for a vast network of law practices throughout the country, huge amounts of corporate business also across the country worth billions of dollars. My own airline, plus heavens knows what else my family have acquired over a period of a couple of hundred years or more.

Dean Carter Baxter looked at me in total astonishment, "are you being serious, Mr Stone?" He asked, "Or is this some excessive prank you have thought up with your friends, which I would have thought was not like you?"

He saw the cold unblinking look I gave him, something my father would have done. Looking hard at me, being very use to young men playing practical jokes, he then realised I was not engaged in a prank or being facetious. The Dean then quickly apologised saying in the next breath.

"Forgive my rudeness I am afraid I am in shock at hearing what you have just told me."

"I understand," came my sympathetic reply.

"It most definitely is not a dreadful prank, I wish it were. When my father informed me of his wishes, which by the way he had already carried out to the last letter without consulting me; the eyes dotted the tees crossed, there was nothing I could do but follow his orders. My father as you may know is not a man anyone disobeys. Ever!"

Dean Carter-Baxter then said. "I know it is none of my business Mr Stone, if you will please forgive me for asking. Did your father give any particular reason as to why he made that monumental decision? Coming to such a massive decision then thrusting it on a totally inexperience youth allowing him such power, simply does not seem normal".

"My father Sir, said he just needed time and space away from everything. He told me he would be away for a period of months, around six months, I am certainly hoping he keeps his word. He has taken my mother's death pretty badly. At the moment he seems quite inconsolable. Had my father been the one to die I would have inherited his empire anyway, as it is I am hoping this burden of madness as you call it, will last only for that short duration. Praying with luck it is certainly no more than the next six months he has mentioned".

Dean Carter-Baxter's face looked blank for a few moments, as if trying to figure out my father's motivation of making such an enormous decision in thrusting upon me such power. In a kindly fashion he went on to say.

"Mr Stone I am at a loss for words, it takes a great deal too either shock or surprise me. Your words have surpassed both of those emotions leaving me to feel incredibly sorry for you indeed."

"Thank you sir, I appreciate your sentiments as well as your kindness." I went on to inform him, "Dean should you determine you need anything which you may regard as a worthwhile addition for the university, then please do not hesitate to inform me. It will be my pleasure to ensure it is purchased".

Dean Carter-Baxter then replied: "Thank you Mr Stone that is very kind of you indeed". He sympathetically continued to say; "If you require any type of help, you can be sure everyone here will do their level best in giving you the finest of advice should you request it. Naturally your confidence will be respected in every way. Until such time Mr Stone you may wish to change your mind, I give you my word of honour this conversation will remain within these four walls".

I thanked the Dean for his time as well as the coffee. We shook hands then once again I crossed the room to the door of his office. As I opened it, I looked back to say goodbye. I could not help noticing the look in the Deans eyes, what were his thoughts? Were they reflecting one of pity or could he have been thinking there goes an immensely powerful young man? Heaven help him!

As it was still pleasantly warm out, I decided to go for a slow walk before going back to my room. I needed to take in some fresh air while trying to sort my thoughts out in conjunction with course work and the business. My mind seeming heavily occupied as to what will be asked of me during the next number of months? How will I handle the heavy burden of responsibility that now lay on my shoulders? What major decisions will be demanded of me? After walking for about half a mile or so I came across an empty bench and took a seat. My mind far from clear about what my life in the short term will now entail. Hoping it will be sooner rather than later when my father decides to return to once again govern his empire.

I was sitting there feeling it was pointless in the short term to even try sorting either my thoughts, or anything else for that matter at the present. Unable to change the situation I was trapped in and could not avoid, my mind being totally blank, my eyes taking in nothing of what they were seeing.

It was at that point I spotted some distance away a young woman in a black dress; she was sitting on the grass with her unruly mop of blonde tousled hair as usual bent over reading a book. Instantly my thoughts sprang back to life. Sitting there looking at this strange girl, for the first time I realised that each time I saw her she was dressed in black. Why had I not noticed this fact before, how on earth had I missed the dull way she dressed? Anyway why should I have noticed how she dressed? So far I had not even seen her face as it was always covered by her incredible head of unruly hair.

Then it dawned on me, this could be the girl that shared rooms with Trudy Hamilton. It is people who are usually in mourning that constantly wear black over a long period of time. I could of course be way off base. This strange girl may for reasons of her own prefer the colour black, that being the reason why she constantly wore it. Whatever the reason that was her problem, for the moment I had enough problems of my own to be thinking about.

I strolled back, having decided I would ask Jeff and Ethan to join me for dinner this evening, though I wanted to go a little earlier than normal. It struck me that I had not eaten properly since breakfast, no wonder I was now feeling hungry.

Ethan was alone when I entered our room, he informed me Jeff had gone to join Miss Hamilton for dinner and later they were going on somewhere to do course work together. Jeff had not stated where exactly that was, leaving my mind to draw its own conclusions.

"Ethan, fancy my company for dinner this evening I am no pretty face but you are welcome to pretend I am?"

We both laughed at my stupid remark; Ethan surprised me by stating: "You know damn well Johnathan Stone I will be escorting the handsomest man on campus being the envy of all the girls".

Ethan again made me laugh; he was such a comedian and the best of company when situations needed to be lighted up.

We washed, changed, and then went down to the dining hall, choosing something fairly appetizing for our evening meal. Finding a fairly discreet table as usual, it gave us the opportunity to take a good look around to see what kind of company we may line up for later.

As we were chattering in walked Jeff with his new girlfriend. They made their way over to our table, Jeff then introduced the girl at his side.

"This is Trudy Hamilton, Trudy allow me to introduce to you Ethan Phillips and Johnathan Stone."

"Good evening Mr Philips nice to meet you," Miss Hamilton said in a pleasant but matter of fact tone of voice. Then turning to me she looked up saying: "Good evening Mr Stone, I have already heard a great deal about you. I feel I know you fairly well, though not necessarily for the right reasons".

"Are you saying Jeff has been telling tales out of school?" I asked.

"Certainly not Mr Stone," Miss Hamilton replied then continued. "Jeff has said very little about either Mr Phillips or yourself. You have Mr Stone managed to build up quite a reputation for yourself without Jeff adding to it. Now if you will excuse us we have quite a bit of work to get through."

Trudy Hamilton was indeed a feisty, attractive young woman with burnished brown hair and lovely brown eyes. Appearing to be conscientious about course work, which left me to think she will go all the way in becoming a lawyer, as well as anyone's lower blanket. That made her a perfect person to encourage Jeff to succeed, if they stayed together.

"Ethan tell me, do you agree with the young lady about my reputation?"

"Rubbish," he replied, "I have never heard any girl say a word about you, let's face it Johnathan they would not talk to me would they? After all I am not your girlfriend," that remark left both of us laughing once again.

Ethan was obviously in good spirits being highly amusing. Deep down I wished he could find someone steady, someone with the same pleasant outlook to life as he had, a girl who would appreciate his kind manner and gentle banter. I could already visualise him happily married with half a dozen children. He is someone I trust and would like with me, both as a friend and colleague once we enter the world of work".

"Fancy anyone"? I asked Ethan.

"No, not really", he replied, "what about you Johnathan is there any young woman you feel like notching up on your belt this evening"?

"No Ethan I am going to give my manhood a rest tonight." That remark made Ethan burst out laughing.

As it was still fairly early I bought another coffee for us both. We should have brought some work down, yet as my mind was so full of other matters I had decided not to bother. Neither Ethan or I particularly wanted to go back to our room, instead we were just about to take a wonder around the dining hall when in walked that strange girl. Still dressed in black and with of course a head of wonderful blonde tousled hair.

I turned to Ethan asking him, "Do you know who she is?"

"Sorry Johnathan," he replied, "not a clue. I have never even noticed her before. My goodness she certainly has a mass of hair, quite like the colour though, as it reminds me of spun gold".

"How observant of you my dear friend, you are of course quite right," I said curtly. My tone of voice surprising even me, I then went on to say in a more conciliatory tone. "I have noticed her before yet so far have not seen her face. Each time I see her she has her head in some book or other with that mass of hair practically covering both her face and book".

"Ethan looked strangely at me for a flickering moment, he had not missed the curt tone in my voice though he said nothing. He continued to remark. "Maybe she keeps her face covered as she is ugly!"

"Ethan how can you say such a cruel thing even if you are right."

We were laughing at our stupid jokes when I noticed Jeff and Miss Hamilton had returned to the dining hall. They walked directly over to the table were the girl in the black dress had chosen to sit. As she still had her back to us once again I was frustratingly unable to see her face. I could though, see the length of her beautiful blonde tousled hair, which tumbled down her back. At least now I knew that she was more than likely Trudy Hamilton's roommate and that she was dressed in black due to being in mourning; not necessarily dressing in that depressing colour for the sake of it.

I was debating whether to go over and introduce myself then decided not to bother, I was not in any mood for any woman this evening, most definitely not a woman whose face I had never seen. Maybe Ethan was right, it could be possible she was incredibly ugly! One of the reasons her face always seemed to be covered. Perhaps tomorrow I will make it my business to take a closer look; after first sleeping on that thought.

The following day came and went, my thoughts being taken up with having decided I was definitely going to open up the old house. With the house not having been used for a long period of time it, would unfortunately need a serious amount of attention. I knew of only one person I could trust to take on the responsibility of that task. I had classes that day so would make phoning Bates my first priority once my last class came to an end.

Due to the difference in the time zones between California and Massachusetts proved perfect, allowing Bates to have his evening meal in peace once having spoken to him. I missed Bates more than I thought I would, the thought of having him live with the boys and I for a few months felt brilliant.

Not having seen the old house was something I must do fairly quickly, along with buying a new car, something I had promised myself in time for the new college year. Once classes were over and with all the best intentions in the world, I decided to postpone my call to Bates until a little later. My curiosity had now got the better of me. The thought of seeing the face belonging to the girl with the blonde tousle hair was haunting me. How utterly ridiculous for someone like myself to even give her a single thought, never mind allow her to play on my mind the way she did.

Annoyingly she was nowhere to be seen in the dining hall. As I felt hungry at least my journey was not a wasted one. Quickly grabbing something to eat I then phoned Bates. Asking him if all was well, I then went on to relate my plans in regard to opening up the old house. Hearing Bates voice made me feel instantly relaxed, a great deal more than I had been for the last number of days.

"Bates I am wondering if you would care to join me and to take full charge of the restoration on the old house".

"I would be delighted Mr Jonathan," came his reply.

I went on to say: "You are going to have your work cut out, I would not mind betting there needs to be a great deal of work done, the old house has been sadly neglected for many years. We are also going to have company, there will be three of us under your feet as Jeff and Ethan have agreed to join me."

Bates had of course known both Jeff and Ethan most of their lives, considering we had been my friends since childhood.

"It will be wonderful to see both you and the boys Mr Johnathan." Bates then went on to ask. "When would you like me to fly over?"

"Now, instantly," I laughed.

"Mr Johnathan, I would if I could," Bates replied then went on to say, "unfortunately my wings are grounded, they have got a bit old and rusted like me," leaving us both laughing at that sentiment.

"Please book yourself on a plane in the morning, I want you to travel first class, so please do not give me any arguments, in fact I will do it now to ensure you follow my orders".

Bates then asked: "It is Mr Stone junior I am speaking to?" Both Bates and I doubled up laughing once again.

"I look forward to seeing you Mr Johnathan and thank you for your kindness, I have never travelled first class it should be quite a pleasant experience for me to try."

"'Till tomorrow Bates, have a safe journey good night".

The excitement of seeing Bates was overwhelming making the day drag on unmercifully slow. No matter how I tried to occupy my mind, I was so relieved when it was time to leave for the airport. Still having no car of my own, I pre-booked a chauffeur driven limo rather than phoning for a taxi. Along with booking the limo I booked Bates into the local hotel, which conveniently happened to be close to the house. Explaining to the manager who I was and that I owned the hotel, the manager asked how long my guest would be staying.

"I have no idea at the present time how long Mr Bates may require his room, you will leave that availability open for him to decide and ensure he is treated with every courtesy. I will call in later when Mr Bates books in".

Bates would probably stay there until he felt the work on the bedrooms and bathrooms had been completed to his satisfaction. As I like punctuality I was pleased the hire car had arrived on time. We managed to drive to the airport fairly quickly with thankfully not too much traffic on the road, which in that instance made a welcome change. Bates was a little delayed as everyone, even today, seems to be before being able to pick up their luggage. At last he walked through the baggage lounge doors, obviously delighted that his long journey was over. We shook hands both pleased to see each other.

"Good trip?" I asked.

"First class," he said smiling. It felt so good to find ourselves laughing again at his silly jokes.

Making our way back to the car we talked about how things were back home. I had already given my instructions to take us to the hotel, so the journey gave me opportunity to ask Bates about my father. I wanted to know when he left the house.

"More or less after you did Mr Johnathan," he replied.

"Bates, did he say anything to you, anything at all about where he thought he may be going?"

"No Mr Johnathan not one single word. He requested a taxi, once it arrived I put his bags in the boot. While doing so he said: "Good bye Bates, should Johnathan require anything, no matter how small, you will please ensure he gets all the help he may need. Without saying another word your father got into the taxi, closed the door, the taxi then proceeded to drive away. Mr Johnathan I am so sorry that I am unable to enlighten you any further."

Replying I told Bates: "Not your fault Bates, I simply cannot fathom out why my father has gone to such extremes of handing over his vast empire to a youth who is still wet behind the ears. It is beyond everyone's comprehension. Yours, the Dean's; I guess everyone at our Head Office as well as across every business we own; most of all mine".

Once again Bates gave me some very sensible advice as he answered my question.

"You know Mr Johnathan, if your father did not feel you were more than capable of handling this vast responsibility. He most certainly would not have laid such a wealth or power at your feet."

"Thank you for your kind sentiments, Bates there is something more I would very much like to ask of you. Unfortunately before I do so I must tell you I will not take no for an answer."

"Most intriguing Mr Johnathan."

By this time we had arrived at the hotel. I asked the driver to please wait until I was ready to return to my hall. Looking at Bates as he booked in, I was sure he was more than ready for a good night's sleep; yet I knew he would be happy in allowing me a little time to divulge to him what I had on my mind. After he had completed the necessary procedures of booking in, and I had introduced myself to the night manager. Bates came over then asked what was it I would not take no for answer to.

Turning to him I asked, "Would you please give me fifteen minutes of your time?"

"Of course," he replied, "Mr Johnathan is there something bothering you?"

"Not exactly bothering me," I told him. "Bates I want to broker a deal with you."

"A deal! What kind of deal?" Bates asked surprised.

"I have decided I no longer wish you to call me Mr Johnathan."

Bates looked taken aback but made no comment as I continued to explain what I wanted to tell him".

"Bates I have known you since I was three, let's face it you have been more of a father to me than my real father. You have taught me so much and I owe you a great deal, though nothing to do with this deal," I laughed. "What I am now going to ask you as well as tell you is this. Bates you know I hold you in the highest regard which has brought me to this decision; I would be honoured when we are alone if you would please just call me Johnathan. In public when people are around if it makes you feel uncomfortable calling me Johnathan. Then Mr Stone will do fine."

"You are without question developing into your father's son," Bates voiced, "but becoming a much nicer person".

"Thank you Bates; I am indeed my father's son, the nice part of my nature I owe entirely to you, you have taught me well. As my father has deemed fit that I am old enough to handle his empire, then I am old enough to choose how I wish to be addressed."

Bates shook my hand then said. "You have a deal Mr Johnathan; sorry Johnathan he corrected himself".

"It would be my pleasure and delight to be on first name terms with you. By the way my name is Leon".

"Sorry Bates," I interrupted, "I would never call you by your first name. I would regard that as being totally disrespectful. Mr Bates or Bates whichever one you choose. It would be like calling my father James something that is quite out of the question".

Bates smiled, gave a little chuckle while nodding his head, then agreed by saying, "Very well if that is how you wish it to be. In return when we are alone Bates will be acceptable, Mr Bates when we have company".

"I accept Bates."

"In that case you have a deal Johnathan," he replied.

"Thank you Bates now I really must go, I am sure you are probably very tired."

We shook hands once again then I wished him good night stating, "I hope you have a decent night's sleep, I will see you in the morning Bates after breakfast".

Chapter 5

The following day I woke up early feeling in a great mood, while washing and dressing I asked Jeff and Ethan if they cared to join me for breakfast.

"Thank you but not this morning Johnathan, I have arranged to meet Trudy," Jeff informed me.

Ethan then wailed, "I have loads of work I must catch up on, before breakfast, during breakfast and straight after breakfast".

Laughing at Ethan I went on to say: "Very well I will see you both later. Straight after breakfast I am picking Bates up, then going over to see the house. After that I am hoping I will have time to pick up my new car, so I have not a clue when I will be back; before dinner I hope".

Quickly making my way to the dining hall, though not overly hungry, I knew I must eat something, as I may not have another opportunity until much later in the day. I joined the queue waiting patiently to be served, in front stood a couple of students, then my heart missed a beat! In front of the students stood the girl with the head of blonde tousled hair. As Ethan had described, it was indeed gleaming like spun gold under the lights. The two students chose what it was they wanted taking their food tray ahead of her.

Still wearing black, though I did notice at least each day the dress she wore was always clean and fresh, this one being even plainer than the one she had on last time I saw her. Moving a little closer to her I could smell her light fragrant perfume, reminding me of spring flowers. I guessed she must have been around five foot seven or eight inches tall, her figure being a little curvy. Most girls were so thin which I hated, sometimes it felt you were having sex with a bag of bones. Still with her back towards me she was about to give me an even bigger surprise, in fact quite a shock!

She slowly moved along the counter to the first person serving and in what I can only describe as the most beautiful crystalline English speaking voice I had ever heard she said, "Good morning how are you?"

There was so much sincerity in her voice I was spellbound.

"Good morning Miss, nice to see you this morning," the man who was serving her answered.

"Thank you," she replied, then continued to exchange pleasantries with him for a few moments more. Moving on to the next person serving who this time happened to be Italian, the same type of conversation was once again exchanged, this time in fluent Italian. As we moved along the counter it was the turn of the Greek boy, being delighted she was speaking to him in his native tongue without fault. Pleasantries were exchanged to the Spanish server, until at last she came to the end of the line.

The final server just happened to be French. Naturally she spoke to him in fluent French, her accent perfect. Listening to her conversing with him, her voice sounded exquisite. He offered to carry her tray to a table of her choice, as her arms were full with a large number of books in them.

"Thank you very much," she said, "that is very kind of you, I am so very grateful".

Listening to her talking in so many different languages with such charm, left me feeling totally mesmerized. Then as she walked towards her table I could see she had long legs that were joined to well-tapered ankles and narrow feet.

As I spoke both perfect French and Spanish at least I could understand what it was she was saying. Having a fairly basic understanding of Italian, with even less Greek under my belt left me feeling more than frustrated. It was her English accent that I found totally fascinating, now without exception I needed to see her face, until I did I knew I would not be satisfied.

Not having the time to investigate any further what had now become of deep interest to me. I ate breakfast quickly, beginning to resent that I had to leave. Who was this intriguing girl? Dear Lord what did she look like? The fact she was English with that beautiful accent, the tone of her voice sounding so musical. I knew instinctively that I could never tire of listening to her talking.

So now I knew her height. Due to her dresses not being fitted it was still hard to judge the exact contours of her figure. The length of her long legs joining a pair of lovely slim ankles. I guessed her feet may have been just a little bigger than my mothers. The colour of her amazing hair, the fact she was multilingual, speaking each language fluently left me enthralled. Her manners I am sure were impeccable, including the fact her place of birth being England. The one thing missing about her that I desperately needed to know, and had so far eluded me dear Lord was her face.

Eating breakfast far too quickly knowing there was so much I needed to do. I had arranged for the hire car once again to pick me up. Apologising to the driver as he stood waiting for me as I was now running overly late. We drove to the hotel where I found Bates also waiting.

"I am extremely sorry for being late Bates, I hope you will forgive me."

"Not a problem, I was just enjoying some fresh air Johnathan," he said, looking for my reaction as he called me by my first name.

I gave him a huge grin, then said: "Your words sound more than perfect".

As we drove towards the house Bates and I started guessing about what we may find. We arrived at the historic, elegant house, which had belonged to my family for well over a century or two, maybe even longer. Not having exact details for the moment, it was hard for me to be accurate. From the outside the house looked to be in pretty good condition. Opening the door the cobwebs greeted us; there were a number of dustsheets covering a few odd pieces of furniture. I loved the wooden floors, which would look amazing once cleaned and polished. Bates opened a couple of the shutters, allowing in much needed light, which enabled us to see at close quarters the general condition of the walls, plaster work, and whatever else may have needed to be done.

We spent a good couple of hours discussing a great many details, which we felt would be necessary in bringing this lovely old house back up to its former glory and ensured it became a comfortable residence to live in once again. Seeing the inside of this wonderful house, I made the decision that once the majority of work had been completed, especially the bedrooms, I would then ask Bates if it was habitable enough to move into. Taking a look at the condition of the house at present told me my father had never spent a day in it, which quite surprised me. How very different we were as people.

At least I knew Jeff, Ethan and I, would very much appreciate and enjoy living here during our following years at Harvard. Bates and I left the house with so many ideas running through our minds. Naturally all our ideas had to be sympathetic to the history and fabric of that wonderful old building. I would leave the entire restoration in Bates capable hands, knowing he will ensure a perfect job would be carried out. Our next stop was to pick up my car.

"Something very large and comfortable", I told Bates, "A car were I can enjoy the company of the opposite sex". Bates as always listening very carefully to all I had to say to him.

With a smile on his face he gently replied, "I appreciate Johnathan you are a very healthy red blooded young man and that you find the opposite sex, should we say, very desirable or would you put it more strongly".

"I would put it this way Bates. All women as far as I am concerned are no more than whores. They want your body and bank account. They willingly go to bed with you, enjoy your body then expect you to pay to take them out to dinner, or any other meal they can get out of you. Some should we say may have the ability to persuade you to buy them gifts, even try to entrap you into marriage if they can! Which heaven forbid I will not commit to for many more years to come? Yes I love and enjoy having sex, my appetite for woman I do not think is any different to that of any other young mans".

"You do practice safe sex?" Bates asked.

"Yes I do, remembering perfectly well what you expressed to me. You know something Bates, not having safe sex, as you put it, is the one thing I am looking forward to once I find the right person. That will be if and when I eventually decide to marry."

"Please forgive me Johnathan for disagreeing with you, but not all women are should we say inclined that way. You may find a delightfully nice girl who just likes to be treated like a lady, one who would expect a gentleman to pick up the bill, buy her a birthday or Christmas present. Maybe you think that is a little old fashion, but it can be the case."

"Bates, I have not met one single girl, woman, or any other word you would care to use to describe a member of the opposite sex, who so far has offered to share a bill with me for food or anything else for that matter? Truthfully, there are at present no comparisons for me to judge by. Women are women. Each one more than happy to give me their favours, which of course I am most grateful for, but I am sorry Bates I do not think the kind of girl you are talking about even exists."

We reached the car showroom to pick up the Lincoln I had decided to buy a few days earlier. I thanked the driver of the limo then dismissed him. The manager of the car showroom appeared to be waiting patiently for our arrival, "Good afternoon Mr Stone nice to see you," he greeted me holding out his hand as I walked into the showroom; then went on to say: "Your car is ready sir if you care to take a look around it then go for a drive".

"No thank you I am in a hurry so will miss taking it for a test drive."

Bates looked at me, saying nothing as usual.

"Very well Mr Stone if that is your wish."

He then went on to say: "We do of course have some paper work to complete then the car is yours".

"Thank you, let us get on with it," came my reply. Within the hour Bates and I were driving towards the hotel, it felt not just exhilarating to be back behind the wheel, but even more fun to be driving a car I had purchased instead of one my father had bought for me.

We were close to a small French restaurant I knew, "hungry Bates, fancy something to eat?" I asked.

"Absolutely" Bates replied. We pulled into the small car park belonging to the restaurant, it was nice to find a decent restaurant that did not require you to pre-book a table during the day. The restaurant was quiet enabling us to talk. After we ordered I decided to ask Bates about what had happened to Mrs Bates and their baby, then changed my mind. Instead I decided to him tell about the strange girl with the tousled blonde hair while we ate".

"Would you say the food is excellent Bates? The company is undoubtedly perfect," I said making us both laugh.

"Johnathan how is your course going? Are you really enjoying it?" Bates asked with concern in his voice.

"Bates," I replied, "if I was just some ordinary young man instead of Johnathan Stone, I would love nothing more than to stay here for the rest of my life. I love everything there is to love about Harvard. 'A seat of learning where dreams unfold and futures begin'. Truthfully I cannot find one thing that I dislike; I dread the day I have to leave, yet I know my life is already planned out for me".

We had eaten well, both Bates and I where now in a relaxed mood. It was then I thought about asking Bates about the loss of his wife and baby. Bates went silent for a few moments, maybe deciding if this was the correct time to convey to me how he came to lose his family. He obviously decided it was, as his voice softened with emotion, he gently went on to tell me about the family he loved and lost.

"Beth and I were far too young when we met. We fell in love as young people do. I had just left college, though for other reasons. The plan then was to work hard enabling us to get a little place together, naturally it did not matter how small it may have been as we had no intention of starting a family. Unfortunately Beth became pregnant and as I was passionately in love with her I had every intention of supporting her. I told Beth that we would marry as quickly as possible and that she must not be upset. We did indeed marry, with very little fuss thank goodness; it is after all what ordinary people living a very ordinary life do. I lost Beth and my son due to complications during childbirth. The heartbreak I felt Johnathan, ran so deep! I decided I would never marry again. Naturally being a man from time to time I to have my need of the fairer sex. Even today you do not have the priority in that department.

"Johnathan, when I came to live in your house, I felt very lucky that your father had taken me on, as I had very little at that time to call my own. When you and I first met you were a huge bonus to my life. The delightful small child I met that day made me think had my son lived, it would have pleased me greatly had he grown to be like you."

"Thank you Bates, I am deeply honoured to hear you say that, of course I am awfully sorry you lost your family. I hope I will always make you proud of me."

Bates then continued.

"I am sure Johnathan it will not be very long before you find what it is you are looking for in a woman, which in turn will ensure one day you have a child of your own; which you will also grow to love."

I dropped Bates off at the hotel, having given him my full authority to purchase everything that was needed for the restoration on the house. Expressing to him that should there be any problems he must let me know immediately.

"We will speak shortly Bates until then take care."

Waving goodbye, I felt quite excited at the thought of showing off my super car to Jeff and Ethan. I loved driving at the best of times, now having this type of car became even more of a pleasure. Perfect for what I had in mind. How many women will this car eventually allow me to entertain? Just for a moment, Bates thoughts about a nice girl struck me. Do such girls exist? They may have done in his world, for the moment they do not in mine.

The following few days proved to be nothing but study work and sleep, as exams were due. The boys loved the car, which naturally pleased me to hear, after all there was nothing about it that was not pleasing. Jeff, Ethan and I went for a couple of drives, including going over to see Bates at the house. The same routine continued, it was vital I prepared well for the first year exams. Even the intriguing girl with the blonde tousled hair seemed to have disappeared of the radar; I guess she also knew how important the exams were.

The end of first year drew to a close; the last twelve months had been momentous. They say it is a good job we do not know what is ahead of us. Who would have guessed within a year I would not only have lost one of my parents, but become one of the most powerful and wealthy young men in the country? Regardless that it was for the present only temporary.

Bates had the restoration of the house well in hand, in fact it was coming along quicker than I had expected. Jeff, Ethan and I, would very shortly be able to move in even though there were still a number of odd jobs remaining. We would naturally try to ensure we stayed out of the way of the crew Bates had employed. To see the completion and refurbishment of this wonderful old house left me feeling exhilarated.

Gradually we were able to start the process of moving in, which became quite a chore, yet lots of fun. Looking at the stuff we transported over to the house, made me question how we ever managed to move around the cramped conditions we were now leaving behind. Living, sleeping and working in those small rooms for a whole year seemed amazing. This old historic house now offered a number of beautiful large airy bedrooms for each of us to choose from, the joy of being able to stretch out was a privilege. It provided a large number of rooms to work in, it also gave the boys and I the privacy we each required should we wish to bring a woman home.

To celebrate my ninetieth birthday I asked Bates if he would like to join Jeff, Ethan and I.

"Thank you very much for asking Johnathan," he replied. "But absolutely not. I will make an early dinner here for the four of us if that would suit you then you must go and have an enjoyable evening out with your friends. You do not need a nursemaid".

Laughing as always at Bates sense of humour, I thanked him then went on to say: "That would be perfect maybe you and I could go out to dinner at a later date".

"I shall hold you to that Johnathan, thank you."

Bates was as good as his word making a splendid dinner, giving the four of us an opportunity to indulge in a great deal of laughing before leaving the house.

Ethan had suggested a couple of places for us to go to where he knew there would be lots of girls.

"Thought we would try to find you a birthday present for the night," he said, regardless that I had told him my policy was that I would endeavour to find my own women.

Jeff went to buy the drinks as Ethan and I made our way to a table. Taking a quick look around Ethan was quite right, there were quite an array of reasonable looking women to choose from.

"Well Johnathan," Ethan asked, "anything in here you fancy?"

"Maybe, we will see later," I replied.

Jeff brought our drinks over settling himself down, "have you seen Trudy"? I asked him.

"Yes she and Lucinda have now relocated to their house," he replied.

Lucinda! So now I had a name to match the other facts I knew about her. I had to find a way of seeing what she looked like. Lucinda! It certainly was a beautiful name meaning; 'The Goddess of light'. Would her face now prove to live up to my expectations, or would she indeed be ugly, as Ethan had previously suggested. All of a sudden I had lost interest in any of the women around the room, my mind focusing relentlessly on my elusive prey, as that is what this girl had now become.

"Jeff, may I ask which library Trudy and yourself would recommend for the coming year?" Both Ethan and Jeff looking at me as if I had just arrived from outer space.

"You all right Johnathan?" Ethan asked. "Why would you want to be thinking and talking about libraries tonight?"

"No idea, the thought just popped into my mind," I replied.

"I will let you know," Jeff promised. "In the meantime Johnathan come on its time to party".

"Ethan found himself some company for the evening, telling us he would make his own way home."

Jeff and I had a couple of further drinks then decided to call it a night.

"Funny Johnathan I thought you may have found someone to entertain you this evening."

"Someone already has Jeff." Jeff looked at me strangely but said nothing.

Jeff called upstairs to both Ethan and I stating he was going over to the library to meet Trudy. "Do either of you fancy coming with me?" He asked.

"Be down in a minute," I replied.

With no response coming from Ethan, we guessed he was well out of it, having retuned home in the early hours of the morning.

At long last, would it now be possible to solve the mystery that had been plaguing me for months? Why did I not feel indifferent, even a little less curious than I actually was feeling about seeing the face of a girl I had as yet never even spoken to?

"We drove over in silence until a few minutes before arriving at the library when Jeff asked. "Is there anything bothering you Johnathan?"

"Not at all," came my reply, "why would you think there is?"

Jeff then went on to relate his thoughts to me by saying

"Johnathan we have been friends nearly all our lives. I hope I know you fairly well so forgive me for saying so but I cannot believe you have lost interest in women. Well not lost interest as such, you just do not seem to have found any lately, should I say as you normally do."

All I could do was to laugh, then went on to reassure him by saying. "Please stop worrying there is nothing for you to worry over Jeff".

By this time we drew up at our destination, as I parked the car I turned to Jeff telling him I loved women as I always had.

"Jeff you know my rules about women, they must be beautiful, dumb and a damn good lay. There are hundreds of women like that, more than plenty for me to choose from as and when I am ready."

"That is a relief to hear," Jeff replied and continued by saying "I was beginning to worry Johnathan, especially as you did not find yourself any company the night of your birthday".

"On the contrary Jeff I found a Goddess to interest me." Jeff raised an eyebrow but did not continue with this line of questioning.

We entered the library, would my mysterious prey at last be here? We walked further into the room until at last Jeff spotted Trudy Hamilton. There, sitting opposite Miss Hamilton with her back to us, was the girl I had come to see. There was no mistaking the head of beautiful tousled blonde hair. My heart felt it had missed a beat, as this time instead of being dressed in black; she was wearing a plain white dress.

Just as we approached the table at which both Trudy Hamilton and her roommate, whom I now knew as Lucinda, we're sitting. Lucinda slowly rose from her chair to find some book or other. Damn, now I would have to wait until she returned. I could not help watching the way she elegantly walked, had she not been a student she could well have been a model. As she raised her head up her beautiful blond hair magnificently fell down her back. Jeff being so delighted to once again be in Miss Hamilton's company, never even noticed my prey move away.

Trudy Hamilton momentarily distracted my attention as she looked up seeing both Jeff and I standing there. Miss Hamilton gave Jeff a quick kiss then turned to me saying. "Good morning Mr Stone happy birthday".

Before I could thank her for her kind wishes, she then continued her voice now quite stern. "When my friend returns Mr Stone, you will conduct yourself, if you are able to, like a gentleman just for once in your life. As I am going to introduce you to a real lady. Let me make it quite plain Mr Stone, she is totally off limits to someone like yourself. Do you understand?"

I had not expected that kind of statement. Not from a woman! Not from anyone! How dare she speak to me in that manner? Had she not been Jeff's girlfriend I doubt I would have capitulated so easily to her wishes. In fact I knew damn well I would not.

Trudy Hamilton sounded like my father giving out his commands. Jeff saw my face as we sat down, knowing full well I was blazing mad at what had just been said to me. Who the hell did Trudy Hamilton think she was? Daring to speak to me like that. Not just to talk to me in that manner, but in that tone of voice in front of my friend. Did she think I was a five-year-old who she thought she could scold? Then dare to go on and tell me what I can and cannot do as far as women were concerned. Those words infuriating me even more. Once I had Jeff on his own I would ensure his girlfriend never spoke to me in that condescending manner ever again. The men in my family give orders, we do not take them!

Seething with anger at Trudy Hamilton's obnoxious statement left me not just furious, but no longer inclined to enjoy anyone's company, I excused myself as I walk away until I calmed down, leaving both Jeff and his overly bossy girlfriend looking at me in surprise.

I found myself walking in the same direction of the girl whose face I was longing to see. Having walked no more than a few yards I stopped. There just ahead of me, sitting at one of the tables with a book as usual opened in front of her was the girl I desperately wanted to meet? Pulling a chair from the table close by which was a little to the left of my prey, hoping I would not disturb her yet wanting to attract her attention. Fortunately for me she was deep in thought in a world of learning and therefore did not notice my presence. Opening my book, as if I had every intention of doing some reading, I sat there very still, unable to take my eyes off her.

The weather being still very close and with all that wonderful hair hanging over her shoulders, she may well indeed have been feeling rather warm. Suddenly, slowly she lifted some of her glorious hair from off her face and neck. Her hands, having long thin fingers, had all the grace and elegance of a ballet dancer. Her gesture now revealing to me what I had longed to see all these months.

Dear Lord! My heart was pounding as I saw her exquisite long neck that reminded me of a graceful swan. She had translucent, clear skin, which must be so soft to kiss. Then looking at her lovely face her parents had named her well, she did indeed have the face of a goddess. I took in every detail from her arched well-shaped eyebrows to her small straight little nose. Her lips perfectly proportioned as cupids bow, they were lips I wanted to possess here and now. The one thing I was missing was the colour of her eyes, covered as they were with thick long black eye lashes. They were still lowered while she sat serenely continuing to read her book.

Sitting there mesmerised just as I had been previously in the dining hall, once again I was utterly spellbound by her. It was as if she had entrapped me with invisible golden chains she had brought with her from Olympus. Entranced I continued to sit. It was of no consequence how long I needed to wait. Now I was as eager as a child waiting for Christmas morning.

All I wanted now was to see the colour of her eyes. Twenty minutes or so later, once again with the same graceful movement, she gently closed her book. With another slow elegant movement just as before, she pushed her hair back off her face allowing me for the first time to see her incredible large blue-grey eyes. I could barely believe the colour of them as they mirrored my own. As Lucinda gracefully stood up I observed the perfect contour of her breasts. She saw me sitting looking directly into her entrancing face. I smiled at her. Her skin turned a soft shade of pink, yet steadily she held my gaze returning my smile. Within seconds my goddess walked away.

I was beguiled, totally intoxicated! Had Dionysus himself tried to drown me, not with wine, but in the ethereal beauty I had just beheld? Why had it taken a year for me to uncover the secret of her indescribable beauty? What a fool I had been to have wasted so much time. Damn Trudy Hamilton, I do not need her to introduce me to any woman, lady or no lady...

What did Miss Trudy Hamilton mean exactly, why did she refer to my goddess as a lady? Does Lucinda have a title as she is English? As that is the only kind of lady I know of. If she does not have a title, then I doubt very much with her face and figure that she had not already had a number of lovers who she has taken to her bed, it was an interesting project for me to find out, better still how fast I will take her to my bed. This time I will ensure I do not wait a year.

Walking back towards the table where Jeff, the obnoxious Miss Hamilton plus Lucinda were sitting. Strangely I no longer had the wish to be formally introduced to Lucinda, nor did I want to re-join Jeff or Miss Trudy Hamilton. As I went to walk past them I looked directly at Lucinda, giving her the most indignant look as I could manage with the thought that she was no different than all the other whores that had so far entered my life.

"Johnathan," Jeff called as I continued to walk past the table.

"I will talk to you at home," I replied, then walked away.

I was about to drive home then changed my mind, feeling still as mad as hell at having been treated like a five-year-old by nothing more than my best friends whoring lower blanket. Who the hell did she think she was, telling me how to behave morally? Especially when she was sleeping with my best friend as and when she felt like it. The fact Jeff was now thinking with his penis instead of his brains, putting up with her rudeness is beyond me. I guess all was not completely lost, at least I had seen what I came to see.

Now I felt deflated, yet did not understand why. Changing my mind again I turned the car around and headed for home. The feeling I had been kicked while down consumed me. As usual it now seemed as good a time as any for me to have a word with Bates. He would try to understand the emotions, which were now filling my thoughts. I found Bates in the kitchen making coffee for the last of the workmen. Naturally surprised to see me, he asked if I would also like a cup of coffee.

"Should we go into the small sitting room or is there somewhere else you would rather talk?" Bates asked, instinctively knowing when I had something on my mind. Somehow he always managed to sense if I was disturbed.

"Thank you, coffee in the small sitting room would be perfect," I replied. "Mugs rather than cups would be welcome," I continued.

"Perfect not a problem, fancy a cookie to go with your coffee?" Bates asked smiling.

"No, but thank you for asking," I replied.

We walked into the small, now beautifully decorated sitting room, which along with the rest of the restoration work had now been fully completed; leaving me to feel absolutely delighted. Bates had ensured everything had been carried out to the very highest of standards.

"The house looks amazing Bates. Thank you so much for the care and time you have taken to ensure we all now have a lovely home to live in."

"Thank you Johnathan that is most kind of you to say so, though that it is not the reason why we are now sitting here."

"No Bates you are quite right, I am as mad as hell at Jeff and his damn girlfriend who I am growing to dislike intensely! To top it all, after having taken me a year; today at long last I saw the face of the girl who I told you about when we stopped at the French restaurant for dinner. Bates she has the face and figure of a goddess, even her name which is Lucinda is that of a goddess. She is everything I could possibly desire in a woman. That for me is the problem. The thought that someone has already made her into a woman and probably she has had so many men in her life. Touching her, kissing her beautiful body, caressing her breasts with their grubby hands. Damn it Bates I feel the gods are tormenting me, driving me insane with jealousy! They send me someone who looks like Aphrodite, yet she is no different to all the other whores in my life."

"Jeff's lower blanket, who likes to give her orders as my father does, had the audacity to tell me she is going to introduce me to a lady, who it turns out to be none other than my goddess. Miss Trudy Hamilton then tells me to try to behave like gentleman towards her, not just to behave like a gentleman but that she is off limits to me. Please can you explain to me why would Trudy Hamilton, of all people dare to tell me to keep away from a woman, who probably already has had a serious amount of untold love affairs? Yet still Miss Hamilton calls her lady!"

"Johnathan, have you thought she may be a lady by birth?" Bates questioned.

"Yes, of course I have given that a passing thought. Her morals though do not reflect her title," I replied.

"If she is a lady by birth then she is a lady regardless of her morals," Bates said then continued. "Johnathan, you may be jumping to conclusions, what do you know about this goddess of yours besides the fact she is incredibly beautiful?"

"Bates, just what do you mean? I have told you all I know of her. Obviously she is as old as I am, there may be a couple of months between us. Her head is always in a book, which must mean she is exceptionally cleaver besides being multilingual. Oh Bates I have been over everything she is, it is what she is not that is driving me mad."

"Wrong Johnathan," Bates said in a firmer voice. "You know very little about this lady who you tell me is called Lucinda. You are surmising that she is, should I say, experienced in love. You used the word probably yet you have no information to confirm that. How can you know anything about her when you have not even been introduced to her?"

"Bates are you trying to tell me that someone who looks like a goddess could in this day and age still possibly still be as pure as driven snow?"

"I am telling you just that Johnathan," Bates replied, going on to say: "Until you find out for yourself you will never know. Should we now talk about Jeff and your dislike for Miss Hamilton? Jeff looks to be happy and content in his relationship with her, and Miss Hamilton in turn sounds like a loyal friend to Miss Lucinda. Johnathan you do have a pretty awful reputation so they tell me, as a man who likes to; if you will forgive me for saying so, bed the ladies then run. Perhaps you could try to have a different outlook on the relationship Jeff and Miss Hamilton have. They do appear to be very much in love. Not everyone Johnathan thinks the way you do, in fact most people have a complete different outlook to life compared to you.

"Your emotions Johnathan have had a pretty rough ride, especially with your father allowing you such power and money and you have handled all that so incredibly well. I am not sure though what it is you are looking for in a woman or why you regard them all with such contempt."

"Bates I am stunned by your revelation, I have never known you to be wrong on anything, yet now you are asking me to believe there may be a miniscule chance that what Trudy Hamilton has said could possibly be true?"

"I would give it better odds than that," Bates intervened.

"Bates you have given me fresh hope, you truly have. I will endeavour to cultivate Lucinda's friendship and yes, I will behave like a perfect gentleman. Not because Miss bossy-boots Trudy Hamilton insists, but because I truly want to know all there is about that exquisite goddess."

"Anymore coffee left in the pot," I asked, I felt a huge weight for the moment had been lifted off my shoulders. "Bates you are amazing, even the anger I felt towards Jeff for allowing Trudy Hamilton to speak to me in that manner is now subsiding. I will of course still have a word with him, Miss Hamilton is not getting away scot free under any circumstances. I do still have my self-respect to consider, which I would never give up for anyone."

"I am so pleased Johnathan that you are feeling in a better frame of mind," Bates replied with a laugh, then went on to say, "I hate seeing you so upset especially when it comes to your personal feelings. The library would indeed be a good place to once again meet Miss Lucinda or Lady Lucinda as the case may be. Perhaps you could invite her out to dinner. You could of course find yourself having to apologise, even do some pretty good grovelling, then hope this certain young lady will forgive your rudeness".

"I have never apologised to a woman in my life, if I am honest now thinking about it I am not quite sure I would actually be capable of doing so. This is a situation Bates I am going to play by ear, if she is a whore it will not matter, on the other hand if she is all I hope she will be; I will endeavour to give her the world."

I decided I quite liked this small sitting room, it was bright yet with a feeling of being cosy. Definitely a room I was going to make my private space. A room I would endeavour to work from, also from now on should anyone wished to talk to me, this was the room they will be invited to do so in. I followed Bates into the kitchen then told him of my wishes about the small sitting room.

"Jolly good idea," he said, "you need a personal room besides your bedroom to call your own."

Bates knew how much I hated offices; regardless I would spend a great deal of my life in one. Maybe offices at work are totally different to having one in your home.

"When Jeff arrives home Bates, please ask him to come and see me in the small sitting room."

"Yes Mr Stone," he answered to which we both burst out laughing.

"Did I really sound that bossy?" I asked still laughing,

"Yes sir, you did," Bates replied laughing. It was wonderful having Bates living with me once again, I dreaded the day when he would have to return to California.

Jeff retuned home late in the evening, Bates informed him that I wished to speak to him, then directed him to where he knew I would be. I assumed that Bates had also informed him that the small sitting room had gained a place of importance in my life. Respecting my wishes Jeff knocked on the door, I shouted to Jeff to come in.

"Hello Jeff had a good day? Please come and sit down as I would like to have a word with you."

"Johnathan, I am terribly sorry about Trudy's outburst this morning. I had no idea what came over her until I questioned her after you left."

I sat there and said nothing allowing Jeff to continue.

"Apparently Johnathan, Lucinda Osborn is a lady in every sense of the word, a lady by birth and still a virgin. Trudy is naturally very protective of her, perhaps you could say overly protective. Trudy is scared she will be taken advantage of by someone like yourself, what she calls a womaniser. Someone who will hurt her then run. Trudy has every intention of ensuring that does not happen, due to Lucinda's personal circumstances, which she did not go into with me."

Listening to what Jeff was now relating to me I asked Jeff if he was telling me the truth, or was he trying to cover up for his girlfriend's rude behaviour?

"Johnathan I am telling you what Trudy has related to me, I see no reason for her to lie to me," Jeff replied. Naturally Jeff would not think of lying to me, funnily in this instance I doubted Trudy Hamilton was lying either.

"Very well Jeff, I want you to give Trudy a message from me. I want you to tell her that if she wishes to continue to enjoy being part of my circle, she will never speak to me in that tone of voice again. I will not tolerate it from anyone no matter who they may be. Talking to me in that manner is off the scale of politeness. I will capitulate for it this time with Trudy being your girlfriend. I will also respect her wishes by giving my solemn promise to behave as a perfect gentleman at all times towards Lady Lucinda Osborn."

Jeff looked at me as if I had lost my mind, little did he realise that is exactly what I had already done from the moment I saw my goddesses beautiful face. Even more so now knowing she was also an untouched virgin!

As far as I was concerned Lucinda now belonged to me.

I went on to say: "You may also tell Trudy if it is a formal introduction she wishes so be it! You will introduce me to Lady Lucinda Osborn by my full surname which you are well aware of".

Standing on formality, which I hated; gave me an equal opportunity to that of Lady Lucinda, if that is what she must for the present be called. Being a very distant relative of a long ago American President, being able to trace my linage should with luck, hold me in good stead. Formality or not I knew I would make Lucinda mine, for the moment I had no idea how, all I did know was that I needed to possess her no matter what Trudy Hamilton thought, or how hard she would try to protect her from me.

One thing for sure, I was not my father and I had no intention of marrying anyone being so young. Lady or no lady! I wanted a great deal more from a woman than just a title. Deciding things would be done my way, I told Jeff I would arrange everything to ensure I was introduced to Lady Lucida Osborn formally.

I asked Jeff if Trudy, Lady Lucinda Osborn and himself would care to join me for dinner at Le Gavoroche on Saturday evening. That I would be delighted to have them as my guests, I will of course ask Ethan if he wishes to join us, who knows he may even have found someone he would care to bring along. Until then I needed to concentrate on my college work and how to make my goddess mine.

My life for the moment was full and quietly calm. I loved athletics, keeping my body healthy enabling me to enjoy women even more. Course work as usual was not a problem to me, classes though a little crowded, were both informative and enjoyable. I loved my home life having Bates on hand to talk to, and I was thrilled with my car. As to my father, I am still hoping he will shortly be home. The thought of being released from the responsibility of running his empire would be such an immense comfort to me, taking a huge burden off my shoulders. That time cannot come quick enough. My main concern for the foreseeable future was the goddess of my dreams and my all consuming desire for her.

The following morning I went to find Bates before either Ethan or Jeff came down for breakfast. I wanted to inform Bates of Jeff's revelation that Lucinda was indeed a titled lady, not only a lady but the fact she was still untouched by any man.

"That of course will not stop me from trying to make her mine should I wish to do so Bates."

Bates looked at me then said, "Take it easy Johnathan, be careful you do not do something you may come to regret. It is not for me to lecture you, but if you would like to take my advice I would advise you to take things easy, as you still know nothing about lady Lucida. Try to cultivate her confidence, it will enable you to find out what kind of interesting even fascinating person she may be. Johnathan, it would be wise to do this before you foolishly decide to fulfil your desires, with time and patience you will eventually come to know all there is to know about this young lady you seem infatuated with and who it seems in return has indeed already enchanted you".

"Why is it Bates you are always right with your sensible advice? It never fails to amaze me how you frequently manage to guide me into taking the right direction. I will once again take on board what you have said. Thank you, now I am starving, definitely ready for my breakfast."

I dressed with great care, wanting to make a lasting impression. My reputation was not at stake but my background was, thanks to Trudy Hamilton's ridiculous attitude. Still if she wanted to behave like a jumped up snob so be it. I had agreed to her terms and would honour them in full.

Jeff had left the house earlier to pick up both Trudy and Lucinda then take them on to the restaurant. Ethan amazingly had found a girl and he asked if he could bring her with him. This was going to be a night of boring introductions; still a deal is a deal.

Bates stood waiting for me at the front door, "if I may say so," he said, "you do look incredibly handsome tonight Johnathan; found yourself a special date?"

Laughing at Bates remark eased a little of the tension I had been feeling since I started to dress.

"Thank you Bates; let's hope I return home a great deal happier than I am feeling at the moment."

"Not because you have misbehaved I hope," Bates replied making me laugh yet again.

"No I have given my word damn it," we both laughed as I left the house. This time driving my car with anticipation at what this evening would bring.

"Good evening Mr Stone how are you this evening," Trudy Hamilton greeted me. I looked at Jeff who then stepped in to correct Miss Hamilton.

"Trudy may I introduce to you Mr Johnathan Robin Jefferson Stone. Johnathan is a direct descendent of President Thomas Jefferson."

The altercation I had with Jeff over Trudy Hamilton was well worth that moment. Her mouth dropped open, her face a picture of exquisite embarrassment. I turned my head to the person next to her. Standing there looking on with great interest as well as looking incredibly beautiful was of course Lucinda. Turning back to look at Trudy Hamilton I politely said, "Nice to meet you again Miss Hamilton".

Trudy Hamilton being totally lost for words simply said: "Mr Jefferson Stone, may I introduce you to Lady Lucinda Elizabeth Alexander Fortescue Osborn".

"I am sorry my name goes on forever," my goddess said with a beautiful smile then continued to say: "Please just call me Lucinda".

"Delighted to meet you Lucinda, like yourself my surname is rather pompous, my background even more so. That is why I am plainly known as Mr Stone; Johnathan to my friends."

"Hello Johnathan I do hope we can become friends."

The last thing I wanted was to be was Lucinda's friend, her lover yes but most definitely not her friend. Ethan was the last to arrive, apologising for being a little late.

"So sorry Johnathan," he said.

"Nothing to be sorry about," I told him. "Ethan are you going to introduce me to your delightful companion?"

"Oh yes, sorry Johnathan this is Poppy, Poppy Penbrook."

"Hello Poppy pleased to meet you."

"Poppy this is Johnathan Stone."

"Good evening Mr Stone, nice to meet you at long last."

I looked at Ethan who smiled then said, "Will tell you later Johnathan, if that is acceptable".

"I rather feel Ethan there have been enough formal introductions, should we go into dinner."

The food was superb, the company perfect, Lucinda intoxicating! I kept my promise by keeping my conversation light, naturally asking Lucida general questions of how she was finding her life at Harvard including her course work. I wanted to know so much about her but this was not the time or the place to ask. The evening ended better than I had expected everyone seemed relaxed having done a great deal of laughing.

As I wished Lucida good night I decided to not just shake her hand but to gently kiss it, her skin so soft against my lips. I would have given a king's ransom to have kissed her further.

"Good night Johnathan it has been interesting meeting you," she said looking directly into my eyes.

"Good night Lucinda, I hope we will meet again shortly." Trudy Jeff, and Lucinda then left, making their own way home.

Only interesting! No woman had ever said that to me before. If that remark was the result of behaving like a gentleman, than what would her comment be if I behaved towards her the way Johnathan Stone normally behaves? Or in her case wanted to behave.

Ethan continued to see a great deal of Poppy Penbrook, he had indeed become quite taken with her. No brains, just a very sweet girl at least that was the impression she gave me. I did wonder where he came to meet her but decided not to ask. It was time I took the initiative to ask Lucinda out once again. I must try to find a way of doing so without alerting Trudy Hamilton, who I came to think upon as Lucinda's guard dog knowing about it, as that is what I felt she had become hanging around her constantly.

It certainly was not going to be an easy task, the way around my problem was to ask Jeff if he would allow me to treat Trudy Hamilton and himself to dinner. I could of course tell him the truth, which would then entail Jeff having to deceive someone he loved. A position I did not want to put him into, or had any intention of doing so. Jeff was delighted to accept my offer. After all how could the pompous Miss Hamilton, not be delighted at the thought of once again returning to Le Gavroche".

I followed Jeff then sat waiting in my car until both he and Trudy Hamilton left the house that both she and

Lucida were now living in. Stepping into the hallway, I asked one of the other students if they would please inform Lucinda I was here. The student returned with the message stating, "Lucinda asked if you will please take a seat she would be down shortly".

After waiting fifteen minutes Lucida eventually came down. She looked enchanting, her attire simple yet elegant. Dressed in a clean, crisp white blouse and navy skirt, her shoes, purse and cardigan were also in navy. I doubted no matter what clothing she wore she would always look as if she had just stepped out of a fashion magazine.

Endeavouring to continue to behave like a gentleman for the time being, I politely said, "good evening Lucida, would you care to join me for something to eat"?

Lucinda then gave a small musical laugh while thanking me, going on to say: "I was expecting you", she laughed again.

"I am sorry you have me at a loss, how did you know I would come over this evening?"

"Elementary! Mr Stone. La Gavroche is not normally a restaurant where Jeff and Trudy would frequent regularly in such a short space of time."

I could not help but laugh at that statement, then told her, "I admire your cleaver deduction I hold my hands up to you. To be honest I needed to find a way of seeing you, not by inviting you to an over pretentious place; but somewhere quiet where we can talk".

"I would like that very much Johnathan thank you, do you have anywhere special in mind?" Lucinda asked.

"Do you like Italian? If so I know a delightful small bistro which serves the most wonderful Italian food."

"That sounds so yummy; I shall take you at your word the food is to die for," Lucinda replied.

"I hope we do not die from it," I commented, which set us both off laughing.

We did a lot of laughing, more laughing than eating. Regardless the food was of the highest standard, but I had very little appetite.

"Lucinda will you allow me to take you out again? This evening has been immensely enjoyable, sadly I still know so very little about you and there is a great deal I wish to know."

"Thank you Johnathan I rather think I should like that very much," she replied. Lucinda then added, "As you are paying for this evening perhaps next time you would allow me to take you out for afternoon tea".

I loved not just the sound of her voice, but the quirky English way she expressed herself.

"Afternoon tea, now that is going to be a new experience for me. I do not ever remember formally sitting down to drink tea," I told her.

Lucida started to laugh and continued to do so for a minute or two then said. "I am so sorry Johnathan I do apologise," then she continued laughing once again. It must have been another couple of minutes until she managed to stop laughing, which by this time I was laughing with her as her laugh was so infectious.

I did not have a clue what we were laughing about until Lucinda regained her composure then said: "Oh Johnathan do please forgive my outburst, I am extremely sorry if I appear rude. I simply have to tell you, people do not just sit formally drinking tea in dainty china cups. Afternoon tea is served with daintily cut cucumber sandwiches and delicious small cakes. It is very much an English tradition which I have been brought up with".

"In that case", I replied. "I look forward immensely to joining you."

On the way home we continued to laugh at silly things we each remembered, until eventually I drew up at her house.

I longed to kiss her but settled by saying, "good night Lucinda".

"Thank you for such an enjoyable evening, I cannot remember laughing so much for a very long time."

I then asked, "May we go for afternoon tea say on Saturday after practice?"

"I shall look forward to that Johnathan," Lucinda replied then continued. "Thank you again it was fun! Until Saturday, good night".

Once more I took her hand and kissed it then told her, "I will meet you outside by the bench near the door".

"That will be fine Johnathan, good night again."

With that I watched her walk into the door of her house. It will not just be your hand I will kiss Lady Lucinda Osborn next time we meet. I will take possession of your lips and make them mine, that is for sure!

While driving home I thought I must ask Bates to tell me all he knew about the tradition of afternoon tea, the thought I was now a step closer to holding my goddess in my arms felt exhilarating. I had arranged a date without Trudy Hamilton intervening in trying to stop me. In fact if Trudy Hamilton ever interfered in my life again, I will call time out on her including losing my long-term friend if I have to. I had no wish to lose Jeff's friendship, but Lucinda had now become so much more important to me, more than a million Trudy Hamilton's.

The rest of the week flew by; I had so much work to complete, including taking calls from our Head Office.

They were checking up I was fine, which was acceptable under the circumstances. I suppose our lawyers meant well informing me everything was running smoothly in regard to our companies. It was of course natural they should. Unfortunately they were calls, which I would rather not have received.

Bates gave me a quick rundown explaining to me the history of afternoon tea, quite interesting I thought; as very shortly I to hope to be enjoying not just the afternoon tea, it would give me the opportunity I wanted of enjoying Lucinda's lips, who knows maybe more.

Ensuring I was on time Bates had everything laid out for me while I took a quick shower. I had booked a table at Malmaison, it was a wonderful French restaurant which served the very best of French food. One of my favourite eating places which I sometimes frequented if I wished to entertain a certain type of woman. Malmaison had purchased the property next door turning it into a small coffee bistro. Offering I am told, incredible afternoon teas, which I hoped Lucinda would find pleasing.

Lucinda was sitting where we had agreed to meet, looking incredibly beautiful as well as chic as she always had since leaving her black clothes behind. Each outfit she now wore was a joy to behold as her taste being impeccable".

"Good afternoon Lucinda nice to see you again everything well with you?"

"Perfectly," she replied then asked. "Have you enjoyed your practice?"

"Absolutely," I replied then told her, "It seems to ensure all my good endorphins are working overtime allowing my body to be in tip top condition."

"Are you ready to experience your first afternoon tea?" She smiled.

"Indeed I am," I said, returning her smile, though thinking to myself; there are far more enticing things I would love to do with you in the afternoon, one day I will show you.

Afternoon tea was actually fun, I loved watching her eat, taking each mouthful so daintily. We continued to talk small talk then laughed about this and that. It gave me the opportunity of finding out in a roundabout way the things we both liked.

"Do you have any hobbies Johnathan?" Lucinda surprisingly asked.

"Only women," came my answer before I could stop myself. "I do apologise I had no right to say that."

Instead of being cross with me, Lucinda started to laugh.

"I suppose for a healthy man it must be quite natural," she tried to say in a matter of fact voice yet found herself continuing to laugh at my ridiculous remark.

I have no idea why but now I felt so embarrassed. "I am terribly sorry," I repeated.

Please do not apologise again," came Lucinda's diplomatic reply, she continued to say, "I am though quite surprised you do not have a hobby of some sort."

"I thought doing sports was a hobby enough," I answered then it was my turn to change the subject.

"Lucinda may I ask you something serious, would you please tell me about your family and how you came to be in America?"

Lucinda looked at me, her beautiful blue grey eyes gazing into mine. In her wonderful crystal clear English accent her voice calm and steady as she asked: "Are you honestly interested or are you making polite small conversation?"

"I am deeply interested," I told her, "I want to know everything there is to know about you".

"Talking about one's self is normally rather boring," she replied. "If you care tell me a little about yourself as I go along, I will tell you a little about me, how does that suit you?"

"You have a deal," I told her.

"Very well," she said.

"First could we please go somewhere else? I rather feel we have now out stayed our welcome. I am terribly full at the moment, unable to eat another thing," she said laughing once more. Lucinda then asked. "Would you please ask for the bill then allow me to pay. I promised it would be my treat."

I stopped her right there by saying. "Absolutely No! I greatly appreciate your generous offer Lucinda, I really do, more than you will know, but no woman will ever pick up the bill when she is with me especially you Lucinda".

Chapter 6

"Lucinda, is there anywhere in particular you would like to go?"

"Johnathan, wherever you would like to take me will be perfect," she replied. The only place I wanted to take her was to my bed, knowing for the moment that was totally out of the question.

I settled going for a drive, "maybe later we could stop for dinner," I suggested.

"That would very nice, thank you so much Johnathan. You have already been very kind, I do not wish to appear greedy."

"Lucinda I do not think for one moment, you could ever be that," I answered.

"This is a lovely car Johnathan, have you had it long?"

"No. I am delighted you like it as much as I do," I replied.

Lucinda then told me how she loved driving and continued to say: "I rather miss having a car for the moment. When I start work I hope I am able to buy a car as lovely as this one".

"I am sure you will," I answered, then ask her if she had one back home.

"No," Lucinda replied, then went on to say. "I sold it along with everything else I owned, enabling me to raise enough funds for the fees I required to come to Harvard."

I suspected Lucinda had obviously decided this may be a good time to share with me, how she came to live in America, as she continued.

"Like yourself Johnathan, I come from a family of lawyers. My grandfather and father were both lawyers attached to the British military. My grandmother Lady Harriet did not work, my mother on the other hand decided she would break with tradition. Most wellborn English girls back then were expected to simply marry and procreate."

This comment caused both Lucinda and I to laugh, she continued: "Mummy was incredibly cleaver enabling her in going to university to become a language teacher".

"So that is your secret," I interrupted. "Now I understand why you are multilingual, your mother was fortunate enough to have a very good pupil".

Lucinda laughed once again, then continuing with her story told me about her grandparents.

"Both my grandfather and granny loved living by the sea, so decided to retire to Cornwall, which is regarded as the English South of France. My father also decided to give up his commission. Finding himself a job with a law firm in the city.

"We lived close to London, which my father hated, particularly in winter. He came home one bitterly snowy evening apparently having had a pretty awful day. Normally he would walk in greeting mummy and I with a lovely smile and kisses. This particular evening he looked cold, drawn and apparently feeling dreadfully tired. He said very little to either mummy or myself, which was so unusual. The three of us would normally laugh and talk about the day's events, especially during dinner. My father continued to say very little that evening until dinner was over. Mummy and I quietly removed the dinner plates. When we returned to the dining room, my father asked me to go to my bedroom as he wished to talk mummy in private. I left the room feeling dreadfully upset as I dreaded what my parents were going to discuss.

"Sometimes at school I heard girls talk about this type of situation when their parent were thinking of parting. I did something I had never done before, I pretended to close the door leaving it slightly ajar wanting to know why my father was so distressed, or if he had decided to leave mummy and I.

"Both of my parents were very pleasing to look at, my father being incredibly good looking. I thought maybe he had found another person he preferred to mummy. Not knowing what my father had to say left me feeling so scared.

"'Elspeth, please come and sit down' my father requested in a grave voice. Mummy decided to sit on a chair rather than sit on the settee next to him. My father then said, 'Elspeth you know how much I love both Lucinda and yourself. I want only the very best for both of you, but I cannot continue to live in this cold climate any longer. I hate the journey I take each day on the dirty transport. I also hate working in the city. I want a better life for all of us, especially Lucinda. We are both highly qualified people who should have no problems finding good jobs'.

"My father then continued. 'Lucinda is academically very clever, she is young enough and will settle into any school. I know she will be a credit to it as she is to us'.

"'Oh darling James', my mother said. 'For one awful minute I thought you were going to tell me that you no longer loved Lucinda and I'.

"'Elspeth you are the love of my life'. My father then got up and went over to my mother. Putting his arms around her he started kissing her long and lovingly. When he released her he drew her to the settee. My father once again giving mummy another very long kiss. Eventually my father released her then said.

"'Elspeth I want to emigrate to America. California in particular. There are a number of excellent firms who practice law. One in particular I have been researching, it has a reputation second to none. In fact Elspeth, I have already been in contact with them. They have offered me a position, which I wish to accept. Elspeth I have also been researching schools for both Lucinda and yourself'.

"'A school for me?' my mother asked surprised.

"'Yes darling. A refined school for you to teach in, and for Lucinda to attend'.

"'You have indeed been a busy bee James, it does though all sound very exciting. It is such a huge step to take James, but if that is what you want. Loving you the way I do; I will support you in this new endeavour.'

"'Oh my darling Elspeth, I had hoped you would agree. Now we must break the news to Lucinda.'

"'I will call her darling,' mummy said. As she went to get up my father caught her arm, then pulled her back towards him. Once again kissing her with such passion it was wonderful to see.

"They were obviously so very much in love, it was such a relief. I must be honest; it was also wonderful to see my father looking so happy once again. Mummy laughed when she saw me sitting on the bottom stair. I had a grin on my face as wide as the Cheshire cat.

"'Lucinda, you have been listening,' she laughed.

"Oh mummy is it really true, we are going to live in America?" I asked.

"'Yes darling it is true, but you must allow your father tell you'.

"'Come in my darling Lucinda,' my father said as I entered the room. 'Please come and sit down as mummy and I have something extremely important to tell you'.

"It was so hard pretending that I did not already know about the wonderful news he was about convey to me.

"'Darling,' my father continued, 'mummy and I are taking you to America to live. To California to be exact, do you think you will be happy there?'

"Daddy I will be absolutely too excited, it is just so marvellous. Thank you I love both of you so much, I am incredibly happy we will still all be together."

My parents understood instantly what I meant.

"'Now it is time for you to go to bed,' mummy ordered. 'Good night, sweet dreams darling.' my parents said in unison.

"I have no idea how I slept that night, I was so incredibly happy that my parents were not going to live apart, also I was terrifically excited that we were going to live in America. We sold our home very quickly, my grandparents were delighted for us, as naturally it meant they could come to stay and enjoy having lovely long holidays in the sun.

"We eventually arrived in this amazing country. My father loved his new job. He said the firm he worked for was indeed very prestigious, having a huge amount of law practices all over the country.

I was most curious to know the name of that original law practice, so asked. "Lucinda do you remember which law practice it was."

"Of course," she answered, "my father stayed with them until both he and my mother were killed just a couple of months before I started Harvard".

"I have no wish to compel you to tell me if you do not wish to do so. I am naturally interested in how your parents died."

In her beautiful English accent her voice calm. Lucinda then went on to tell me that her parents had been killed in a car accident.

"I am so sorry Lucinda, I had no idea you had sustained a double tragedy as horrific as that. I partly understand how you must have felt, as my mother was also killed in a car accident. It happened nine months after I had started Harvard."

"Oh Johnathan, I am so sorry for you. It is horrid loosing ones parents whether it is one or both."

"Thank you," I replied, at that moment I wanted to take her in my arms as if to protect her. Instead I asked, "Lucinda are you feeling hungry yet? We could go to have an early dinner if you would like that".

"No thank you, not just yet. Perhaps after I have told you what it was you wished to know," she answered.

"If that is what you would like to do that is perfectly fine by me," I replied.

I pulled over into a parking spot, which had a pretty view of a small lake just in front of us. The sun was gradually setting, casting its spell on everything we observed, It had already started to turn the whole vista into many shades of pink as if by a magic.

"It is lovely here", Lucinda commented, "My parents would have loved a place like this."

Then she continued to tell me her story.

"My father first went to work at Stones, they have been a law firm for over a century, maybe more. Have you heard of them as they have the same name as you?"

For a few seconds I was completely taken aback at this information. Instantly deciding I had no intention of explaining to Lucinda, that for the present I owed Stones. Instead I just said, "Yes; my father works there also".

"Really? How interesting," Lucinda said looking at me in a strange way, she then continued to say. "My mother died instantly at the scene of the accident. Fortunately I did manage to get to the hospital just before my father passed away".

"My parents had quite a large insurance policy. Together with the sale of their home, including selling the majority of the things we owned plus our cars, taking everything into consideration, I fortunately managed to raise the fees that I needed to enable me to go to Harvard. Stones also donated a large sum of money, which was amazingly kind of them, that allowed me extra money for clothes and food. It ensured I would not have to scrape the bottom of the barrel, so to speak. So there you are, you have my life story". Lucida laughed.

"Thank you for telling me, I hope discussing your loss with me was not too painful. I did not mean to be intrusive, I just wanted to know more about you."

"Lucinda smiled then went on to say. It can be a little worrying being alone but I have Trudy, she is such a wonderful friend and is very protective of me.

I love her dearly, she never allows me to be on my own during holidays or high days, which I am enormously grateful to her for. I know you had to buy her dinner this evening to ensure we could spend a little time together, which was so very, very kind of you, thank you for that."

"How about you and I now going for dinner ourselves?" I suggested.

"I would like that very much now," Lucida replied.

I drove the car to Mistral's, another French restaurant I knew. Normally you are expected to book well ahead as the restaurant is exceptionally popular. I phoned across to see if they had a table available, on hearing I needed one it was reserved instantly. Sometimes I loved being Johnathan Stone, especially on a night like this.

Dinner was superb, the food cooked to perfection. I told Lucinda a little about myself, trying terribly hard not to reveal the true extension of my background, particularly as it stood at the moment. The evening slipped away so fast, too fast. Each moment I spent with Lucinda was like eating nectar with the gods.

As I drove back to her house, my mind desperately searching for a way that would allow me to kiss her. Each thought I turned down as I had no intention of frightening her. I pulled up walked around the car to help her out.

"Thank you," Lucinda said as she stepped out, "would you walk with me to the door?"

"Of course it will be my pleasure," I answered.

Lifting her head up to my face she softly said: "Thank you again for a lovely day Johnathan, you really have been incredibly kind".

I looked down into her beautiful eyes then told her. "I have loved every moment being with you, it has been my pleasure entirely".

I now desperately wanted to possess her lips.

Dare I ask her to give me just one kiss, as that is what I would settle for right now? Why am I even thinking about asking her, had she been any other woman I would have taken what I wanted. Too late I heard myself say her name.

"Lucinda, would you mind if I asked you," she stopped me. Putting her fingers to my lips, which I kissed, she then said.

"Yes, just one kiss."

I felt ecstatic. Had Psyche allowed her to read my mind as she was willing to surrender her lips, giving to me what I had longed for all these months?

Slowly lowering my face towards her, for one awful moment I thought Lucinda had changed her mind as she took a tiny step away, then very slowly she came forward again. Lifting up her lovely face towards me, her eyes now half closed, her lips found mine. Hovering, barely touching they were like the wings of butterfly, which had been captured in a silver web, fluttering to be released.

Within moments she drew away, looking up at me once again. Her next words nearly blew my mind.

"Johnathan," she asked, "do you French kiss?"

I looked at her astounded, my brain barely taking in her words. Collecting my thoughts, I smiled; my voice becoming hoarse with emotion. "Yes" I replied: "Yes I French kiss."

"Then would you please give me a French kiss, I rather think I should like that."

Of all the hundreds of woman I had kissed, not one had ever asked that question. I felt my heart pounding thinking. Dear Lord let me get it right, let it be perfect. I took Lucinda gently in my arms, lowering my face towards her, she once again met me half way. Raising her beautiful face to me closing her eyes as she did so. My lips found hers, so tender so willing. Slowly she opened her mouth; carefully I gave her the French kiss she desired.

We kissed across eternity, as that is what it felt like. It was beyond any kiss I had ever experienced, never wanting it to end. Eventually Lucinda withdrew, standing there her eyes still closed for a few moments more. When at last she opened them she said.

"Thank you that was so lovely Johnathan. It has been a truly wonderful day, good night."

With that Lucinda walked into her house.

Standing there alone I felt the gods had cast me from paradise. They had at least thrown me a few crumbs of kindness in allowing me the knowledge that I now knew Lucinda had never been kissed by any man. While I had kissed her I had not taken possession of her lips. Lucinda on the other hand had taken possession of my soul, which would never be mine again.

I had no idea how I arrived home, remembering nothing of the journey. All I could think about, was that a goddess had stepped off Olympus and had deigned to kiss a mere mortal.

We had made no further arrangements to see each other. That for the moment did not matter, I would see Lucinda in class, or one of the libraries we used. Trudy Hamilton may well indeed be her best friend, but I will never again allow her to come between Lucida and myself.

Walking into the small sitting room I remembered what Lucinda had told me about the generous donation Stones had given to her after her father died. I had never heard my father mention about anyone having been given that type of donation before. I was now most curious as to why Lucinda had received such a donation. I would certainly look into it later. Having no wish to talk to anyone I made my way to my bedroom, would I sleep? Yes deeply, having after all these months been successful in kissing Aphrodite herself.

My studies occupied my mind for the next few days, there was so much work I needed to cram in before the Christmas break. My thoughts drifted as always towards Lucinda. This time I needed to know if she would be joining Trudy at her home in California. When Jeff retuned home I asked him if he knew of their plans.

"Yes Johnathan," he replied. "Trudy, Lucinda and I, are flying back for the entire holiday. I believe Ethan is also joining Penny at her home, did you know she also came from California"?

"No Jeff I had no idea, I guess it is going to be just Bates and I who will remain here."

This evening the house seemed quieter than usual, both Jeff and Ethan had gone to meet the girls. For some reason I felt edgy, usually I was quite content with my own company. Could it be the fact I was missing Lucinda's company. Or was it simply the case, that for the first time in my life I was not going to spend Christmas with my mother. Damn my father for being away. Even his company along with Bates would be better than having no family at this time of year".

Bates came as far as the sitting room door, which I had left open. "Dinner is ready if you are Johnathan," he informed me.

"Thank you Bates," I replied. He had prepared a small table for the two of us in the small morning room, which adjoined the kitchen. We talked about a number of inconsequential topics, making polite conversation. Towards the end of dinner Bates asked, "is there something bothering you Johnathan?"

How did he always manage to sense when I was troubled? Laughing for a moment I went on to tell him he was clairvoyant, then continued to divulge my thoughts to him over Christmas.

We were just about to discuss the situation when the phone rang. Bates went over to answer it, his face suddenly becoming visibly shocked, his colour draining away. His next words made me freeze, as he said: "Good evening Mr Stone how are you? Yes sir, Mr Johnathan is here with me. One moment sir I will put him on".

Bates and I looked at each other; not daring to believe my father was phoning after all these months.

"Good evening Johnathan how are you?" My father asked in his usual inimitable manner.

"I am fine sir," I replied.

"Have you made any arrangements for over the Christmas period?" he then inquired.

"No sir none at all."

"Then I would like both Bates and yourself to return home. I have things I wish to discuss with you. I will send the plane at the end of term, it may make your journey easier."

"Thank you sir, it will be very much appreciated," I answered.

"Your welcome, I will see you both shortly, good night Johnathan."

"Good night sir," I said. With that he replaced the receiver.

"Damn him Bates, he is already laying down the law. Maybe he has forgotten, as things stand at present it is my airline not his. Bates, I will no longer stand for you calling me Mister Johnathan in front of him. I am my own man and damn well old enough to choose how I wish to be addressed. I am financially independent of him thanks to my mother. As I do not need his money he had better blasted well get use to the idea? If he refuses to, he and I will for the first time be having serious words, a situation I know he definitely will find rather uncomfortable."

"Johnathan, there is no point antagonising him. He is after all your father and I am just one of his employees."

"No Bates, you are so much more than one of his employees, you have been and are like a father to me, more than he ever has. If he does not wish to accept how I feel, then we will both leave his house, on the other hand considering it is my house he can be the one to leave."

"Johnathan, I could never allow that to happen, I owe him a great deal and you are after all his son. While I appreciate as well as understand he can be extremely difficult Johnathan, he does love you in his own way. He has also expressed how incredibly proud he is of you. Perhaps we can find a way of getting around this situation. How about calling you, Mr Stone junior in front of him."

"I will think about it Bates I am making no promises. At least we will be home for Christmas, maybe I will get to see Lucinda if she can escape from her guard dog."

"Johnathan, I have told you before Lady Lucinda is very lucky indeed to have a friend like Miss Hamilton."

"I know Bates, I know. Bates do you think we could all fly back together or do you feel I should ask my father for his permission?"

"I should think Johnathan it would be the correct thing to do in asking him, especially due to insurance."

"Very well, I guess this would as good a time as any to test the water. Next time I will be the one to make any decision about my plane, tomorrow I will tell him I want my friends with me, I will ensure that is my first task".

It was not until the following afternoon that I phoned my father, then returned to tell Bates, there will be seven of us returning home."

"Well done Johnathan," Bates said with a smile, then continued. "At least it will give you some time to spend with Lady Lucinda".

"I am concerned Bates at what further changes my father will put into place once we are home."

"Try not to worry Johnathan we will find out quick enough."

* * *

Going home should have been great fun, yet my mind seemed fully taken up by my father's return. At least I would have Lucinda to myself for a few precious hours. Once we arrive home I thought I will phone her asking if she would join me for dinner at the weekend.

My mind drifted for a few minutes. The awful feeling of emptiness swept over me. Very much in the same way it did on the return journey home, after being told my mother had died. It was Lucinda's gentle voice that brought me back to reality.

"Johnathan, you seem very quiet, is there anything you would like to share with me?" She lovingly continued to say, "I am just wondering if I have perhaps said something to annoy you."

"Lucinda you could never annoy me," I said drawing her closer then lifting her beautiful face to mine; kissing her the way she loved to be kissed.

I had no wish to tell her of the predicament I had to endure for the present. As we departed from the plane I said to Lucinda; "I told my friends I will arrange to meet you all later". Then taking Lucida in my arms wishing I could take her with me I kissed her goodbye.

I dragged myself away to the car where Bates was waiting remarking to him, "five star service Bates would you not agree?" Trying to lighten my sprits as the chauffeur proceeded to put our cases into the boot of the vehicle my father had sent.

Bates laughed recognising my sarcasm, going on to say. "I am sure everything will work out fine Johnathan. You have shown your father that you have managed his empire perfectly well, and with great confidence."

"Thank you Bates, you are tactful as always. In this case I have done very little. We have brilliant employees who my father has chosen well. I will just be so relieved when I am able to sign his empire back to him."

We drove home in silence. Bates, understanding of how worried I was, allowed me the luxury of not having to be polite in making small talk with him. As we entered the gates, the thought of having to face my father brought on that awful feeling of nausea once again. On the other hand I was strangely pleased he had arrived home for Christmas.

During his long absence Bates had left a skeleton staff to ensure the house had been taken care of. Once he knew my father had returned, a full complement of staff had quickly been installed to take care of his every whim, we were greeted by our housekeeper as well as a couple of new members of staff, who proceeded to take our suitcases.

"Good evening Mr Johnathan, how nice to see you again," the housekeeper said as pleasantries were exchanged.

I must stop this Master or Mr Johnathan business, as I hated the blasted title. Within minutes came the dreaded summons of my father wishing me to go to his office.

Knocking once again on his office door, I now realised I hated that damn room. If my father does decided to move out of the house, the first thing I will do is have that damn room dismantled turning it into a junk room would be a good idea.

"Please come in Johnathan," my father's voice called out. He was as usual sitting at his desk, which over the years I had grown to hate.

"Good evening Johnathan," he said as he rose to shake my hand. "You are looking well, had a good flight? Is Bates with you"?

"Yes sir, to both questions," I answered him.

"I am interested in how Bates, came to be with you, but you can tell me about that in a few minutes," he continued. My mind was made up in that moment; I was not going to give any ground with regards to Bates.

"You are looking a great deal better yourself sir since we last met."

"Thank you Johnathan, I feel a great deal better, tell me how is your course work going; well I hope?" He enquired.

"Brilliant, thank you," I replied.

I then went on to tell my father about having opened up the old house. "I am rather surprised sir, you did not use it yourself when you were at Harvard, it is a wonderful old house making a perfect base to work out from".

"You are quite right, I am rather surprised I did not do that myself, I actually stayed in the hotel," my father then questioned, "Is that the reason Bates came over to Boston?"

"Yes sir, he ensured a marvellous job was carried out. Not just ensuring the work was done extremely well; I missed Bates living with me. In fact I want him with me permanently"!

My father had never before heard the serious and determined tone that was now in my voice. He looked at me with what I would call one of his steady gazes, then surprised me by saying.

"You have always got on well with Bates, ever since you were a small boy. I always felt I could trust him to take care of you, especially when I had to be away on business. I am pleased now you are a man; you are able to enjoy that same relationship with him. Johnathan, if it means so much to your wellbeing to have Bates with you. So be it."

"Do you really mean that?" I asked.

Once again the emotion of feeling like a small child who had been promised a treat came over me. More importantly I did not want any confrontation with him.

My father continued to say: "Of course I do Johnathan; I have trusted Bates with your life, practically from the moment he joined this household. Knowing he is taking care of you while you are at Harvard, is in fact a brilliant idea. Now I have a number of matters I wish to discuss with you".

Inwardly I felt ecstatic! Nothing could be more important than knowing Bates would now be with me, when it was time to return to Boston.

"Johnathan," my father's voice brought me back to reality. "You have done a splendid job during the last months, which leaves me feeling very proud of you. Therefore I have decided to allow you to continue running the business for a further six months. I will not be away this time should you feel you require any help, but continue to work as I normally do in our head office. I want you to get the hang of all the business in case anything should ever happen to me. Johnathan, I gave this matter a great deal of thought while I was absent. I understand you still have your studies, and appreciate this is a difficult time for you, which is why I will be at the other end of a phone should you need me."

Once again I sat there stunned! Just as I did the first time my father told me about owning his empire. What the hell was he still playing at and why? I could understand and appreciate some of what he was saying, in case something untoward should happen to him. It was just the thought of being responsible for so much which was terrifying. I had no intention of arguing with him, as I knew it would have been hopeless. I decided there and then to show him his young pup had grown teeth by saying.

"Very well sir, if that is what you still want. I must admit I had hoped you would have taken back your empire."

I had never heard my father laugh out loud at anything I had said before, I guess there is always a first time for everything.

"So you regard our businesses as an empire? Well I guess Johnathan you could indeed be right, and you are for the present the Emperor of it all, making you a wealthy, powerful young man that I am excessively proud of."

"Thank you for your generous compliments," I replied. "While we are talking, there is something I am most curious about."

"Oh what is that?" my father asked.

"I believe Stones had a Major Osborn working for them, he and his wife were killed in a car accident a few months before I started at Harvard. I have been told that Stones donated a tidy sum of money to Major Osborn's daughter, enabling her to attend Harvard". Then repeating Lucinda's words I went on to say. "Without scraping the bottom of the barrel so to speak. I had no idea we would normally donate in cases like that".

"You are quite right Johnathan, we do not normally do so. I made the exception as Major Osborn did not have a great deal of insurance put in place, due of course to the fact that he had only lived and worked in America for a few years. Major Osborn was a brilliant lawyer who worked exceptionally hard for Stones, in return Stones decided to help his daughter. Have you met her?"

"Yes sir," I replied, "she is both beautiful as well as brilliant. I am sure she will make a first class lawyer, as her father once was. Stones will do well to have her work for them".

"Johnathan, may I ask, do you have any personal interest in this girl?"

"For the moment. Yes, as she is part of my circle of friends."

I had no intentions of being drawn into answering further questions about my relationship with Lucinda.

"Is it serious?" My father asked.

"No sir, the only thing that is serious at the moment are my exams."

I hated not telling him the whole truth, which for the present time I felt I was none of his business.

"Glad to hear that" he said looking at me with his eyes half closed.

Then out of the blue once again my father surprised me as he went on to say: "Women are to be enjoyed Johnathan when you are your age, nothing more".

"Yes sir," I agreed: "I am rather tired, would you mind if we talk again tomorrow?"

"Not at all," my father answered, wishing me good night.

"Good night sir and thank you," I replied. I closed the office door thrilled in the knowledge I had found the ability, in showing my father I was becoming a man: who could if necessary bite back. Wait till tomorrow when Mr Johnathan becomes Mr Stone.

* * *

I made my way up to Bates' rooms as I wished to speak to him before he went downstairs. Knocking on his door I could barely contain the excitement I now felt. The thought of being able to convey to him, that if he wished to, he could be with me for the rest of his life, which was brilliant.

"Come in," Bates called, "good morning Johnathan, I had no idea it would be you," he said with a look of surprise on his face as I walked through the door.

"Bates I have some fantastic news to divulge to you, at least I hope you will regard it as fantastic." I then went on to tell him of my father's decisions in allowing him to be with me always should he so wish.

"I am positively stunned! Are you sure he meant it?" Bates asked.

"I stood up to him Bates, telling him I wanted you with me permanently. I was shocked when my father capitulated so easily, He went on to say: 'Of course Johnathan if that is what you would like, and depending of course on how Bates feels; I could think of nothing I would like more'".

"Looking at me a little startled Bates answered: "Thank you Johnathan, I must admit I am feeling rather overwhelmed".

"Bates this will always be your home, I give you my faithful promise. Even when I eventually have to marry, I will ensure my wife whoever she may be, understands how important you are to my life. If she does not wish you to be part of my life, then as far as I am concerned; she will never be mistress of my home."

Bates turned his back to me then walked towards his bathroom, saying as he went: "Will you please excuse me for a few minutes?"

"I sat looking around the room that held so many happy memories for me. I loved this room, as it was Bates world not my fathers. I then noticed the new furnishing Bates had bought at my request, replacing the old settees that were beyond shabby. Strange he must have searched hard in trying to maintain the continuity of the furniture that had originally been here, as the new furniture was incredibly similar. Bates returned asking me if I was ready to go down for breakfast.

"Just before we do," I answered him, "there is something else I must tell you. Bates I still own the empire! My father has decided to allow me to continue running the businesses for a further six months".

Bates shook his head, just as he did the first time I had told him about becoming responsible for so many people's welfare.

"At least this time your father will be home," Bates replied then continued: "Should you require his help day or night, he is no further away than a phone call"

"That Bates is exactly what my father said, though he did not mention the night time bit," which made Bates laugh. "Come on Bates lets go down to breakfast I need to prepare for round two."

"May I ask what you mean Johnathan? I thought you had sorted your problems out with your father?" Bates said looking a little worried once again.

"Bates as I told you, am sick to the back teeth of being called Master or Mr Johnathan. You and I have a very special understanding. My mind Bates is made up regardless of what my father may think, from now on the rest of the staff will addressed me as Mr Stone".

My father joined me for breakfast, which I found unnerving yet welcoming, it had been nearly a year since we last breakfasted together. Now strangely I no longer felt afraid, maybe as I was willing to stand up to him, or could it simply have been I felt rather sorry for him being alone.

We ate breakfast fairly silently, my father reading his paper, then cook addressed me asking. "Master

Johnathan is there anything else you would like". My reply was to change things dramatically.

"Yes I said firmly, from now on I would appreciate it if the rest of the staff, including yourself would address me as. Mr Stone!"

My father dropped his paper, just sitting there looking at me for a few moments then said: "You have indeed become a man, welcome to my world Mr Stone". He then resumed to read his paper without another word being spoken between us. Bates looked across the kitchen catching my eye then winking, giving me the widest of smiles while nodding his approval.

I interrupted my father saying, "When you have finished breakfast sir, I would like a few minutes of your time".

"Certainly Johnathan", my father replied then asked. "Is it private? Or could we discuss it in the conservatory?"

"The conservatory would be fine," I told him.

There was definitely a change going on; my father rarely frequented our lovely conservatory. Now instead of just using his office, he had decided at long last to enjoy the relaxing atmosphere of that room also.

He joined me for coffee later in the morning asking what was on my mind. "I have a couple of questions I would like to ask you," I replied.

"First I am wondering sir, what you had in mind with regards to Christmas? Are we going to put up a tree this year or would you prefer not to bother? Secondly would you rather go out for lunch or dinner in the evening, or have dinner at home? Perhaps you would like to invite some guest over?"

"Johnathan what would you like to do?" my father asked.

"I am happy to go along this year with whatever suits you," I replied.

"In that case Johnathan I would like to go out for Christmas lunch, just the two of us," my father then carried on to say. "I am not too bothered if you wish to have a tree up, perhaps just in the hall this year. We will continue the tradition of handing out presents to the staff on Christmas Eve," or would you prefer the afternoon?"

"I am fine with whatever you decide," I replied.

My father then asked: "Do you have some friends you wish to spend some time with or would like to ask over"?

"I have made no arrangements at present, so have no idea what my plans will be until I have spoken to the boys".

"Very well Johnathan, we will leave our Christmas arrangements as they stand for now. Johnathan, there is something furthermore I would like to tell you. You may remember me mentioning to you that after your mother died, I no longer wished to remain in this house."

"Yes sir I remember," I answered.

"I have decided Johnathan I am going to have the top floor of our main office turned into a penthouse. It will allow me a fresh start and plenty of space to live in without the constant memories of your mother. It will also allow me to be on hand for the business."

I was quite surprised at this piece of news. Trying to be as tactful as I could, I gently said to him.

"I am sorry sir, I had no idea how painful it must be for you now my mother is no longer with you. I understand you wishing to build a new life for yourself. Are you sure that a penthouse, rather than a smaller property is the correct way to go about it?"

"For the moment Johnathan, yes. If in the future I find it is not the correct solution for me, I can of course alter my plans by buying a smaller property. The penthouse can then be used should we need to work late into the night. It will save from having to book into a hotel, or have a long drive home."

What my father was saying made common sense. I had no idea then how the penthouse was going to eventually change my entire life forever.

I decided to buy Lucinda a gold bracelet with her name engraved inside. While in the jewellers along with Lucinda's bracelet, I bought Bates and my father gold cufflinks with matching tiepins. Jeff and Ethan were to receive cashmere sweaters and for Trudy and Poppy cashmere cardigans, as they were so luxurious and Boston so cold in winter I added further sweaters to my list for Bates, Lucinda and myself.

I missed seeing Lucinda more than I had realised, I missed holding her in my arms, kissing her beautiful face and tender lips. I did not want to introduce her to my father just yet, so decided not to invite her over to my home. I phoned across to Trudy's to ask would she come to dinner with me. It would give me the opportunity to give her my present; maybe she would allow me to put the gold bracelet on her adorable wrist. Unless of course she decided not to open the box until Christmas morning.

I would have very few precious hours with Lucinda during the holidays. One of the evenings would be taken up with the boys, ensuring they also had their presents in time for Christmas.

At least it would not be too long before we all once again flew back to Boston. When we arrive back to the house I will invite Lucinda for dinner. It will at least ensure we have a great deal of private time together. I wanted to take my relationship with her a step further. The thought of undressing her, caressing her beautiful breast then kissing them should have made me feel ecstatic, yet for some unknown reason I felt deflated. I am sure once I have her in my arms I will feel differently.

"You look very handsome this evening," Bates informed me, "I can assume you are taking a certain lady out to dinner".

"You are quite right Bates, I have missed Lucinda more than I thought possible. Sadly as I will not be seeing her on Christmas day, I must ensure she has her Christmas present beforehand."

"Are you going to introduce her to your father sometime during the holiday?"

"No absolutely not, by the way I hope you like your present Bates," I said wishing to change the subject of Lucinda coming to the house.

"I am sure whatever it is you have bought for me will be perfect, thank you Johnathan," Bates replied.

Lucinda looked every inch of the lady she was, as we drove to one of the finest restaurants in town, to Lucinda it was just another place to eat, as usual she fitted in so perfectly.

Presenting her with her Christmas present she looked at me saying: "How extraordinarily kind of you Johnathan, may I open it now?"

"I would love you to," I answered. On opening the box carefully Lucinda gave a little gasp.

"Oh Johnathan, it is beautiful! Thank you."

"It is not as beautiful as you," I told her, then asked, "Will you allow me to fasten the clasp on you?"

"Of course," she said as she held out her delicate hand slipping the bracelet onto her arm. I wish it had been a magical gold chain I was clasping on her arm, ensuring she belonged to me forever.

The evening as always passed far too quickly, I longed for it to never end. Delivering Lucinda safely back to Trudy's, I hated the thought of not seeing her during the Christmas break. Taking her in my arms, giving her the French kisses she loved I desperately wanted to explore her body, knowing for the moment I still dare not.

"Good night Johnathan. Thank you again for not just a wonderful evening, but for my beautiful bracelet I shall treasure it always."

For the first time in my life I hated Christmas. I missed my mother and all the traditions she normally ensured were put in place, even opening the generous Christmas presents both Bates and my father bought me failed to lighten my spirits. Except for spending some precious time with Lucinda, I would be more than pleased to return to Harvard.

The holidays drew to an end, but not before time as far as I was concerned. Saying goodbye to my father was not as uncomfortable as it had been the last time we parted. He actually seemed a little more amicable, maybe as he knew his pup would now bite back. The new Chauffeur drove Bates and I back to the airport where my private plane sat waiting for us. When the others joined us, except for Lucinda they all seemed a little sad to say goodbye to California.

Ethan and Poppy now appearing to be very much a couple, Trudy and Jeff were talking of getting engaged during the summer vacation. In a matter of months we will become third year students, I hope by then to have achieved my ambition of getting Lucinda into my bed. Only time will tell if I have been cleaver enough to conquer her. The game resumes once we return Harvard.

Chapter 7

Leaving California the weather was warm and sunny, arriving in Boston the weather had changed dramatically becoming bitterly cold. Everyone's spirits seemed low once we landed, was it my imagination about the others, or was it my spirits that were feeling low? Whatever it was, Lucinda in some way was connected with the way I felt. Bates had organised a couple of cars to take the girls and ourselves home. Feeling out of sorts, tired and worried meant it was not a good time for me to talk. I knew I would not be receptive to wise advice even from Bates. Perhaps tomorrow his advice would be more welcome.

The following morning Bates greeted me by saying: "You look as if you have had a rough night Johnathan, something troubling you?"

"Yes Bates I have had a rough night, I have barely slept, so yes there is something troubling me."

"Would you like your breakfast first before you talk," Bates asked politely.

"I am tired, in fact I am very tired Bates to the point I may just go back to bed."

Bates showed his concern by asking: "Are you sure you are feeling well Johnathan, or is there some further issue that is causing you to feel so disturbed?"

"I have no idea what is actually upsetting me," I replied. "I am unable to clearly focus on the problem. There is something obviously troubling me".

Bates, polite as always asked: "Could it be something to do with still being responsible for the businesses?"

"No Bates," I replied. "It is not the businesses that are bothering me. Neither is it my course work, which I am thoroughly enjoying. Christmas was sad without my mother, but it is not that either."

Bates looked very concerned for a moment or two then very gently asked, is it Lady Lucinda, Johnathan?"

How perceptive of him he hit my problem spot on.

"Yes! Bates, you are right. It is Lucinda that is causing me to feel uneasy."

"Would you prefer to return to your bed or would you like to talk?"

"Honestly Bates, I would like both; the problem being I cannot sleep. If you do not mind a little of your time would be most welcome."

"Where would you like to talk, here or in your little sitting room?" Bates asked.

"The sitting room please."

"That is an excellent idea," Bates replied, he then asked. "Perhaps a pot of coffee would be welcome?"

I laughed: "Yes Bates a pot of coffee would be most welcome."

I walked to the little sitting room, funny how its name stuck, as everyone now calls it that. Bates followed bringing in the welcome pot of coffee with two decent size mugs, which I much preferred to china cups. Bates sat on the opposite chair then poured our coffee, as he did so he said, "Johnathan you do not need to feel embarrassed. I have been in love myself remember."

"Bates I am not sure if this is anything to do with love, I am very fond of Lucinda, and yes I wish to take my relationship with her further. I desperately want to make her mine; kissing her on her lips is now not enough? I want to kiss her the way a woman should be kissed. I want to make her into a woman before another man touches her."

"Are you telling me Johnathan, you are not in love with her?"

"How can I be Bates? If she allows me to take her to my bed then make love to her, after which she will allow any man to take her to his bed."

"Johnathan, Lady Lucinda is a beautiful woman. Are you saying she should never have another man in her life to love her, once you have eventually decided you no longer have use for her?"

"Yes… No!" I said confused. "I do not know Bates how I feel, all I do know is that I want her. I want her more than I have ever wanted any woman. My body aches for her when I am in close proximity to her. I want to devour every part of her body, especially when I am kissing her. It takes every ounce of self-control not to touch her. I cannot go on like this. If she gives herself to me it will be the greatest disappointment of my life, if she refuses to give herself to me I will go insane."

"Have you talked to Lady Lucinda about your feelings?" Bates asked.

"No Bates, not yet, it is something I intend to do next time we are together. I was going to ask her to come over here."

"You mean here to the house?" Bates asked surprised.

"Yes. I thought I would invite her here for dinner, then see if she would stop me or not making her mine.

Even getting to first base with her would be incredible, yet devastating."

"Johnathan you surely cannot expect Lady Lucinda to say no to first base as you call it, she is after all a human being and not a nun. With all due respect, she has the emotions of a human being just as you have; or any other woman who maybe in love."

"Bates how do you know she is in love with me? She has never as yet said she was."

"People like Lady Lucinda would never mention they were in love, until the person they are in love with tells them first."

"I cannot tell her that, you know I do not want to marry any woman, certainly not for a great many more years to come."

"What you are then basically saying Johnathan, is that you just want to possess Lady Lucinda until such time, you decided to go and find someone else that takes your interest?"

Once again I heard myself saying: "Yes Bates. What I want is to possess her, and no I do not want another man ever to touch her. If like Zeus, I could take her to Olympus keeping her at my side for eternity I would. As I am no Greek God, I will settle for taking her up to the top floor of our head office which as you know is like a glass tower, keeping her there magically chained to me forever instead."

"You would keep her in your glass tower without marrying her? Is that what you are telling me?" Bates asked.

"I do not know what I want Bates, I just know my feelings for Lucinda are intense. Of all the many women I have been with, not one has ever made me feel this way."

Bates gave me a very broad smile, and then said, "I suspect Johnathan that deep down, you could just be in love!"

"Rubbish, absolute rubbish. Bates I would know if I was in love. If I was in love as you call it, I would want to marry, which as I have told you is something I have not planned for the foreseeable future. Sorry you are wrong in this case, your judgement is way off this time."

"Very well Johnathan, we shall see what develops."

We finished our coffee, Bates leaving the rest of the pot with me. I was surprised Bates making such a bad call about my feelings, how could I possibly be in love with a girl who I just wanted to have sex with.

I invited Lucinda over for dinner the following weekend, I needed the house to myself so asked both Jeff and Ethan had they made any particular plans. Both were going to meet their girls, I would have been more than happy to pay for them to go out to dinner if I had to.

Bates made a simple but delicious meal, which I knew Lucinda would enjoy. I offered Bates my car for the rest of the evening.

"Thank you Johnathan, I shall look forward to driving your Lincoln."

I dressed carefully hoping when it came to undressing me that Lucinda would find my clothes easy to slip off.

"Please Johnathan," Bates advised. "Take things easy, remember Lucinda is still a virgin, do not frighten her. First base is what you should be settling for, not the whole way".

"Thank you for your advice Bates" I replied, "as always I will do my very best".

"I am sure you will Johnathan, that is what I am worried about".

"Enjoy your ride; as I hope to enjoy mine!"

With a sharp tone in his voice and a look of anger in his eyes Bates went on to say.

"Johnathan you never struck me as a bloody fool," then he walked out.

Damn! I had never heard Bates talk to me in that way before, how dare he interfere or tell me how to treat Lucinda. His words felt like having a bucket of ice-cold water thrown in my face. The trouble was he was damn well right. I could not now ask Lucinda to have sex with me. Instead I suppose I will have to settle for just caressing and kissing her beautiful breasts. Maybe she would allow me to go a little further if I pleased her, who knows what will eventually happen.

Watching the clock tick away pacing up and down, I felt a little nervous until Lucinda arrived. At last her taxi drew up, stepping out well wrapped up against the cold she looked like an angel. Wasting no time I took her in my arms covering her face with kisses, then kissing her as always with passionate French kisses just as she loved them. Oh Lord. How I loved putting my tongue inside her sweet mouth, pressing my lips on hers. Eventually she pulled away smiling so happily. Looking at her a little more intent than I had previously, her face now flushed. I began to wonder was Bates right, was she in love with me; or was it just the passion of the way we kissed that made her look even more beautiful this evening?

As we stepped into the hallway, I asked if she would you like to see the rest of the downstairs rooms.

"Oh yes please if you do not mind, it looks a wonderful old house from the outside." Lucinda then went on to say, "Jeff mentioned to Trudy your family have owned this house for over a century or more. You have ensured a fantastic facelift has been carried out. The interior is now truly wonderful."

"Thank you Lucinda that is most kind of you to say so."

We spent a further good fifteen minutes taking a quick look at the other downstairs rooms, then I asked.

"Should we walk back to the small dining room? Bates has laid the table in there for us, I hope you enjoy his cooking."

While we ate, as always we did a great deal of laughing about the funny tales we each remembered. At the end of our meal Lucinda requested, "Please allow me to help clear the dinner plates away."

"If you wish Lucinda, we can do it together, then it will not take too long."

We were nearly finished when I took Lucinda in my arms. I could not get enough of her, her kisses were intoxicating. The passion I was now feeling for her spilled over, my heart beating heavily as my hands now slowly found her breasts.

"Stop Johnathan, please." Lucinda demanded, her words bringing me back to cold reality. Her next words were to send me into the depths of despair.

"I cannot Johnathan, become any deeper involved with you. I am so terribly sorry, but I must keep my emotions strictly under control,"

"May I ask why?" my voice sounding devoid of any emotion, it sounded as ice cold as my father's when he was cross-examining.

"Yes Johnathan you may ask," Lucinda continued: "Do you remember me telling you about the night, my parents were killed in that awful car accident? Just before my father died, I gave him my word of honour promising him I would complete my degree, before I became emotionally involved with any man."

"'Not all men are honourable my darling child,' he said gasping for breath. 'My darling I am so sorry I have to leave you. Please Lucinda I must ask you to promise me,' he said again labouring to breath. 'Lucinda once you have your degree, no man can ever take away your livelihood, until then I beg of you do not give yourself to any man. If in the meantime you may one day find your true love my darling. If he loves you he will understand exactly what it is I am asking of you.'

"I promised daddy. In fact, I solemnly gave him my word I will wait until such time, my degree is in my hand. My father closed his eyes, then slipped away in my arms.

"Now do you understand Johnathan? I understand you are a red blooded young man who needs a woman in his life, but I cannot give you what it is you want. I think under the circumstances it would be sensible for us to part, on good terms if we can. It has been more than wonderful knowing you and the times we have spent together. You have given me so many happy memories, thank you again. Thank you also for my lovely present, I will treasure it forever. Now if you would please fetch my coat then call a taxi, I would be most grateful."

I called a taxi then handed Lucinda her coat, not a further word was spoken between us, until Lucinda said goodnight as she made her way to the taxi.

I paced up and down until Bates returned. He looked at me then said: "By the look on your face Johnathan, you look as if you have lost a great deal."

"Once again Bates you are quite right," I told him, my voice full of anger. "I have lost Lady Lucinda, she was a lady to the end. Even without me getting to first base can you believe that"?

"Like to talk?"

"No thanks Bates, from now on I am going to stick to whores. At least you know where you stand with them. I am now going out to find myself one for the night and every damn night".

* * *

The weeks turned to months, which passed with glacial slowness. Seeing Lucinda in classes, roughly knowing her routine when and where she would be, or which particular library she would use on certain days. I tried to ensure I did not go when I thought she would be there, though most times without success. Unable to study together was simply more than I could bear, not a single word or smile passed between us during those long empty months.

Living without her kisses, was living in a hell of my own making. There was now no longer laughter in my life, just a huge void of loneliness. I studied in automatic gear without giving a thought to what I was reading. Towards the end of the last class of the last day of term, I looked across at Lucinda. I could not help but notice she was looking pale and drawn as well as having lost weight. I had no idea what the tutor was saying; I was just so pleased when the class eventually came to an end.

I started walking away when I heard a commotion going on behind me. Turning round I saw the students crowding around someone who had obviously passed out. Then I heard my name being called, Johnathan get here now. It was Jeff's voice shouting me. Collapsed on the floor was Lucinda, "get the hell away from her," I shouted at everyone. I picked her up in my arms and carried her to my car. I drove like a bat out of hell to the hospital. Jeff and Trudy followed trying to keep up with me. On arriving at the hospital I asked for Dr Neil Gregory, or Dr Timothy Holland to report instantly to the emergency room. The nurse looked at me, my tone of voice was enough for her not to argue. Neil came within minutes bringing with him a team he obviously trusted.

"Johnathan we will take over now," he said in his calm voice. "Please go to the waiting room where I will join you shortly."

Instead I went to the main desk to tell the sister on duty to get the Jefferson Stone suite ready. "I am sorry sir" she said, "I cannot do that without permission."

"You have ten seconds to comply with my wishes," I told her, "or get your coat and get the hell out of my hospital. I am counting now – Ten. Nine. Eight".

"May I ask who you are sir," the sister then asked?

"I am Johnathan Jefferson Stone and this is my hospital."

"I do apologise. Your suite will be made available instantly, Mr Stone."

"Thank you," I replied, my voice devoid of kindness, I sounded for a moment as if I was indeed my father. Jeff and Trudy joined me in the waiting room, Trudy totally ignoring me as if I had the plague. Jeff had not said a great deal to me over the last few months, the atmosphere at home had sometimes being rather tense.

"What the hell is keeping them"? I asked.

"Calm down Johnathan," Jeff quietly advised. "The doctor will be here shortly." Another twenty minutes passed before Neil walk in.

"How is Lucinda," Trudy asked. Neil turned to me to tell me that Lucinda was suffering from dehydration and exhaustion. "We need to keep her in for a few days," Neil stated.

"I have had my suite made ready for her," I said.

"That's fine Johnathan she will be taken good care of," Neil informed me.

"Make sure she is, and that she has everything she needs Neil, Lucinda is the love of my life."

Trudy and Jeff stood there unable to believe what they had just heard. Jeff hesitantly then said, "I thought you and Lucinda had split up."

I looked at both of them, wanting to take my pain out on someone. In a voice Jeff now recognised when I became angry or frustrated, a voice now sounding as cold as ice I told them. "It is of no consequence what either of you thought, all you need to know is that Lucinda belongs to me, now and forever."

Jeff knew better than to say another word. Trudy followed Jeff's example, still in shock that I had professed my love for Lucinda.

Neil was about to leave when he was joined by another doctor, now it was my turn to be deeply surprised. The pretty doctor that had just walk in was none other than Poppy Penbrook.

"Poppy! I had no idea you were a doctor, Ethan has never said."

"Hello Johnathan, I am so sorry to hear about Lucinda. I am sure with Neil looking after her she will be well in no time."

"Thank you Poppy I hope you're right."

I turned to Neil then asked: "When are you taking her upstairs?"

"Very shortly Johnathan, she will be fine, try not to worry."

I turned to address Trudy, "I will ensure Trudy that Lucinda has everything she needs, please do not bring her anything in, unless she specifically asks for a particular item".

"Johnathan," Poppy interrupted, "we have given Lucinda something to enable her to sleep for a little while, it will do her the world of good. For the present she does need a great deal of rest".

"I understand, thank you Poppy."

Turning to Neil I told him: "When I am not here, I want a nurse with Lucinda at all times. Day and night until she is a great deal better. If you will now excuse me I will wait for you upstairs, in the meantime I have some phone calls to make, and to ensure everything is perfect for a very special lady".

* * *

"Good morning your ladyship, how are you feeling this morning? My name is Karen, I am one of a number of nurses that will be taking care of you during your stay in hospital."

"Good morning Karen, please will you just call me Lucinda as I hate formality. Would you please be kind enough to tell me where I am? Unfortunately I do not quite remember how I managed to be here."

"Of course Miss Lucinda," Karen replied adding the miss rather than your ladyship, regarding the need to still be polite. "You are in the Jefferson Stone Hospital. Your young man brought you here after you collapsed in college two days ago."

"My young man? I am sorry Karen, I think you must be mistaken as I do not have a young man."

"Oh you most definitely do Miss Lucinda. Mr Johnathan Stone, jolly handsome he is as well if I may so," Karen continued to say, "I guess he must love you very much, as he stays here most of each night just in case you wake up. Have you seen the wonderful things he has bought for you? No man would buy such exquisite things for his young lady unless he loved her. He has incredible good taste, each beautiful item, must have been seriously expensive that is for sure".

"Karen I do not understand what in the world you are talking about?"

"Allow me to show you Miss," the nurse said as she walked over to the floor to ceiling units, which cleverly disguised a complete set of wardrobes. Not just wardrobes, inside were shelf units, drawers and a shoe rack. On Karen, opening the wardrobe doors as well as a couple of the draws. Lucinda gasped at the array of exquisite nightwear, underwear, and day clothes. Plus whatever else a young lady may need on a day-to-day basis. It all appeared like a vision out of an Aladdin's cave.

"Oh Karen how lovely everything is. Karen what do you mean Mr Stone stays most of the night while I sleep?"

"He sits in the chair and reads, Miss Lucinda," Karen explained, pointing to the chair situated next to her bed.

"When does he leave?" Lucinda asked.

"Mr Stone leaves in the early hours of morning Miss, usually when he is happy you are sound asleep. He then ensures one of the nurses on duty comes in to stay with you. He has given strict orders, you are not to be left on your own until you are well."

"Could you please tell me what is actually the matter with me?"

"I will tell you," Poppy Penbrook said, as she entered the room.

"Poppy how wonderful to see you, what are you doing here?" Lucinda asked.

"I am one of your doctors Lucinda," Poppy replied.

"Poppy I had no idea you were a doctor, how long have you been one? Why did you never say? Does Johnathan know you are a doctor?"

"Slow down Lucinda," Poppy laughed: "Yes Johnathan knows I am a doctor, he has specifically asked for me to be on the team that is looking after you".

"Poppy would you mind telling me what is wrong with me?" Lucinda asked cautiously.

"I was just coming to that," Poppy replied. "You were suffering from dehydration, as well as exhaustion. I am sure you are making excellent progress, you will probably be discharged in a few days".

"I feel fine right now, and would like to return to my studies," Lucinda argued.

"Your doctors Lucinda, would simply not consider letting you go, at least not for the moment. Do please bear with them and try to understand they have your best interest at heart. Lucinda is there anything you require?"

"Yes Poppy, I want to know what Johnathan Stone has to do with me being in this suite; as well as being responsible for buying all these expensive items. Poppy you know I could never afford to re-pay him?"

"Lucinda it was Johnathan that brought you to the hospital when you collapsed. He has made sure you have the finest team in the hospital to take care of you," she continued saying: "I find it difficult to believe that you do not know how much Johnathan loves you".

"Loves me!" Lucinda exclaimed, "Poppy are you mad? The only person Johnathan Stone loves is Johnathan Stone".

"Oh no Lucinda, you are quite wrong, he even told Trudy and Jeff that you are the love of his life," Poppy revealed.

"He told them I was the love of his life! Are you sure Poppy?" Lucinda asked.

"I am absolutely sure Lucinda," Poppy gently replied.

"That is just too amazingly wonderful, I have missed him so terribly. Thank you so much for telling me."

"You are welcome Lucinda," Poppy replied then asked. "Now, would you like to take a shower and try to have some breakfast? We can talk again once you have eaten if you feel up to it".

"That would be perfect, thank you again Poppy."

"You are welcome dearest, must fly for the present, goodbye Lucinda I will call in again later," Poppy remarked as she made her way out of the room.

"Would you like me to help you Miss Lucinda?" Karen asked.

"Thank you that is very kind of you," Lucinda answered, as she slowly lifted her legs over the edge of the bed. "Perhaps you would like to choose which one of those amazing nightgowns I should wear today that some mythical prince has delivered on his magic carpet for me."

That remark left Karen laughing for quite a while.

* * *

"Good morning sister, how is Lady Lucinda? Did she enjoy a peaceful night after I left?" I inquired phoning across to the hospital.

"Lady Lucinda is doing well Mr Stone, she has showered and had breakfast. Will you be coming in later today to see her?" The sister dared to ask.

"Absolutely not! I want her to sleep as much as possible, you will restrict visiting for everyone to no more than an hour during the day. Do I make myself clear?"

"Very clear Mr Stone," the sister replied, her voice trembling a little.

"I will come in later this evening as I normally do."

"Very good Mr Stone, is there any message you would like me to pass to her Ladyship?" She asked quietly.

"Thank you no… yes… maybe you would just say I phoned."

"Very good Mr Stone."

It was late afternoon when Bates asked: "Johnathan will you be going to the hospital this evening?"

"Yes Bates I will."

"Do I take it Lady Lucinda is feeling greatly improved?"

"Yes, they tell me she has manage to shower today."

"That is excellent news," Bates answered.

"Bates, would you please ask Ethan to come and talk to me in my sitting room? Perhaps you would like to sit in on this conversation, I rather feel you will be as pleasantly surprised as I was."

Ten minutes later Ethan and Bates returned to the little sitting room. Bates obviously intrigued as to why I wished to talk to them together.

"Please sit down both of you, there is something I would very much like to ask you Ethan."

Ethan looked at me with a smile, as he knew near enough what it was I wanted to know.

"Ethan why did you not tell me Poppy was a doctor? I was completely surprised at seeing her at the hospital. When did she qualify?"

"Let me stop you there Johnathan, before you continue to ask any more questions," Ethan requested, then went on to explain all I wanted to know.

"Poppy is three years older than me, she qualified this year. I wanted you to like her for herself and not because she is a doctor."

"Let me stop you there Ethan," I said in return making us both laugh.

"Please allow me to tell you, I have liked Poppy from the first evening you introduced her to me. I thought she was a charming, delightful person who I hoped would grow to like you, my dear friend. I will hold my hands up and tell you, I never for one moment thought she had two brain cells in her pretty little head. That did not matter to me as long as you were both happy together. Now I must eat humble pie. As well as being a lovely sweet person, she is obviously one exceptionally clever lady, who Lucinda thinks is adorable."

"Thank you Johnathan, I deeply appreciate that you not only like Poppy, but have entrusted her to help look after Lucinda."

"Ethan you are my best friend, all I am concerned about is your welfare. I sincerely hope your relationship with Poppy turns into something very special, if that is what you both wish."

"Now if you will excuse me Ethan, I have some business I wish to discuss with Bates."

"Thank you Johnathan, both Poppy and I are most grateful to you; please pass on my love and best wishes to Lucinda when you next see her."

"I will Ethan thank you, I will speak to you later," I said as he left the room.

"I am greatly surprised," Bates said on hearing about Poppy.

"I thought you might be. Bates there is something serious I wish to talk to you about. There is something I need to reveal to you in regards to my feelings. Bates I am scared."

"Johnathan?" Bates spoke my name in a concerned tone.

Interrupting him again I went on to say. "Bates if I make one more false move, I will lose Lucinda for good. Please can we talk?"

"Of course we can Johnathan, coffee in here?" Bates asked.

"Thank you that would be perfect," I answered. Bates went to make the coffee retuning with a welcome pot including two mugs as usual. After pouring the coffee he sat patiently waiting for me to tell him what was on my mind.

"You know you were right Bates, I do love Lucinda. I love her deeply. That unfortunately is the quandary I am in. Due to the solemn promise she gave to her father; she will never allow me to make her mine until she has her degree. I cannot live that long Bates without, should I say, without the touch of a woman. I have no idea what to do about the difficult situation that I now find myself in".

"Johnathan, maybe you should try to talk about this situation with Lady Lucinda," Bates advised.

"Bates, when Lucinda and I last spoke she said she understood that I needed a woman in my life. Unfortunately she could not be the one, which is why she broke up with me."

"Johnathan, I am afraid this is a situation that no one except Lady Lucinda and yourself can, and must sort out," Bates replied.

"Bates I cannot talk to her, not about this. Not about making love with another woman, when I am supposed to be in love with her. Bates you are the one person I trust, the one person who understands my feelings. Please do try giving me some wise advice?"

"Johnathan may I suggest we leave this matter for the present, at least until Lady Lucinda returns to good health? A solution may have been found by then. Your lovely lady is no fool Johnathan, do not underestimate her common sense."

"Thank you I will do as you say for the present."

Later in the evening I drove over to the hospital longing to take Lucinda in my arms, then kiss her once again the way she loved being kissed; the way I now loved kissing her. How I have missed her warm lips, her loving smile. Yet feeling deeply troubled knowing her kisses would not satisfy my sexual needs, certainly not until she had her degree. I found Lucinda asleep. Quietly going over to the chair I sat next to her looking down at her beautiful face, gently taking her hand in mine raising it to my mouth. If I could not kiss her lips, I could at least brush my lips across her delicate soft hand. Kissing her palm then turning her hand over to kiss the top of it. As I kissed each of her long thin elegant fingers. I must have disturbed her as she whispered, "Johnathan".

"I am here my darling," I told her.

"I have missed you so much." Lucinda replied.

"I know darling, I have been so lonely without you also. May I kiss you?" I whispered.

"Oh please do," Lucinda answered.

It was paradise kissing her once again. Had it been for an eternity it would not have been long enough. When I did release her, Lucinda closed her eyes falling into a deep contented sleep.

The pressure of trying to sort my feeling out continued to grow. Knowing on one hand, I desperately needed to find a way in trying to explain to Lucinda my emotions, yet for the moment unable to do so, not wishing to cause her one moment of despair. My needs were growing to enable me to release my sexual feelings. I am after all still a red blooded young man who has not taken an oath of celibacy. Should Lucinda find out there have been other women in my life, I doubt she will ever forgive me. Maybe Bates was right, maybe she will understand. The gods are indeed tormenting me as I hold Aphrodite in my arms each day, yet I cannot touch her. How do I go about resolving the predicament I am now forced to face?

* * *

"Bates, Lucida is being discharged from Hospital this afternoon, I will naturally go to pick her up. I hate the thought of her returning into Trudy's care instead of mine".

"I am sure Trudy will take great care of her," Bates ventured to say.

"Yes I know she will, that is the trouble. Trudy will smother her like a lioness protecting her cub," I replied.

"So Miss Hamilton and yourself do have something in common at long last," Bates said smiling. I just stood there laughing at that welcome remark.

"Do you know Bates both love and laughter have returned to my life? I was so lost, so empty, without Lucinda being in my life."

"Hello darling," Lucinda said as I entered her room. "You are just in time for afternoon tea before we leave".

I could not help but laugh.

"Lucinda my darling, I guess I am going to have to get used to having a lifetime of afternoon tea with you." Hearing her musical laugh at my stupid remark was sheer heaven to my ears. Lucinda looked at me holding my gaze as only she could.

"Johnathan, I want to have a serious talk with you," Lucinda's said, in a voice that was calm though devoid of any emotion.

"Lucinda what is the matter are you not feeling well?" I asked now concerned.

"Johnathan I am perfectly well thank you, it is nothing to do with my health."

"Then my darling, has someone upset you? I can tell something is bothering you from the sound of your voice."

"Johnathan no one has upset me, please do listen to what I have to say," Lucinda said, trying quietly to explain before I interrupted her again. "Jonathan I have been giving a great deal of thought to your situation."

"My situation darling? I do not understand what in the world are you talking about."

"Johnathan, as much as it pains me to say this to you..." I stopped my goddess instantly by kissing her. For one awful moment my heart froze, I was thinking was once again Lucinda going to tell me; that she had changed her mind about our relationship.

"Johnathan," she continued. "You are a handsome healthy young man. It was terribly wrong of me to expect you to be without having the type of women you may obviously need from time to time. I cannot break my vow to my father, I must wait until I have attained my degree before I can give myself to someone I love. Therefore I am prepared to do you a deal, if you agree".

I felt the blood drain from my face, hesitantly I asked. "What sort of deal do you want me to agree to?"

"I want you to agree Johnathan, that when you have sex with these other women, you promise you will never ever kiss one of them."

I could not say a word for a few moments as I was stunned by Lucinda's words. Taking both her hands in mine, kissing them as I looked deep into her beautiful eyes. I then said: "I promise my darling on all I hold sacred, you will be the only woman I will ever kiss again". With that I took her in my arms, my voice hoarse with passion as I told her: "No woman Lucinda, could ever mean as much to me as you do. There is no one my darling, who could ever kiss me the way you do. You hold my heart in your hands and always will". With that I kissed her a little more passionately than perhaps I should have done, but she understood how I felt.

Driving Lucinda back to Trudy's made me wonder how it would feel when one day I would drive her to our home for the first time. For the moment it all seemed far too far into the distant future. It felt wonderful we were now together once again. I would be able to study with Lucinda or hold her hand in class. When we used the libraries or ate together, I could take her in my arms and kiss her when I wished to. We could go for picnics, or afternoon tea if that is what she wished, dinner in the evening and a great deal more kissing after that. Just having her close to me would be more than marvellous. It would give us time to get to know one another, maybe I would now tell her about owning Stones.

I could still not understand why my father did not wish me to sign his empire back to him though he was now basically running it again. Our studies became more intent during the third year, with Lucinda by my side it seemed to fly by. We returned to California for Christmas; this time I ordered the plane not my father. The seven of us flew back with the atmosphere being highly charged as Jeff and Trudy, were set to become engaged the day before Christmas. Jeff would not allow anyone to see the ring he had bought until the day of the engagement, Trudy's family had decided to give the happy couple a small intimate party for close friends and family.

In some strange way I wished I had been able to buy Lucinda a ring, maybe become engaged. Perhaps thankful it was my friends instead, I guess I was not quite ready for the responsibility of taking on a wife or the bonds of marriage. Things were just fine as they were, I had what I needed as far as other women were concerned, and Lucinda as well.

It felt incredibly strange coming home knowing my father no longer lived there. The penthouse had been completed a couple of months earlier and my father decided to move in there straight away. Now I had full control of my home I gave orders that after Christmas the entire house was to be redecorated the way my mother originally had it before she died. I asked Bates, as much as it would pain me being without him for a few weeks, if he would please ensure everything was carried out to my liking?

"Bates I would like all of my mother's furniture returned and placed the way it had been originally."

I decided that for the present I would continue putting a tree up in the hall, with no family to share a main tree, it seemed pointless to do otherwise. Bates and I decided to go out for Christmas lunch, later I would join my father with a few of his friends on Christmas night, I was growing to feel resentful of spending my time with just Bates and my father. I realised I now wanted Lucinda with me as I missed her company on special days like Christmas or Easter.

My father phoned when I arrived home. "Johnathan I would like you to come across to the office tomorrow if you have no plans", he requested.

"That's fine," I agreed, "I will call around ten thirty if you have no appointments".

"Perfect Johnathan, I shall look forward to seeing you," he said, before hanging up.

"Funny Bates, my father's request still always sounds like a command."

"At least Johnathan, you will get to see how the new penthouse looks," Bates replied.

"Bates, it is just a space to live at the top of a glass tower."

It turned out to be an amazing experience going into our head office as its new owner. Naturally none of the staff new that I was their boss, at least not for the time being. I had asked my father not to tell anyone he was expecting me. The security guard stopped me naturally asking what I wanted.

Looking at his security tag, I said, "good morning Ben," then told him my name was Mr Stone. Mr Johnathan Stone. Ben looked at me smiled then stated, "Oh really and I am prince charming".

"Then good morning you're royal highness," I replied. Ben this time a little more hesitant, yet still not convinced asked for some form of identity. Happy to give him some, the look on his face was worth being stopped for.

"I am so sorry Mr Stone he apologised, I had no idea."

I did not give him time to finish whatever he was about to say. "Not a problem, you were just doing your job, by the way Ben; I own Stones, I am actually your boss."

With that I took the lift up to the main offices laughing inwardly. This was fun. Whether my father liked it or not I decided I was going to have a little more of the fun I had just enjoyed. Walking out of the lift into main corridor, which fed a great many offices on each side, I decided to find one that was being used by a number of young lawyers, who were at present in a meeting. Opening the door they all turned round to look who had dared to intrude on them. One then asked in a condescending voice, "are you lost"?

"No not at all," I answered.

"Then are you looking for someone"? He questioned.

"No," I replied again. "I was just interested in what you were discussing," I told him.

"Young man leave this room immediately or I will call security," he dared to tell me.

"May I ask your name before you do?" I requested.

"No you may not," he replied.

"Then at least allow me to tell you my name. It is Johnathan Stone, and I do not like my employees talking to me, or any other person in that manner. Now would you like to give me your name?"

The look on the faces around that table was just to much as they sat there stunned. I have no idea how I stopped myself from laughing. The young man who had been rather rude was not a great deal older than myself, could not apologise enough.

"Just be a little more considerate in the future," I told him, before I left the room.

I decided this time to find the boardroom, which generally the older lawyers used. This time I knew I had to be a little more cautious; they would sure as hell eat this pup for breakfast, boss or no boss. Sure enough they were all in the meeting, I was surprised my father was not in there with them. I quietly walked in hoping not to disturb them, at least not too much. There was a chair right next to the door, which I immediately sat on. I had hoped they may have thought I was one of the secretaries, unfortunately I was not smart enough to fool any of them.

The most senior of the gentlemen looked at me then said. "Good morning young man, as you have made it your business to come into this room without first being invited, would you like to now tell these gentlemen as well as myself, what is your business here?"

"Good morning," I answered, "I must apologise for disturbing you, I was just curious about the way you conduct your business".

"Interesting to hear that," the senior lawyer who had spoken to me replied. "Are you a lawyer?" he asked.

"No sir, well not yet," I told him.

Then why would you be interested in what we are doing in this meeting?" His voice now serious. I knew in that instant it was time I divulged who I was. Taking a look around the room at each of the men as they sat there obviously intent at what I would say next. I stated.

"It is just that I own this company, so I was a little curious how you actually conduct our business." Once again there was deathly silence for a few moments, then everyone around the table stood up. "Johnathan! Is it really you?"

"Yes sir it is really me."

Each of the lawyers then came over to shake my hand.

"Johnathan it is marvellous to see you? How long will you be here for?"

Many interesting questions were now being asked of me. I told them I had called to see my father, and really must not be late. I promised I would talk with them again once my meeting with my father was over.

"Gentlemen if you will now please excuse me, I really must go."

I left the room having had a great deal of fun, which I would relate to Bates later. I took the lift up to the next floor, on stepping out I found myself directly in a hallway allowing me to look out onto a fantastic panorama. The ocean, the mountains and the city all spread out in front of me depending in which direction I chose to look. I could without doubt understand my father enjoying the view in regards to work, but living here, that I could not understand. Still that was his choice and it was not for me to argue with him about.

"The penthouse is amazing sir, you have indeed ensured a brilliant job has been done."

"Thank you Johnathan, please come and let us sit," my father said as he walked over to the very large settees next to the windows; which in turn gave a marvellous panoramic view across the ocean.

"Your studies, they are going well I hope?" He asked as usual.

"Fine sir," I replied.

"May I ask about your personal life?" He enquired.

"That too for the moment, is also fine," I replied.

"Are you still seeing Major Osborn's daughter?"

"We are still just good friends sir, I like Lady Lucinda, but there is nothing deeply personal going on, we are not having an affair if that is what you are asking."

"Well maybe one day Johnathan you may come to like her who knows, she incontestably comes from very good stock."

He then changed the subject. "I still have no wish Johnathan, to make you a prince instead of an Emperor. I am here if things should go wrong, and I am constantly delighted in the way you handle everything as well as your life. I cannot for the moment see why I should take away your crown. I am enormously proud of you and the way you take both the business and your college work in your stride."

"Thank you sir," I said, "I just find it hard to understand your decision".

"Does it trouble you very much?" my father asked.

"No sir," I told him. "Funnily enough I am now rather enjoying the gift of power you have given me."

"I hope you understand Johnathan, I may one day resume the leadership of the empire as you call it, but certainly not for the present. It has an excellent young Emperor doing a brilliant job, and for me that is all that matters."

"Thank you," I said, then asked. "May I tell you what I did before coming up? I do hope you will not be too annoyed about."

I went on to relate my tale, which my father found very amusing. "I did promise sir I would go back down stairs to talk to our senior lawyers, would you care to join me"?

"Delighted to Johnathan, it is about time everyone met the fantastic boss they have at present. Let us keep them on their toes."

On returning home I related to Bates the full tale of what had happened in the offices.

"Bates, even my father laughed, which I was not expecting. His praise of me seems to be growing, it is as if I am now talking to another man. Bates, do you think there could be another woman, which is causing this change of attitude in him."

"No Johnathan, I do not for the present think your father would ever marry again. He is very like you a highly handsome red-blooded man, there is no saying of course he does not perhaps enjoy the company of a woman."

"I suppose you are right as always Bates. May I ask you something very personal?"

"Depending what is it you wish to know," Bates cautiously asked.

"Bates when your wife and son passed away, did you find solace in the company of another woman right away?"

"Yes Johnathan I did, I am not proud of myself for doing so, but yes I went to a bar a couple of nights after losing Beth and the baby. I drank until I became should we say blind drunk, then started to walk back home. Some woman in a black sedan who was also drunk, stopped and picked me up. That car was big enough to have sex in that is for sure. I have no idea who she was or even what she looked like, I do not know how I even managed to make out with her, I just know I did, when I got out she threw me a wad of money, which I left in the gutter. I was so disgusted with myself; I guess Johnathan death sometimes does that to a man."

"I am terribly sorry Bates that you lost your family,"

"I have a family Johnathan I have you, which makes me extremely lucky."

"Thank you Bates. I hope my father managers to find some happiness soon, after my mother I suspect he will be a hard man to please. Like you he may never marry again."

Christmas came and went and it was time to return once more to Boston, I said my goodbyes to both my father and Bates. I hated the thought of leaving Bates behind, but he was the one person I knew I could trust to ensure my home was refurbished as it once was. Bates knew every inch of the house so would ensure all of my mother's things would be placed as she had them. Once everything was completed Bates would then re-join me in Boston.

The weather was seriously awful when we arrived, hating the cold that greeted us further soured my mood, adding to the thought of having left Bates behind, I decided to move the boys and myself into the hotel until either Bates re-joined us or the weather improved.

At least staying in the hotel our needs would be catered for, our rooms cleaned, food on tap, we were grateful for small mercies.

Bates last words to me being, "you just worry about your studies as well as Lady Lucinda".

"I will, I promise," I told him.

"Then take care of yourself, I shall hope to join you soon," Bates conveyed, the tone of his words having a little emotion in them.

It was another two months before Bates flew in to re-join me. Jeff, Ethan and I were so pleased to see him, which in turn eventually allowed us go back our lovely home.

"You have been sorely missed, not just by me but by the boys also," I informed him. "You could have at least brought some sunshine with you," I said making Bates laugh.

"How is your lovely lady Johnathan? I hope you are looking after her the way you should?"

"Yes Bates, I promise you I have not put a foot wrong. I do find it hard to believe she is so understanding."

"You just make sure you do not break your agreement to Lady Lucinda. Remember there is always someone to upset the apple cart, some little witch who will be more than happy to inform her should you break your word."

"Bates when I eventually make her mine, there will never be another woman in my life. That I swear."

Spring came and went, we all buckled down as this year's exams were vital. Jeff and Trudy were now talking of marriage. Trudy naturally wanted a big white wedding out in California, it would take them at least twelve months to plan. Ethan's relationship with Poppy was now on a very firm footing, like Jeff and Trudy, they could not keep their hands off each other. Why had I chosen to fall for a girl I could not touch? I wanted desperately to spend my nights with Lucinda instead of some high-class whore. I wanted to go away for weekends with her, but knew it was useless to even ask. Instead I had to be grateful for the few crumbs Lucinda gave to me. I kept my promise to her by never kissing any of the women I employed. On rare occasions I would pretend it was Lucinda I was making love to, instead the latest whore I had paid.

Another year to go before Lucinda became mine. Why in hell had her father extracted such a promise from her?

"To protect her from men like you," Bates informed me.

"To protect her from men like me," I repeated.

Chapter 8

With the summer vacation starting Jeff and Trudy with Lucinda in tow flew back to California.

"We are going to start the ball rolling for our wedding Jeff informed me. By the time we qualify next year, all the preparations for the wedding with luck should be in place".

"How long do you intend to be away?" I asked.

"Around a couple of weeks maybe longer, why?" Jeff replied.

"I had hoped to have spent the entire holidays with Lucinda," I answered.

"Sorry about that Johnathan, I guess like all girls Lucinda included they become excited about weddings," Jeff replied then went on to say, "especially with this one being Trudy's. I know Trudy is thrilled to bits, must say so am I. I can hardly believe it has been nearly three years since Trudy and I first met, now at long last we are planning to marry, Johnathan, you will honour me by being my best man."

"Of course I'd be delighted to, I would not have it any other way," I answered.

"Brilliant at least that is one problem easily solved."

"Jeff then surprised me by saying. Rather thought you and Lucinda may have become engaged by now."

"Enjoy your trip Jeff, give my best to Trudy."

Recognising my tone of voice, Jeff was wise enough not to say another word. He knew he must be very judicious about any mention of my relationship with Lucinda. My feelings for Lucinda were off limits to everyone.

He was of course quite right, we should by now have been very much involved with each other, there was nothing I would have liked more. Damn the promise she gave to her father. The one positive outcome of this situation was that I knew Lucinda would not renege on a promise, even one she may find hard at present to enforce.

That thought unfortunately, did not make me feel any better on the lonely nights I desperately wanted to make love to her. Driving to the airport made me wish I was going back to California with the others. Taking Lucinda in my arms, kissing her as passionately as I dared. Then having to say goodbye to her, left me feeling empty even desolate. I hated the very thought of letting her out of my sight, regardless that I knew Trudy would take good care of her. Not seeing her beautiful face for two, maybe three weeks, was more than I thought I would be able to bear. Damn Trudy Hamilton and her wedding plans. As far as I was concerned, she was doing nothing more than taking Lucinda away from me. Poppy and Ethan decided to fly down to Florida for a couple of weeks, being left alone to entertain myself, was definitely not my idea of fun.

"Bates pack a bag for you and me we are going home. I have endured my own company long enough."

Being without Lucinda, though it had been no more than a couple of days, made me feel not just lonely as I thought I would be, but incredibly miserable. I did not care whether Trudy Hamilton thought I was intruding or not, I needed Lucinda's company even if it was just for a few hours here and there.

I ordered my plane for an early evening flight; Bates ordered the cars to and from the airports. I guess when I arrived home I would then get in touch with my father.

Bates put a stop to that thought by saying to me: "Johnathan, if I may say so it would be advisable to phone your father before you leave".

"As always Bates you are quite right. Picking the phone up knowing it was very early in California. I firstly apologised for disturbing him, going on to inform him. "Dad I just wanted to let you to know I am on my way home for a couple of weeks".

"That sounds excellent Johnathan, I shall look forward to meeting you. Will you come to the office, or shall we meet somewhere else?" My father answered sounding most convivial.

"I would love to come to the office sir if you do not mind, perhaps we can go out to dinner later."

"That sounds perfect to me," my father agreed then asked. "When do you intend to come into town, tomorrow, or the day after? I will hold that particular day free for you."

"The day after tomorrow,' I told him, "if it is convenient for you".

"That will be just fine, I will see you around ten thirty; have a good flight Johnathan, until then goodbye."

"Goodbye sir," I replied, my father then replaced his receiver.

"Bates, did I just speak to my father?"

"I am sorry Johnathan I do not understand," Bates replied.

"I swear Bates, the man I just spoke to, whilst he sounded like my father, his attitude did not attain to being anything like him."

The housekeeper opened the door to greet us: "Hello Mr Stone, so nice to see you again".

I loved her calling me Mr Stone, this being her first time in doing so, previously it had always been Master Johnathan on arriving home. All though I was tired, I wanted to see what Bates had done with the house. As I walked through the rooms everything was not just pristine, but perfect, just the way I loved it. My mother's furniture back where it should be, I had missed seeing it around the house since her death. Now my home felt like home once more.

Finding Bates before going to bed was now a necessity as I wished to thank him, luckily he was chatting in the kitchen having a nightcap.

"Thank you Bates you have once again ensured a splendid job has been carried out; I am most grateful to you".

"My pleasure entirely Johnathan, now you can think about bringing your young lady to see where you normally live when not in Boston," Bates said with a smile.

"Good night Bates I am off to bed."

Walking upstairs I knew unquestionably I had no intention of bringing Lucinda to my home, regardless of how fond I may be of her, or any other woman for that matter. This was my space, which I am not prepared to share with any member of the opposite sex; unless of course they worked for me.

"Not slept too well?" Bates asked the following morning.

"I am fine," I told him: "Perhaps a little tired from the long journey".

I knew in my heart of hearts that statement did not ring true, my thoughts being private and I had no intentions of sharing them. I did not need or require any further lectures at the moment in regard to Lucinda, from Bates or anyone.

I went to look around my father's office. Opening the door without knocking first, felt fantastic and leaving the door open felt even better. All his expensive law books, which must have cost a fortune, remained intact on the shelves. On his desk lay a sealed envelope that was addressed for the personal attention of Mr JR Jefferson Stone. Inside was a letter from my father. On reading his words I was both shocked and surprised.

"My dear Johnathan, no one could ask for a better son, you know how very proud I am of you. Therefore I would like to gift to you the sets of law books, which I am sure you are at present observing. I hope they will be of some small service in the future. They are given with all my love. DAD.

This was indeed far from what I was expecting, I had never received a letter from my father in my entire life. To now receive one with so much conviction of pride written into it was amazing.

On entering this room, which had been his private space from the day he had bought this house, I thought he may have had the room stripped bare. Instead to now find such a gift, given obviously with immense sincerity, was beyond my comprehension. I sat down and not for the first time tried to figure out my father's behaviour, yet still unable to even begin to understand his nature.

It would now be impossible for me to strip this room as I had intended. Instead I would use it to study in should I have the need to, accompanied by this amazing array of law books. They will naturally be most welcome in the future, should I eventually become a lawyer. The rest of my father's things I can only surmise had been taken across to the penthouse.

I decided to phone Jeff to see what plans had been put in place for Trudy and himself, as well as their families for today. He would not be risking Trudy's wrath in telling me what I wanted to know as they think I am still in Boston. At least Trudy would not for the time being try to interfere when I asked to speak to Lucinda.

"We are having a number of wedding planners coming over," Jeff informed me, "So I will be spending the day at Trudy's. My parents are dropping over for lunch it should be quite a pleasant time for all."

"Delighted for you, hope all goes well,, I replied then asked. "Could I please speak to Lucinda?" The phone went quiet for a few moments; Jeff came back on to tell me. "Sorry Johnathan, Lucinda is a little busy for the present, she is apparently helping Trudy to choose flowers of sorts. Why not phone back later this evening, I am sure she will be free after dinner."

"I am sure she will," came my cold reply.

With that I put the phone down. How dare that jumped up pedantic bitch, try to keep me from talking with Lucinda, never mind seeing her.

"Bates I want a chauffeur driven limo now; make it a Rolls Royce! A silver one at that."

Bates looked at me knowing I was as mad as hell. He had better sense these days not say a word when I spoke in that manner. Returning to my dressing room, changing my clothes with care, if I owned an empire then

Trudy Hamilton was going to see how an emperor dressed and behaved when angered.

We arrived at the main gates of Trudy's home, the chauffeur telling the gate man his passenger was Mr Johnathan Jefferson Stone, the best man. We were waved in instantly. As the chauffeur drove up the long drive Trudy's house came into view, my passing thought being, not bad, but nothing as magnificent as my home.

The car came to a halt at the front entrance; the chauffeur was about to jump out to open the car door. I thanked him telling him: "I am still more than capable of opening my own door, but please wait for me".

On ringing the doorbell, the front door was opened in seconds by Trudy's butler.

"Good morning sir are you here to see Miss Hamilton," he asked.

"No," I replied, "I am here to see Lady Lucinda Osborn".

"Oh please come in, I will tell her Ladyship you are here."

"Thank you, but I will tell her myself along with Trudy and Jeff," I replied, "I assume everyone is in the main sitting room?"

"Yes sir," the butler replied.

"Thank you, I can find my own way."

"Very well sir," and with that the butler disappeared.

I stood discreetly behind some overgrown potted palm for a few moments taking in the scene before me; Trudy was sitting between her mother and future mother-in-law, all three being deep in conversation. Jeff was animatedly talking to his father and future father-in-law. Lucinda sat on her own browsing some wedding magazines. Seeing her sitting alone looking a little lost made me feel even angrier than when I had earlier put the phone down on Jeff.

Closing the magazine Lucinda looked up and saw me. I put my finger up to my lips, telling her not to say a word, then indicated to her to come over to where I stood. Putting down her magazine she walked over very slowly, so not to raise suspicion of my presence, with the grace most women would envy.

I gently pulled her out of sight, then took her in arms, I found her beautiful, sweet, tender lips. Kissing them for what seemed far too short a time before Lucinda quietly asked: "What are you doing here Johnathan, I thought you were supposed to be in Boston?" I kissed her again and again not wanting to stop, eventually telling her how much I had missed her.

"I wanted my darling to spend the whole summer with you, instead your guard dog has dragged you away from me."

"Oh Johnathan, please do not talk about Trudy like that," Lucinda begged. "Trudy is terribly kind which I am most grateful for, and I am deeply indebted to her for being so."

"Trudy is certainly not kind to me, as she would not allow me to talk to you this morning," I replied.

"We were trying to choose flowers," Lucinda told me.

"I do not give a damn about Trudy's flowers or whatever else she wishes to choose for her wedding. All I want Lucinda, is to spend my time with you. Now I am here you will be surplus to Trudy's requirements."

Taking Lucinda once again in my arms. I rained kisses down on her beautiful face and lips.

"I think we should tell the others you are here Johnathan," Lucinda pleaded. "Please, as I do not wish to appear rude."

"Very well, but I will not take no for an answer, not from Trudy or anyone else where you are concerned. Do I make myself clear?"

"Yes darling, I understand," Lucinda said smiling.

"Then give me one last kiss before we return to the sitting room. Now Lucinda I want you to walk back in as if you have not seen me, I will then follow a few moments later."

"Johnathan, what are you up to?" Lucinda asked.

"Making a grand entrance for Miss Priggy boots," I replied.

"Johnathan you are incorrigible," Lucinda laughed.

"I know darling, but it can be such fun sometimes."

Lucinda returned to the others while I went to find the butler.

"Mr Johnathan Jefferson Stone," the butler announced in his pompous voice, addressing me by my full title. Everyone stopped what they were doing, obviously surprised at the butler's announcement of my presence.

"Jeff came over looking totally shocked, "I thought you were still in Boston Johnathan".

"Decided to jump on my plane and fly to see my friends," I replied. Trudy Hamilton looked furious, knowing full well I would now take Lucinda away from her. To all intense and purposes Lucinda appeared to be no more than a play puppy for her anyway.

I was introduced to each of the respective parents. Trudy's parents appeared very pleased to meet me, and why not. Their daughter was now a friend of an excessively rich and powerful young man, one of the finest this country had to offer. Jeff's parents of course, I had known me since I was a small boy.

"Johnathan dear boy delighted to see you, you are looking a great deal better than when we last met at your mother's funeral. Tell me how is your father keeping?" Jeff's father asked.

"He seems to be picking up sir," I told him.

"Good, very good, please pass on our best wishes if you would."

"I will indeed, sir," I replied: "Now if you will all please excuse Lucinda and I, we will leave you to your plans." With that I took Lucinda by the hand and left the room.

It was wonderful having Lucinda to myself for the rest of the day, as well as the evening. Unfortunately neither Jeff or Trudy were pleased about me taking Lucinda away. Not that I gave a damn what they thought or felt, in fact my resentment of Trudy was growing as each year passed. I found her insufferable with her love of formality, even though she was not bad mannered as such. I disliked the fact she spoke her mind outright without first being a little more diplomatic, especially when she was damn well right. Most of all I hated every moment Lucinda spent with her instead of me.

The limo drove us into town where I dismissed it. Lucinda and I had lunch at a low-key bistro, in the evening we went for dinner to a wonderful French restaurant, which my father had highly recommended. We laughed about all sorts of ridiculous things, including the prank I had played when I went to see my father at the office. Lucinda looked at me quizzically, I had stupidly given the game away by telling her of the fun I had at the expense of the other lawyers.

"So your father does own Stones," she said.

"No Lucinda," I replied. "He does work there as I told you; I own Stones." Looking at the shock on Lucinda's face, I had no choice but to tell her the truth. "I think Lucinda I had better now explain the full story. Before I do. I would like to extract from you a promise that you will tell no one, at least not for the moment."

Lucinda looked at me for a few moments, then quietly asked: "Are you kidding me Johnathan, as I do not think this is something to kid about?"

"No darling," I replied, "I am not kidding you".

Again Lucinda looked at me, holding my gaze, saying nothing for a further few moments. "Very well then, I promise I will tell no one your story."

By this time I had ordered another car, enabling me to drive Lucinda back to Trudy's. It had been a wonderful evening, except for the fact I now regretted that I had revealed to her about owning Stones. I had to hope Lucinda would hold good on her promise to me, as she had her father. It seemed that the men in her life, in some way or another, always managed to extract promises from her, telling her it was for the best as they cared about her. Damn her father and damn my father for putting me in this position.

We arrived at Trudy's, pulling up to the front door, I held Lucinda in my arms then told her. "I must go to see my father tomorrow, the moment I am free darling I will call over for you, until then I will miss you terribly." Each time I kissed her goodbye was becoming harder and harder to let her go, regardless of our agreement that I could have other women in my life. It was Lucinda that I was desperate to make love to, not them. Watching her disappear into Trudy's home I told myself by this time next year Lucinda, I will be your lover.

* * *

The following morning I entered our glass tower once again to be greeted by Ben, I felt so happy at the thought that the sooner this meeting was over with my father, the sooner I would be holding my goddess in my arms.

"Good morning, how are you Ben?"

"Good morning Mr Stone, Ben replied.

"How is your family?" I asked.

"They are fine Mr Stone, thank you for asking."

"Good I am pleased to hear that." As far as I am concerned the little people in my company were to be treated with all the dignity and respect that any of our top lawyers receive.

Taking the lift directly up to the penthouse, this time I was greeted by my father's sectary. My father had decided to have a desk installed just outside his private office, which lead into his living quarters. His sectary Mrs Atkins had been with him since I was a small boy. He completely trusted her as he did Bates.

Mrs Atkins was a small, plain but very charming woman, probably in late middle age with impeccable manners. She practically knew as much about the business as my father did. The main thing she did not know, that for the present I was the current owner or did she?

"Good morning Mr Stone, so nice to see you again."

"Hello Mrs Atkins nice to be here, how are you and your family?" I inquired.

"We are all doing well, thank you for asking," she replied.

"What do you think of your new work space?" I asked her.

"So much nicer than the downstairs office, in fact rather grand. The views are amazing! It is a wonder I get any work done sir," she said, laughing.

"I fully agree with you Mrs Atkins the views are indeed stunning," I then went on to ask her if my father was free.

"Yes sir, he is looking forward to seeing you."

"Thank you Mrs Atkins, it is a pleasure seeing you once again, I am sure we will speak later. Oh before I go in, if you have a pot of coffee going that would be very welcome."

"My pleasure Mr Stone I will bring it in shortly," Mrs Atkins replied kindly.

I walked into the office then opened the glass doors to the private living quarters. "Good morning dad, you are looking very well."

"Good morning Johnathan so are you."

"I hope you do not mind sir, I have asked Mrs Atkins to bring in a pot of coffee."

"Not at all my," father replied.

Taking a quick look around the vast open area that was now my father's living quarters, I commented to him about it, by saying: "This is an amazing space you have had made. Fantastic would be a better word to describe it, so are the views. Are you settled in here now?"

"For the present Johnathan," my father replied. "I must admit it can be a little overwhelming on my own at night. I rather feel the penthouse is somewhere you may enjoy once you are married. It is after all very much a family space. If I am being honest maybe you would like to move in here when you marry".

"I have no intention sir of marrying for a very long time."

"Tell me Johnathan, do you still see Lady Lucinda Osborn?"

"Yes sir, she is still part of my crowd."

"Does she as yet have a young man in her life?" My father asked.

I did not want to lie, so told him half the truth by saying: "Lady Lucinda continues to hold her promise to her father, in that she will not become involved with anyone until she has gained her degree".

"That makes her a very special, rather unique young lady in this day and age; would you not agree?" My father questioned.

"Yes sir, it does indeed."

Changing the subject I went on to say: "Thank you very much dad for your exceedingly generous gift. The law books are magnificent, there is no mistaking they will positively be of great help to me in the future".

"I am delighted Johnathan you are pleased with them. It is my pleasure to make a present of them to you. Johnathan, if you wish to stay at the cutting edge and become a top lawyer you will find you will need to study the law, practically each day, for the rest of your working life. I hope the set of books I have gifted you, will in some small way help you to do just that".

"As I said sir, I am indeed positive they will. I am also exceedingly grateful for your wise counsel I will bear in mind all you have told me."

My father was delighted to hear reply. "Anywhere in particular you would like to lunch?" my father enquired.

"Anywhere you wish sir, as long as the food is edible."

Both remarks making my father laugh, we spent a rare very enjoyable day together, talking business among many other things and I found myself actually learning a great deal from him. In the evening we went to one of my father's favourite French restaurants for dinner, he seemed more relaxed in my company than he had been for many a long year. Maybe he felt he could now relate better to me as I grew older. Or simply the fact I was the emperor for the moment not him.

Whatever the reason may have been, by the time I dropped him off at the office we had enjoyed each other's company immensely. Just as I went to pull away, he stopped me by saying: "I am being sincere Johnathan when I tell you how very proud of you I am. I could not have wished for a better son." With that he turned and walked into our glass tower. I had not planned to spend the whole day and evening with him, this time I was rather glad I did.

The following week I returned to the office, my father having decided to officially introduce me to all of the staff. The senior lawyers once again delighting in seeing me. Comments of, 'you have a fine son there James', or 'you must be proud of him', 'he has grown into a handsome pup', 'chip off the old block' and 'I am sure he will make a damn good lawyer James like yourself'. My father appearing puffed up with pride, as I continually replied: "I try to do best sir, I get my good looks from dad".

"You do indeed young man, you certainly do, one of them stated. The compliments were nice to receive, though I am not normally receptive to flattery; or allow it to cloud my judgement.

On returning downstairs to the offices where the junior lawyers work out of. The atmosphere became a little more strained. I guess it was time to try and make amends, they were after all my employees, trying my very best to be as charming and as pleasant as I could, eventually managing to work things out. I did though have to eat a little humble pie, but well worth it in the end.

There were of course a large number of women working in the offices, some being very pretty.

"Nice looking girls for you to enjoy," my father said.

"What about you dad," I said laughing. "Have you met anyone you may like to become involved with?"

"Johnathan," my father replied his voice not sounding quite like ice, just fairly cool. "That topic is off limits."

"Yes sir," I answered him with a smile, yet as my father being a damned handsome man. I hoped it would not be too long before he allowed some attractive woman to draw his attention.

I continued to see Lucinda as and when it was possible. The four of us spent the evening together just before it was time to return to Boston. It gave me the opportunity I wanted to inform Jeff of my arrangements that Lucinda will of course be flying back with me.

"If Trudy and yourself would care to join us you are most welcome. I will be taking Lucinda back of course whether you both come or not".

"Thank you Johnathan, but Trudy and I have return flights already booked, as does Lucinda", Jeff answered.

"Jeff I have just told you Lucinda will be flying back with me, regardless if you have booked ten bloody flights back for her, do I make myself clear."

Jeff's reply shocked me: "I have no idea Johnathan why you are so obsessed with Lucinda, to the point of upsetting Trudy. You deliberately came out to California knowing how important this trip was to the three of us, you knew we intended making plans for our wedding".

"There are two of you marrying," I answered. "You are marrying Trudy, you most definitely are not marrying Lucinda. So there is no three of you planning a wedding. From what I have seen Jeff, both your mother as well as Trudy's, have more than managed to have their input into your plans, without the need for Lucinda's opinions".

"Naturally it is only Trudy and I who are marrying," Jeff moaned, then went on to say: "By taking Lucinda constantly away from Trudy, you are depriving her of having her best friend with her."

Now mad as hell! I told Jeff: "Do not give me that bullshit, Lucinda is no more than a well-bred puppy dog for Trudy to play with, as and when she feels like".

"Johnathan do not let me hear you say another derogatory word about Trudy, I mean it. We have been friends all of our lives. I have no wish to fall out with you over a woman, particularly one you have never even slept with."

Jeff now sounded as angry as I felt, he continued in the same tone of voice: "Johnathan, you know full well you will probably never marry Lucinda once you have taken her to your bed, you would do her a great service by giving her up. In doing so you will allow Lucinda to find a man who will love her enough to eventually marry her, not someone like yourself who will treat her at the end of the day like all the other whores you go with. As far as Trudy and I can see Johnathan, Lucinda is nothing more than a game to you, giving you a great deal of perverse pleasure".

Jeff and I had never had an altercation in all the years we had been friends.

"You sound more like Trudy every day," I retorted, "and she assuredly has you brainwashed, or is it she is just a good lay that you put up with her bullshit. Neither of you know anything about my feelings for Lucinda".

Now incandescent with rage I told Jeff: "Get the hell out of my sight, you should both learn to mind your own damn business".

By this time Trudy and Lucinda had returned to the table. I grabbed Lucinda's arm storming out, with her looking terribly upset.

"Johnathan what has just happened? "You sounded so angry," Lucinda remarked as we drove back to Trudy's.

"I have told you before Lucinda, I am my own person I do not need anyone. I run a multi-million dollar empire having done so since I was eighteen. It entails me being responsible for hundreds of people's livelihoods. The firm's top lawyers tell me I am doing a damn good job to. On top of that I am studying my backside off to become a lawyer. Lucinda that is something I have to be to ensure I am good enough to run my companies. I will not accept anyone interfering in my life. Not now, not ever; especially my darling, where you are concerned".

"Johnathan please, I cannot believe you have just fallen out with your oldest friend over me."

"Lucinda, you are and always will be mine, you belong to me. I will not allow Trudy, Jeff or anyone else to tell me I should give you up. I have never discussed with Jeff the arrangement we have. I have honoured that arrangement Lucinda and will never break it. You hold my heart and my soul in your beautiful hands. Lucinda I will not lie to you; it is becoming harder as each lonely night passes, unable to take you to my bed fulfilling the need I have for you. I understand your reasons though I hate that I have to respect them, Trudy it seems does not understand. Lucinda does she know of our agreement?"

"No Johnathan, I have never spoken to her about it."

"No wonder Trudy thinks I am not good enough for you. I have no idea who she thinks would be good enough, maybe some English Prince. All I do know Lucinda, there are very few men in this country that can give you what I can give you. You know I will spend the rest of life trying my best to give you everything you could ever desire".

"Johnathan I am terribly upset that I am the cause of this awful fallout with your oldest friend," Lucinda replied then continued to say: "Please we must find a way of working this problem out. I promise I will have a serious talk with Trudy tomorrow. Maybe she will then come to understand my situation".

Lucinda then asked: "Please kiss me darling I love you so much".

For the first time I did not kiss her. I was still as mad as hell at Jeff. My voice still full of anger I told Lucinda. "I have no wish for you to discuss with Trudy our private life. It is absolutely none of her damn business, or Jeff's. I will be most upset with you if I find you have degraded yourself in doing so, I like my private life, being kept private. Lucinda do I make myself clear".

"Yes Johnathan, I will respect your wishes if that is what you want. How are you going to make up with Jeff? I cannot bare the thought of Jeff and yourself not being friends after all these years."

"Lucinda leave Jeff to me, this is a man's thing not something for you to lose any sleep over. Promise me Lucinda, you will not allow Trudy to bully you, mistreat you or be rude to you in any way. If she does then you must phone me instantly. Do I once again make myself crystal clear? I will not allow anyone to insult you not even for a moment."

"Oh Johnathan, I love you so dearly, thank you. I am so grateful and appreciate that you wish to protect me."

My anger slowly began to dissipate, knowing Lucinda was dreadfully upset about the whole fracas. I looked into her beautiful eyes, which now looked sad from worry, then said: "Thank me by kissing me this instant". And with that I took Lucinda in my arms and smothered my goddess' face and lips with kisses.

* * *

"Please will you find Lady Lucinda?" Trudy ask her butler. "Would you ask her if she would please join me in the morning room?"

"Of course miss," the butler answered. Lucinda came down stairs to find Trudy already eating breakfast.

"Good morning Trudy I believe you wish to speak with me."

"Lucinda come and sit down you look simply dreadful, are you feeling ill?"

"No Trudy," Lucinda replied, "I am just terribly upset that Jeff and Johnathan have had this terrible fall out over me".

"Oh Lucinda it is not just over you. Jeff and I love you dearly, you know that darling. Johnathan Stone is indeed Jeff's best friend, but he hates the fact Johnathan is behaving terribly towards you, Lucinda you must know that Johnathan Stone is a womaniser: he always has been. He thinks because his daddy is one of the richest men in the country, he can do as he wishes including giving him the right to behave in any way he wants towards women. He takes every little whore to bed he can lay his hands on, as and when he feels like. I am not saying he does not pay them well, I have been told he is at least very particular using high class ones of course. The trouble Lucinda is that he is not seriously interest in someone as decent as you". Trudy then continued: "Lucinda darling, Jeff is quite right, once he gets you into his bed he will discard you, just as he does every other woman. I understand Lucinda he has said he loves you. If he really loved you darling, he would surly behave with a great deal more decorum than he does at present including courting you".

Lucinda knew she dare not tell Trudy the truth, having promised she would not say a word. Instead Lucinda continued: "Trudy you do not understand, I love Johnathan. I always have and always will love him. I remember seeing him for the first time in the library, he looked every inch the type of man every woman dreams about. Handsome, tanned, and athletic. Even though at that time I had no knowledge of his wealthy background, I just knew I loved him. He could not see me looking at him under my hair, when he came into view I could barely breathe. I had no idea who he was until one day not long after I saw him in the dining room. He was talking to a couple of girls, eventually they went to the little girl's room so I followed them. There the two girls were talking about him, one saying to the other, 'I would love to get into Johnathan Stone's pants'. The other girl replied, 'I would rather he got into mine'. To which the first one answered: 'Maybe with luck we will both have our way,' then they left still laughing".

"Both girls were so beautiful Trudy, not for one moment did I think Johnathan would ever look in my direction, or regard me as attractive. Most assuredly not interesting enough to talk to. After a period of months very slowly I began to notice, he would frequently watch me when he was either in the library or in the dining room. You have no idea how thrilled I felt, daring to hope he may indeed possibly find me interesting enough to talk to after all. The day you introduced me to him. I knew then I had lost my heart to him. Trudy, I am hopelessly in love with him, he is my world. I have absolutely no interest in any other man, when I am ready to become a woman I will give myself to him and no other, in his own way he already is very protective towards me."

Trudy Hamilton then commented, "Lucinda you have astonished me, I had no idea how deep your feelings for him were, I should say are for him. I know Lucinda he was both very kind and generous towards you when you were in hospital, but I must be honest dearest, Jeff and I are very worried should he hurt you again".

"Johnathan has never hurt me Trudy. It was I who fell out with him, not the other way around. Johnathan has said he will always look after me, which is wonderful to hear when you are unfortunately on your own. What you do not understand, neither does Johnathan it seems, is once I have my degree I am independent of everyone. I will not need any man to provide for me. Please Trudy, please ask Jeff to make up with his life-long friend, I am sure he will understand. Jeff and Johnathan love each other like brothers; I do not want to be the cause of their fall out."

"Jeff will certainly be as surprised as I am Lucinda, like myself I doubt he has any idea that your love for Johnathan runs that deep. Very well, I agree to go along with your wishes. If you are sure you are happy to continue to accept the situation that Johnathan has a great number of other women in his life for the present. Trudy then continued, I will explain your feelings to Jeff."

"Please Trudy it is all I ask," Lucinda requested then asked, please make Jeff understand how I feel, it is so vitally important to both Jeff and myself, not just to make up with his friend, but to respect my deep love for Johnathan, as he means everything to me. When you have told him do you think Jeff would reconsider about flying back with us? Please Trudy do try to persuade him? I am sure there is nothing Johnathan would like more."

* * *

"Good to be back Bates, I can hardly believe I shall shortly be starting my final year."

"I am not looking forward to winter, that is for sure," Bates replied.

"I agree with you Bates, I just hope the weather holds, allowing us to fly home for Christmas. It was a close call last year."

Johnathan, I am sorry Jeff and Trudy did not fly back with you."

"So am I Bates, so am I. Unfortunately Jeff cannot understand that Lucinda belongs to me. I refuse to go into any detail with him why we are not a couple as he and Trudy are. Quite honestly as far as I am concerned Bates, his attitude stinks. He has become more of a prissy miss, than the Miss Bossy Boots he is going to marry. How he, or anyone, dare tell me to give Lucinda up is beyond me".

"Do you think he will move his things out?" Bates asked.

"I hope not. Unfortunately the feelings between us at present are pretty rough."

Tactful as ever Bates then asked: "Would you consider try talking to him?

"If he apologises to me yes, if not then I guess that will be that. Our friendship will be over, which would leave me feeling incredibly sad.

"I had hoped Bates both Trudy and Jeff would have come to work for me once we returned to California."

Looking me directly in the eye Bates then asked: "Johnathan, does Jeff have anything to apologise to you for?"

"What do you mean Bates, of course he does, he is suggesting that once I make Lucinda mine, I will no longer be interested in her".

"And will you? Bates inquired.

"I cannot believe Bates, you have just asked me that question. You know full well how much Lucinda means to me."

Bates searched my face before he stated. "I did not ask you how much Lady Lucinda means to you

Johnathan, I asked you once you have taken Lady Lucinda to your bed, will you still want to marry her?"

"Bates you know full well I have no intention of marrying anyone for a very long time, just as Lucinda knows."

I could hear the anger rising in Bates voice as he continued: "Does she really Johnathan? Or does your Lady believe once you have your degree you will indeed make her yours. Not just by taking her to your bed, but by the expedient of making her your wife. Let's face it you have allowed her for the last number of years to believe you love her".

I interrupted Bates by saying, "you are talking as much rubbish as Jeff".

Bates now vented his anger, his voice cold as ice as he replied. "Am I, am I really Johnathan. Maybe you would like me to leave as well as Jeff for saying so?"

"You can please yourself Bates if you wish to leave go ahead. I will never give Lucinda up for anyone."

"I am not asking you to give her up, I am asking will you do the decent thing by her or not."

"Bates, I have no wish to continue with this conversation, it is none of your business or anyone else's. Now if you will excuse me I am going to bed."

"Johnathan, do not walk away from me while I am talking to you, not this time. I asked you a question and I want an answer," Bates tone of voice remind me the way my father would sound when cross examining in court; or when he appeared severely angry with someone who had displeased him. This shift in his usual calm demeanour caused me to snap back at him.

"You may sound just like my father, but you are not my father," I continued in the same angry tone of voice: "What gives you the right to speak to me in that manner?"

Furious at my attitude Bates replied. "My self-respect Johnathan, something you are obviously very short of at this moment in time. Be very careful how you answer me. I will take none of your bullshit even if I do work for you. You are at the moment treading on very thin ground".

Bates was right I was on thin ground. I had never heard him talk to me, or anyone in that manner.

Changing my tone of voice, I asked Bates: "If you do not mind I would appreciate it if you will excuse me, may we please talk about this in the morning. I am extremely tired and upset over Jeff."

"Very well Johnathan, we will talk in the morning, but I will not change my mind about Lady Lucinda. Or your behaviour towards her".

"Good night Bates."

"Good night Johnathan," Bates replied in the same cold voice as he had used before.

I reached the door then turned around, looking at Bates then said: "A pot of coffee would be good in the morning".

Bates looked at me for a few moments then answered: "A pot of coffee will be waiting for you".

I thought I knew Bates so well, I guess you never know someone one hundred percent. Never having seen or heard him so angry, the whole experience left me feeling somewhat traumatised. The fact he was even prepared to walk out after all these years came as such a shock to my system, especially knowing he had a home with me for the rest of his life. Not just a home, but a job I knew he loved. What possessed him to want to throw it all away for the sake of a girl I wanted to have sex with?

I knew he would not let me off the hook this morning, but why should I have to marry to please Bates, Jeff and Trudy or anyone for that matter. Even my father understood that I did not want to marry for a long time to come. Yet each time he saw me he would always enquire about Lucinda. Why! Why was he also damned interested if she was still part of my life?

What was so wrong, having waited for four years, then taking Lucinda to my bed without the commitment of marriage? Lucinda was obviously happy with this agreement, she had never questioned it, so she must be content with that thought. Lucinda knew once she had her degree, our love life would be totally different; I had kept to my word of kissing no other woman. Lucinda in turn had kept to the ridiculous promise, which she had made to her father. I must admit some nights I wished it was Lucinda in my bed that I was having sex with, not some expensive whore; that is not quite true, most nights now I wish I was making love to Lucinda, not just having sex.

Funny, I am not one hundred percent sure what the difference is, is there a difference? Maybe I should ask Bates, would he know? If so I am sure he would be more than happy to enlighten me.

"Good morning Jonathan," Bates said looking tired.

"Good morning Bates, you look as if you have not slept very well."

"Actually Johnathan you are quite right," Bates replied. "I have had a great deal on my mind, so no. I have not slept too well."

I knew I must diffuse the atmosphere between us, therefore it was for me to apologise. "Bates, I am very sorry about last night. I should not have spoken to you the way I did, it was uncalled for as well as damned rude of me to have done so."

"You are quite right it was damn rude, but your apology is accepted," Bates then gently said: "I know Johnathan and understand it is none of my business, or anyone else's for that matter what you do with your life. I have watched you grow up into a fine young man with a great deal more pressure on you, than you should have at your age, I know and understand you do not need anyone to dictate the terms to you, being your own master. I also appreciate and understand that people are easily replaceable in your world of work. What I do not understand is how you think you are able to go through your life; without the love and trust of people that are close to you. Everyone needs love Johnathan, no matter who they may be, from the poorest man to the richest, I do not mean just sex, Johnathan. I mean real love. Bates continued, Johnathan, have you ever given some thought to what real love is?"?

"Yes... No..."

"Which is it?" Bates asked then went on to say. "Do you think just taking a woman to your bed, having good, maybe even great sex with her is love?"

I looked directly into Bates eyes for a good few moments, knowing his answers would be honest.

"Bates, I was actually going to ask you just that; Is there a difference? Bates, I have learnt how to perfect the art of undressing a woman. I have learnt how to pleasure them in every way. Yet after all these years, it seems I do not have the ability or have not learnt how to recognise true love. Am I now being confronted with it? I know my father loves me, as I know you do. The way you ensured I was always safe as a boy, or the way my wishes are carried out to perfection now I am a man. Surely that has to be a form of love and trust isn't it"?

"Yes Johnathan, it most certainly is. I am therefore at a loss to understand what the unknown reason is you seem unable to recognise how much Lady Lucinda is in love with you?" Bates then patiently waited for my answer.

I replied as openly as I could telling him. "Lucinda tells me she is in love with me, yet she know nothing of the world of men. How can I ask a young woman to commit to me, to put it politely when she may not like the act of love? I need a woman in my life who enjoys the pleasures I enjoy."

Bates took his time answering me, then replied in a very firm voice.

"If you feel that way, why are you still determined to hang on to her, why not just let her go? Or are you refusing to admit to yourself that you are totally obsessed with Lady Lucinda. Tell me Johnathan is she indeed no more than a big game to you? Is that the reason you are refusing to let go, at least until you have made a woman of her. Johnathan if you feel you cannot, or will not commit to her that in itself shows both disregard and disrespect for someone you are supposed to care deeply about. Do you not think you are being totally selfish towards her in continuing to allowing her to believe you are in love with her and will always take good care of her? As that Johnathan is what she does indeed believe of you."

"I know Bates, I know she loves me. That is why I have no wish to cause her any further anguish, and yes, I am totally obsessed by her".

"So what you are basically saying Johnathan, is that you are in love with her, but scared to commit, am I right?"

"Yes Bates, if being obsessed with Lucinda means I am in love with her, then yes, I am madly, hopelessly, deeply in love! Lucinda is everything to me."

"At long last Johnathan you are facing your real feelings. I am delighted you have actually come to face the truth.

"Well said indeed Johnathan, I am also pleased to hear you have at long last admitted your true feelings to yourself and for Lucinda." Both Bates and I turned around to find Jeff walking into the kitchen.

"I am sorry, I do not normally listen to other people's conversations," Jeff said with a smile on his face. "I was actually coming to see you to hand you my keys. I am so delighted that I did something out of character by standing listening as the door was open. It was very rude of me though in this case I make no apologies for doing so. On the other hand I truly am sorry that we had unpleasant words. You are my oldest and best friend Johnathan, and I love you dearly. Trudy and I love also love Lucinda, we both care immensely for her. We hated what we thought you were doing to her."

"Johnathan you do not need me to tell you Lucinda is one of the nicest sweetest girls anyone could wish for as a friend. The fact everyone adores her, as she is so loving, on top of being sensitive and beautiful. You know full well Johnathan, Lucinda could have any man she wished. The fact she is besotted with you, makes everyone around her worried. Well it did until now, I cannot wait to convey to Trudy your true feelings about her. I am sure, in fact I know Trudy will be as delighted as I am, on hearing you are madly in love with Lucinda after all. By the way I think I will keep my keys for the next few months, if you do not mind?"

"Like some coffee?" I asked Jeff.

"Love some," he replied.

"Jeff I would be most grateful if you said nothing for the moment of this conversation to Lucinda, or at least you may tell her just the part where I truly love her."

"Delighted to agree with you Johnathan, now you must allow Trudy and I to take both Lucinda and yourself out to celebrate. First I must go and do some serious unpacking," Jeff said finishing his coffee laughing.

When Jeff left the room I turned to Bates once more, sounding perhaps a little more worried than previously. "Bates supposing Lucinda does not like love making, what in hell am I going to do then?"

"Johnathan, can I ask you a very personal question?"

"Yes Bates absolutely," I replied.

"When you are kissing your lovely lady, how would you say she responds to your kisses? Would you say she accepts them, or would you say she thoroughly enjoys you kissing her?"

"Good question Bates, very good question, why did I not think of it. The fact Lucinda loves French kissing which is rather intimate, must mean she would probably enjoy love making."

"There you go Johnathan, you have answered your own question, I seriously do not think you have anything to worry over".

"Why is it Bates, you always have the correct solutions that manage to put my mind at rest."

* * *

Preparing for our last year was an utter joy, Ethan and Poppy had returned from Florida, having decided to become engaged. Ethan related to me his news making me laugh as usual. He had asked Poppy on the first day of their holiday if she would marry him, then told her: "I will have to wait though until I have my degree in my hot little hand".

"I am so delighted for you both, you must allow me to take you out to dinner to celebrate. Ethan may I know when and where you intend to marry?"

"Back home in California next year," Ethan replied continuing to say, "naturally with our families and friends around us. Johnathan you will be my best man?"

"Of course, as long as you do not choose the same day as Jeff," I laughed.

"I assume Ethan you will come and work for Stones alongside me won't you?"

"I would love to Johnathan, I had always hoped you would ask your dad about allowing me to work at the best law practice in America."

"There is no need for me to ask my father Ethan, for the present I own Stones, as well as the rest of my father's empire. You may as well now know the truth, just in case I am your boss when we leave Harvard."

I went on to relate to Ethan the full story of how I became one of the richest most powerful young men in the country.

"Johnathan, you are joking."

"No Ethan, unfortunately I am not."

"Do the others know?" Ethan then asked.

Dean Carter Baxter has known from when I returned to Harvard after my mother's funeral, naturally Bates, and the firm's main lawyers new from the beginning. I guess I had now also better tell Jeff. I kept it from you both for various reasons, mostly not feeling sure about a damn thing at that time, thinking it would be for no more than the six months my father had stated."

I went on to ask Ethan about Poppy: "Will she wish to continue to work after you are married?"

"Yes of course," he replied.

"Ethan, Stones own a slightly smaller hospital out in LA in comparison to the Jefferson Stone hospital, would Poppy consider working there?" I inquired.

"Johnathan that is fantastic of you, thank you so much; I am sure Poppy would be over the moon."

"Good that is both of your jobs settled. Not a word Ethan, please not even to Poppy until I have spoken to Jeff."

"I understand Johnathan and thank you again."

"By the way Ethan, Lucinda does know as I could not keep my big mouth shut. I told her about the great fun I had, on the first day when I went to visit my father at the office."

That remark make Ethan laugh: "When we are all together I promise I will relate the full tale to you."

A couple of days later I asked Bates: "Will you please ask Jeff, to come and see me when he comes in? I will see him in my little sitting room as usual".

Jeff retuned home late that evening, "sorry it is so late Johnathan," Jeff apologised as he walked through the sitting room door, which was always now left open. I actually hated closed doors except for my bedroom door. I had no idea as to why, I just did. Jeff sat down opposite, making the predicament of telling him that I owned Stones a little easier.

"Jeff there is something I wish to convey to you. I feel the time is right and that you have the right to know about me owning Stones."

Actually it was now no longer a predicament for me. I loved being the young emperor; I was certainly not going to relate those thoughts to Jeff, so I continued saying.

"I have no idea Jeff when my father will resume the chair, he has so far not made up his mind. Until he does, I am guided by him and a panel of our very top lawyers."

Jeff's reply was so pompous, he was becoming more like Trudy Hamilton each day: "I am indeed shocked Johnathan by your news, someone as young as you, running a multibillion dollar company like Stones?"

"I have been told Jeff, that so far I am making a damn good job running my business. Jeff allow me to explain it in different terms; if my father had been killed instead of my mother I would automatically have taken up the reigns of the business anyway."

"Never thought of it like that," Jeff informed me.

"Johnathan, you never fail to surprise me he continued, first over Lucinda, now the fact you have been running a multibillion dollar business, since you were eighteen. That is mind blowing. I must sincerely apologise to you. Once again it seems I have not quite understood, the position you have found yourself in during all this time. Of course even though it was no fault of your own, Johnathan it must have been hard not telling anyone, I am most grateful we are still friends".

"Thank you Jeff, I hope we will always be friends. You meet a great many people in your life, but true friends are so very few and far between. One thing I will always be grateful for is that neither Ethan or yourself have ever lied to me. Quite frankly I would rather suffer having an out and out row with you, as I could think of nothing more despicable for a friend to do, than to look me in the eye then lie to me. Tell me Jeff, are both Trudy and yourself coming to work at Stones when we return home? I need a team around me I can trust implicitly."

"Trudy and I would be honoured, thank you Johnathan. By the way what about Ethan and Poppy, will Ethan be joining us?"

"You bet he will, I will ensure Poppy has a job at the hospital, a good doctor is hard to find".

Chapter 9

"Bates I am starving this morning, I could eat for my team."

"I hope not Johnathan," Bates laughed then told me, "your figure would soon be far from athletic if you did".

"Maybe I am just feeling rather exuberant at the thought I am starting my last year. I suspect it is going to be busier than ever. Bates I am hoping we manage to pull out all the stops. Achieving our degrees means everything to all of us, particularly more so to Lucinda as you can imagine. Last year many of my fellow students had already dropped out."

Bates looked at me as a father would look at a son, then said, "I do not think you will have anything to worry over Johnathan. I am sure everything, will continue to be just fine. Especial with Lady Lucinda to inspire you. I never told you that I also wanted to be a lawyer when we last spoke about Beth".

"No Bates you never even touched on that subject, please would you tell me now?" I pleaded.

"Very well Johnathan, if you truly feel you are that interested."

"Beth became pregnant for the sheer expedient I did not practice safe sex... I knew I could not afford to continue to stay at law school, so naturally dropped out.

My mother could not financially help top up the amount of money I needed for my fees. I never met my father, as he was a married man. My mother had fallen head over heels in love with him when they first met, and was until the day he died. Sadly she knew from the beginning he would never divorce his wife. My mother refused to discuss with me who he was, both to protect him and me. He had been a generous provider as I was growing up. He ensured I had a good education up till then. He died just before the end of my second year at law school."

"That must have been devastating for you," I replied.

"Yes and no," Bates sighed, then continued with his story. "I loved Beth so much, leaving law school at that time, I simply regarded it as the right thing to do. Marrying Beth and finding a job to support us was far more important. Funnily enough I actually still have my law books tucked away. I saw no point in giving them to you, as the magnificent set you now own, far outclasses them."

"Bates, you must show them to me. They are an integral part of your past, and I am always interested in everything you did or do. I thought you said you knew nothing of the law?"

"Not having qualified, Johnathan, I know very little about the law, certainly in comparison to you," Bates replied.

"Oh Bates how I wish you had indeed continued your studies, who knows maybe we would have worked together once I qualify, It would have been absolutely splendid."

"Johnathan we do work together, in fact more closely than all the other people in your life at present. I look after you and you entrust me with your inner most thoughts. I hold your confidentiality in regard to many things, which matter to you, including most projects you feel needs my attention for the type of detail you like. You do not only trust me with material things, you entrust me with your emotions. Being able to confide in me especially when it comes to discussing your personal life, if I may say so that in itself is such a huge honour. Most importantly of all the affinity we have for each other, is something most people never achieve in their entire life. That Johnathan is what makes our relationship so special."

"As always you are quite right Bates, I do hold you in the highest regard."

Bates smiled at my reply. I then asked him: "You will show me your law books later tonight won't you?"

Once again I felt like a small child being promised a treat: "If you are seriously interested in seeing them Johnathan, then yes I promise I will endeavour to show them to you this evening," Bates replied with a huge smile.

There were even less students this year, I was quite taken aback just how many never returned. At least the five of us were still together. What a dream team we will make once we start work, what a dream team Lucinda and I will make. I will teach her everything there is to know about love, everything my goddess should know. Besides lectures and everything connected to course work I had decisions to make regarding what to do about the house once we returned home. Something I shall have to discuss with my father at a later date, I would not be foolish enough go against his wishes, in regard to a beautiful property that had been part of our family for many generations.

The Lincoln I will sell and buy something a little different. How strange, already I was dismantling one life while working to build a new one. This new life except for Lucinda, had been planned for me from the day I was born. Bates I knew, would be pleased to return home to the sun, as will I in a great many ways. I never seemed to adjust to the appalling cold weather that descends on Boston during the winter. I know that I will sorely miss my life at Harvard, having loved everything there is to love about it. I suppose it is now time for me to grow, to take up my responsibilities of running what should have been my father's empire. As time goes on, he seems more and more entrenched in allowing me to become the permanent owner, of what is indeed a vast business empire.

The weeks and months were passing incredibly quickly, the season's changing from pleasant autumn to the cold of winter, which would soon herald the start of preparations being put in place for Christmas once again. This was to be our last trip home for the Christmas holidays. This year I was going to give Lucinda something special. I had decided I would buy her a pair of diamond earrings, the most exquisite I could find, in the form of bows. My mother had left many beautiful pieces of jewellery, which would be perfect for Lucinda to wear, but her first pair of earrings I wanted to come from me.

Taking no chances I drove to the finest jewellers in Boston, explaining in detail to the salesman exactly what it was I wanted. "Perfect but not ostentatious, if necessary you have my permission to send direct to Cartier's. I want the most perfect pair they have, which of course must be made with the finest diamonds, immaterial of the price."

When Lucinda belongs to me, I will cover her from top to toe in diamonds. As no one piece so far has been created that could ever be as exquisite, or outshine my goddess. The rounds of Christmas dinners, and parties began in earnest. We worked hard and played hard. This would also turn out to be the last winter vacation in which the six of us would fly anywhere together for many years to come.

I phoned my father to inform him I would shortly be flying home.

"Johnathan when you arrive back, I would very much like to talk to you in person, it is a personal matter, nothing to do with the business."

"You sound very mysterious dad, I told him, are you keeping well?"

"Yes Johnathan I am very well, it is nothing to do with my health as such," he related.

"You are sure?" I once again inquired.

"Yes Johnathan, I promise I am keeping in tip top condition. I am going to put the phone down, I look forward to seeing you when you arrive home."

"After he replaced the phone, I began to feel uneasy; a feeling that would not disperse, until I sat with him having coffee. Once again while waiting to see him, I was preparing myself for another unpleasant surprise, which unfortunately, seems the norm these days when he tells me he has something to discuss in person.

I had hoped this Christmas was going to be different from the previous Christmases, one that would be so much happier than I had experienced in a very long time. I gave instructions for my home to be decorated the way my mother had always arranged it. A huge Christmas tree in the sitting room, as well as in the front hall. Plus of course all the other decorations, around the house my mother had loved during the season.

Another decision I made this year was to spend Christmas day with Lucinda, this time I would accept no interference from Jeff and Trudy. Naturally I hoped they had come at long last to realise it was pointless to argue with me in regard to anything to do with Lucinda. Lucinda is now most definitely my concern, the fact she was staying with Trudy, as usual, instead of in my home was bad enough. I had no choice about that decision this time, next year will indeed be so different. For the present I will at least have Lucinda spending Christmas day with me. I had no idea if my father would also come for Christmas dinner. When we talk I will invite him, then conveying to him that a very special lady, will be joining us.

Our flight home was full of laughter and love, Jeff and Trudy were like an old married couple, happily content it seemed with each other's company rather than overly passionate, which Ethan and Poppy appeared to be, they looked so madly in love. I had always hoped. Ethan would find someone who would love him the way he should be loved. Of the three of us Ethan was the one who was most sensitive, the most amusing. Poppy being a doctor did not need to marry anyone for money, like Ethan she came from a very wealthy family and she naturally hoped to go a great deal further in her chosen profession.

My feelings towards Lucinda were continually growing; she had taken possession of my soul after our first kiss. My obsession for her increasing with each day, she held both my heart and my soul. Not just my heart and soul, but every atom of my being. The fact she had extracted a promise from me never to kiss another woman, was unreal, beyond belief for a man like myself. Still having kept to our deal, never once even wanting to break it surely it meant I loved her. The kind of love I had fought against for so long.

I had promised myself I would never allow any woman to make me her husband, at least not for many a long year to come. Now this untouched, exquisite girl, held my happiness in her elegant delicate hands, I knew without her my life now would not just be lonely, but unbearable. I had just a few more months to endure this torture, which I had amazingly agreed to; before I am able to make Lucinda into the sex goddess I wanted her to be. Until then I will have to be satisfied with her passionate loving kisses.

"Bates, I am worried how I will find my father this morning."

"I should think Johnathan you will find him in tip top condition," Bates replied.

"I hope you are right Bates. I hate it when he springs unexpected surprises on me; they are not just irksome in some small way, but inordinately worrying. You know full well Bates, the surprises he springs are usually gigantic."

"At least Johnathan," Bates went on to say: "This time it is not the business, and he has said he is in good health".

"Heaven knows what it is then, or what he is now up too," I replied: "I will let you know as soon as I can. In the meantime I am just about ready to go."

"Good luck Johnathan, though I doubt you will need it," Bates said, managing to find words to give me the confidence I needed in respect to my father.

Walking into the main hall at the office, I was once again greeted by Ben, wearing a beaming smile on his face: "Good morning Mr Stone, so nice to see you".

"Hello Ben, nice to see you once again, I believe the boss is waiting for me."

"You are the boss, sir, Mr Stone senior though is waiting," Ben, laughed.

"You are indeed quite right Ben, thank you for reminding me." I said laughing.

Stepping out of the lift Mrs Akins greeted me, also with a smile on her face. Everyone seemed in such a relaxed mood today, just what was going on?

"Good morning Mrs Atkins."

"Good morning to you to Mr Stone," she replied with a big smile on her face.

"Mrs Atkins how is my father? I mean how is he in regard to his health?"

Mrs Atkins looked at me and gave me another of her sweet smiles, probably already knowing what it was my father would very soon divulge to me: "Your father is in jolly good health, Mr Stone. You have absolutely no need to worry on that score I can assure you".

"Very well Mrs Atkins, I will take your word for it." Then what score was she talking about I wondered.

"Mrs Atkins, pot of coffee would be nice please."

"Certainly Mr Stone one coming up sir," Mrs Atkins replied.

I found my father as usual, sitting looking out at the ocean. I guess it had become his favourite spot, the view indeed being magnificent. "Good morning dad how are you feeling?" I asked, still with some apprehension.

"Good morning Johnathan, I am very well thank you, and you?"

"Dad I am just fine, but I am not going to lie, I have been quite concerned about your health ever since you told me there is something you wish to discuss with me in person."

"Johnathan my health is just fine, and yes I do wish to talk to you about a personal matter, very personal in fact. A matter I did not wish to discuss over the phone."

At that moment Mrs Atkins knocked on the closed glass doors, entering with the usual tray of coffee.

"Thank you. Mrs Atkins the coffee is most welcome," I told her. Mrs Atkins set the tray down, then withdrew, gently closing the glass doors behind her.

"Would you like to pour Johnathan?" my father asked.

The suspense was killing me, I handed my father his coffee then asked, "Please will you tell me what it was you feel I need to know?"

My father looked at me, the kind of look I have now grown accustom to, which was his way when he wished to import to me something of a serious nature or make a full blown statement. Once again he did not let me down. This time conveying what he had to say in a somewhat gentler manner, which was indeed unusual for him. I most certainly was not prepared for his following statement, yet eventually I suppose it had to happen.

"Johnathan I have met someone I am growing rather fond of, the lady in question is called Meredith Lake. Meredith is a widow who I met at a lawyers dinner a few months ago. Her husband was a lawyer who worked out of one of our other offices. Meredith is the same age as myself; she is a very attractive, charming woman whose company I thoroughly enjoy. I have explained to her Johnathan that I have no intentions of ever marrying again. You and the business are, and will always be, my number one priority. I have every intentions of living with Meredith, but not here. We have decided to buy a house together, not overly large as we are both getting on, plus of course neither of us having young children. I would very much like you to meet her, perhaps before Christmas. Johnathan whether you like her or not I will not give her up."

"Dad have you been reading my mind," I laughed: "I cannot believe you have just said that. I guess I am very much a chip off the old block".

"Less of the old, young man, I am still a very active healthy sexy man, who can still give a woman, a great deal of pleasure."

"I bet you are sir, it would seem there is hope for me yet," a remark which left my father and I laughing. "Dad I would delighted to meet your new lady, I cannot tell you how pleased I am for you. I was sir, going to ask you if you would care to come over to the house this year for Christmas dinner. I hope would will bring Mrs Lake with you as she would be very welcome."

My father stopped me right there.

"Thank you Johnathan, I would love to have dinner with you, but I have no intentions of setting foot in that house again. Please forgive my feelings, it is nothing to do with you personally."

"I understand sir," I looked at my father apologising instantly then continued to say. "I am sorry the house still holds so many memories for you which it appears must still cause you pain, it was insensitive of me to ask."

"No Johnathan, you are not at all insensitive, it is not your fault the way I feel."

My father then asked: "Johnathan, would you please join Meredith and myself for Christmas dinner? I thought we could go to one of my favourite restaurants".

By extending this invitation to me he left me with no choice, this time I had to come clean and tell him the truth about Lucinda. I was not prepared to lose one second of her company on Christmas day, not even for my father. Therefore I went on to reveal my secret.

"Dad while we are talking about special ladies, there is something I would now like to tell you. You are not the only one who has a special lady in their life. I had every intention of introducing my very special lady to you on Christmas day. I would still very much like to introduce her to you. If you do not mind me bringing her with me when I have the pleasure of meeting Mrs Lake. I hope we can also join you for Christmas dinner, as I have no intention of spending one second of Christmas without my lady."

"Johnathan, firstly I would like you to call Meredith by her first name in future."

Then with a gleam in his eyes, as if he had just won some big court case, my father went on to say: "I would be enchanted Johnathan to meet your mysterious lady. Now do tell me who this lovely lady is, and how she has captured your heart".

"What makes you say she has captured my heart?" I asked, rather astounded by what my father had just said.

"Johnathan, you would never introduce me to any woman, no matter how beautiful she may be, if you were not madly in love, and I mean in love! Nothing to do with sex or her being a good lay."

"Dad you have totally amazed me, I had no idea you were as perceptive to my emotions as you obviously are."

"Well... Johnathan, are you ever going to tell me who this lady is. Or better still, perhaps you would allow me to guess," he said mischievously.

"Come on dad you cannot possibly guess who this incredibly wonderful person may be."

"Allow me the benefit of the doubt Johnathan, if I am wrong then of course you may tell me."

"Very well sir," I said laughing, "but no more than one guess".

"Johnathan, I have waited a very long time to meet Lady Lucinda Osborn, I am sure she is not only excruciatingly beautiful, but must also be amazingly fascinating. The fact she has honoured the promise she made to her late father makes her a very special, intriguing young woman as well. Would you say I am reasonably right in my assumptions?"

"Dad how in the world did you know, it was Lucinda. I am stunned, this is one of those rare occasions when I am at a loss for words."

"I have suspected for a very long time Johnathan, that it was Lady Lucinda you were interested in. May I ask, has she still kept to her promise?"

"Yes sir, she has, I replied.

"Then you are indeed an extremely fortunate young man. So very few women would honour such a promise for such a lengthy period of time, especially when they are in love. I had suspected for various reasons, that Lady Lucinda was the one girl who would eventually capture your heart. That my dear Johnathan, is part and parcel of being a good lawyer. Something I hope, you will eventually acquire with time."

My father further continued to say: "I am right am I not Johnathan, you are hopelessly in love with your lovely Lady. You do have every intention of marrying her, once you both leave Harvard and return home?"

"Yes sir you are quite right, "I answered him.

"Johnathan, I do not think you could have chosen better. I shall be incredibly proud to have Lady Lucinda Osborn as my daughter in law."

"Thank you sir, I am sure she will be just as delighted to have you as a father figure in her life, sadly as her father is no longer with us."

"I will make all the arrangements for Christmas Day, as well as for dinner in the evening. Should we say in a couple of day's times? I am sure the four of us will have a splendid evening together, each meeting the others new lady, it could not be more perfect."

"Thank you sir, I will look forward with great anticipation in being able to having dinner with Meredith and yourself. Dad I hope you do not mind me asking, does Meredith have any family of her own?"

"No Johnathan, sadly for her she does not. One thing I am sure about when she meets you, she will grow to love my son and his future wife as much as I do."

"Thank you dad, that is very kind of you to say so."

This statement of feeling about me surpassed all others he had mentioned over the years. He then continued: "Johnathan once I move out of here, this penthouse will automatically become your office. Do you think you would enjoy working out of here, even though I will be here some of the time?"

"I think that will be excellent sir, there is so much I need to learn about our businesses. I could not think of a better teacher."

"Thank you for your most welcome compliment, I am not always the easiest of people to work for. Sorry

I should change that to, I am sure my boss is though," his words making us both laugh again.

"So it was Meredith who for many weeks had evidently brought out the convivial side of my father's character, more so than I knew could be possible. He sounded, as well as appeared a man easier within himself, definitely a great deal more human than he previously use to be. It will be a pleasure, and one I am now looking forward to in meeting Meredith Lake. Whatever magic she possesses it must indeed be special, observing how my father for the moment seemingly has changed.

I could not wait to tell Bates, he will be in for a huge surprise. Returning to reality I enquired: "Dad would you like to go for lunch, or are you meeting a special lady?"

"I am indeed Johnathan meeting a special lady, but thank you for asking."

"Very well sir, if you will please let me know what arrangements you decided on for dinner. I will go and do some Christmas shopping. Oh just before I go sir, does Mrs Atkins know about your new lady"?

"No Johnathan. I was not prepared to inform anyone, until I had spoken to you, actually if on your way out you would please ask Mrs Atkins to come in I will convey to her my news".

"Delighted to do sir, goodbye, "I said feeling more relieved than I thought possible.

"Mrs Atkins, my father would like a word with you, he does seem in very high spirits would you not say?"

Mrs Atkins looked at me with a twinkle in her eye, then winked. "Your father Mr Stone has, should we say, been in very high spirits, since he started asking me to order, wonderful boxes of roses for a certain lady over the last few months". I could not help but burst into laughter then told Mrs Atkins, she was wonderful.

"My father, Mrs Atkins simply does not seem to know how well you understand him. Or how much you know about his life. Thank you, you are a treasure. I think he is now about to tell you, who you have been sending those boxes of roses to."

With that I left my office laughing all the way home.

"Bates I have wonderful news to tell you over a pot of coffee."

Bates asked with a smile on his face, "Johnathan and where would you like it?"

"In the morning room will do very nicely", I replied, another room that he and I had shared many happy hours in when growing up.

"Bates you are not going to believe what I am about to tell you." I then went on to relate to him all about Mrs Lake. "Bates I am astounded, yet it was to be expected sooner or later. My father is not the type of man you could possibly ever call a monk. Unfortunately I also had to tell him about Lucinda sooner than I had intended to. What has amazed me is the fact he guessed it would be Lucinda who had captured my heart. Rather uncanny if you ask me, no wonder he is a brilliant lawyer, he does not seem to miss a trick".

"Your father is indeed a very perceptive man," Bates replied then went on to say: "I am genuinely pleased Johnathan, you have at long last told him about Lady Lucinda. It will make things so much more comfortable all round".

"Bates, I hope he likes her as much as you do."

"Johnathan, she will have him eating out of her hand, wait and see if I am not right," Bates answered.

"One thing for sure Bates, Lucinda most definitely has me eating out of her exquisite hands. Now I must go and phone her to inform her, she will not only be dining with her future boss, me of course", I said laughing, but her future father in law. Without saying another word to Bates I then changed my mind, telling her she will be meeting my father and his new lady.

* * *

I picked Lucinda up from Trudy's, "you look beautiful this evening my darling," I told her. Lucinda was wearing a simple little navy cocktail dress, the simplicity and cut of the dress was perfect, showing off her wonderful figure. I hated Lucinda in black, though of course there would be times when she would have no alternative but to wear that depressing colour.

"Johnathan, how exciting to be meeting your father and Mrs Lake."

"My darling I would not mind betting they are just as excited to be meeting you."

My father and Meredith Lake were indeed eagerly awaiting our arrival. My father had given a great deal of thought about this evening, pulling out all the stops. He had chosen a five star restaurant, the décor being luxurious, serving the most perfect of French food.

"Good evening Dad, hope we are not late?"

"Not at all Johnathan," he replied. "Johnathan may I introduce you to Meredith Lake, Meredith my dear this is my son."

"Good evening Mrs Lake," I said being polite, "my father has said I must call you Meredith".

"Please do," she replied.

I was curious to see what sort of woman had replaced my mother in my father's affections. At first glance Meredith and my mother were similar yet worlds apart. Meredith was an elegant well-dressed woman, as my mother had been, but she didn't have the glamour that my mother had to go with it. I am sure as the evening wears on I will see the many differences between them. For the moment it was my turn to introduce to my father to... My goddess.

"Dad may I introduce to you, Lady Lucinda Osborn."

"Delighted to meet you at long last Lady Lucinda," my father said with great charm as he took Lucinda's hand, kissing it, trying his best to put Lucinda at ease. Lucinda, as always, perfectly happy perfectly comfortable, no matter whose company she was keeping, answered him by saying: "Delighted to meet you Mr Stone," her clear cut English voice casting a spell over him, my father was now apparently mesmerised by her, as I was on first hearing her talk.

He then went on to ask. "Will you be joining us when you have acquired your degree?"

"I do hope so Mr Stone," Lucinda replied.

"I hope so to my dear," my father counter replied, going on to tell Lucinda about her father which totally surprised me.

"Your father was a brilliant lawyer who did a great deal of good work for the company. He was sadly missed after the tragic accident which took both of your parents away from you."

"Thank you for saying so, that is very kind of you Mr Stone," Lucinda responded. "May I also take this opportunity, to once again thank you for the wonderful donation Stones gave to me? It has helped tremendously in allowing my years at Harvard, to be a great deal more comfortable than they would have been without it".

"I am delighted my dear we were able to help in some small way. There will always be a job for you here should you wish it," my father conveyed to Lucinda once again, as she had obviously enchanted him as she does everyone.

"Now allow me to introduce Meredith to you."

"Hello Lady Lucinda, delighted to meet you," Meredith said.

"Please I would like you both to just call me Lucinda. I hate formality unless there is no other way around it."

We spent a delightful evening together. It was good to see my father relaxed and in good spirits. I envied him at the end of the evening as he would go home to Meredith's bed. How I longed for the night that I would be taking Lucinda home to my bed, knowing I would feel ecstatic when making love to her. Instead once again, I will have to just settle for her loving passionate kisses.

* * *

"Good morning Johnathan, have you slept well?"

"Yes Bates I have thank you"

"Well are you going to tell me about your father's new lady?"

"I wish Bates you had a new lady in your life, it would be so good for you."

"Maybe Johnathan when we return home next year I will think about it. Not that I have been deprived of feminine company as and when I have felt the need for it. One thing you must understand Johnathan, I have told you before, Beth was the love of my life no one can replace her. I have no wish at the present to ever marry again."

"I do understand Bates, I would just love you to have someone special in your life once again. Even if it is just, should we say steady regular company?"

Bates smiled at my effort to be polite. "Johnathan, I am still waiting to hear about your father's new lady."

I described Meredith roughly to Bates. "Naturally Bates, she is a very lovely looking woman, well-mannered, soft spoken, and has no children of her own or any family for that matter. I dare say, she is very much in love with my father, after all he is a very attractive man. Bates, you are also a handsome man, not to dissimilar to my father. Which is why you would soon find someone to interest you once again".

"You are most amusing Johnathan most amusing," Bates said laughing.

I called for Lucinda early Christmas morning. Trudy's family were still in the process of unwrapping their presents. Jeff had still not arrived, which I found rather amusing. He will now be in hot water with miss bossy boots, especially with me arriving there before him. The butler announcing me with so much pomposity, it took all my self-control not to laugh. Trudy' and her family were enjoying the season to the full.

Lucinda's eyes lit up as I walked into the room.

"Hello darling, Merry Christmas," I said as I took Lucinda into my arms, gently giving her a kiss. It was rude of me not speak to Trudy's parents when I first entered the room, yet I did not give a damn. Eventually greeting them and the rest of the company they had invited. Pleasantries exchanged, I excused myself along with Lucida, telling Trudy we would see her later. All I wanted was to have some private time to enable me to give Lucinda my present. Then taking her in my arms kissing her, then kissing her some more.

I drove Lucinda to my home, something I never thought I would do for many more years to come.

"Johnathan your home is stunning," Lucinda gasped as it slowly came into view from the top of the long drive. "I had no idea you lived in such a beautiful house."

"One day darling it will be our home, do you think you will be happy here."

"Of course I will Johnathan. I will be happy wherever you wish to live."

Taking Lucinda by her delicate hand, kissing it as we walked into the main sitting room. I retrieved the beautifully small wrapped box from under the tree, which Bates had decorated amazingly well this year. Handing Lucinda her present, she slowly gently opened it up. Everything Lucinda did was both slow and gentle, part of her lovely patient nature.

"Oh Johnathan," Lucinda gave a gasp of surprise on opening the box. "What an exquisite present," she said looking down at the diamond earrings, which sparkled like a pair of stars. "How incredibly kind of you."

"They are not as exquisite as you my darling," I then asked Lucinda if she would allow me to put them on her. "Lucinda you look even more beautiful if that is possible, are they comfortable my darling?"

"Johnathan they feel perfect, thank you again."

I kissed her ears, her hair, her face then her tender lips.

"If I do not stop Lucinda I will lose control," I told her, gently pulling away from her ethereal face.

"Johnathan thank you for respecting my wishes, it is occasionally difficult for me as I love you so much."

"I understand my darling. In a few more months you will be mine forever. Now we must call Bates to give him his present, then go on to keep our appointment with my father and Meredith."

Christmas was indeed wonderful, my father seemingly very happy now Meredith had entered his life. Bates appearing delighted as he prepared for our return to Boston, knowing this would be the last winter he needed to spend in a cold climate. Most importantly of all, Lucida and I managed to spend a great deal more time together, which for me, was heaven.

My plane was made ready to return all of us to Boston. I went to say my final goodbyes to my father.

"Will you be returning for Easter?" He asked.

"No sir," I replied: "Next time we meet, I hope I will have my degree in my hand".

"I am sure you will be very successful in your exams," my father said as we shook hands.

"Thank you sir I will do my level best. Please give my best wishes to Meredith," I requested.

I was just about to go through the glass doors, when my father stopped me. With a smile on his face he said, "I look forward to seeing you in summer counsellor, even if it is a little premature to say so. I am more than sure I will have the pleasure of continuing to call you that".

Counsellor. It felt amazing to hear that word, I hope my father is right; I had wanted to be a lawyer ever since I can remember. Whatever it took, during the next few months. I must work harder than ever if I was to succeed.

Regardless that the weather had drawn in, our amazing captain once again landed the plane perfectly on time. The weather at present was not quite as bad as last year. At least Bates being with me ensured the house would be warm and welcoming in double quick time. I kissed Lucida goodbye promising to see her very shortly. Dear Lord, how I hated being parted from her. How had she managed to reach into my very being I have no idea? Bates was right, she had calmed the wild young man that I once was.

Lucinda did after all, have the ability to inspire me to study harder and longer than I had ever done. It was what I indeed needed to enable me to succeed, as it was imperative for me to do so. I already owed her so much, I wanted her so badly my body ached for her. With my degree in one hand, and Lucinda in the other. I will tell her; no show her just how much I needed her.

The house was quiet as Jeff, Ethan and I were now studying for our finals, lost in a world of knowledge, knowing our future lives depended on it, at least for the lives we wanted. It was crucial we passed, although unlike a number of students we did not have to take some other job to survive, should we fail we would at least be in a comfortable position enabling us re-sit our exams. Lucinda and Trudy naturally being in the same predicament in their house, in Lucinda's case I knew she would sail through her exams. My goddess was not only incredibly beautiful, she was academically far beyond any of us.

We had decided we would see each other at the week-ends for lunch or just to talk over coffee. Occasionally meeting up for dinner on a Saturday evening, then once again going our separate ways. This pattern of activity continued practically until the exams themselves. I guess we were all a little apprehensive by this time. Probably feeling no different to how thousands of other students were feeling, who over the years had stood trembling in their shoes, as we do now in ours.

"Bates do you think my father will fly out here if I pass?"

"I see no reason Johnathan why not. You may find he will bring Mrs Lake with him, I know she would probably love to see Harvard". Bates as always giving me encouraging words.

"Bates you will come to the commencement ceremony. I would dearly love you there, it is important to me that you are. Lucinda would also love you to be there as she has no family of her own to enjoy the day with."

"I could think of nothing I would like more, I am sure you will both do very well, and yes I am honoured you have asked, thank you Johnathan".

Chapter 10

"Hello Bates, how are you keeping?"

"Hello Mr Stone, nice to see you again, Johnathan tells me, you are keeping very well."

"I am Bates, thank you for asking, may I introduce you to Mrs Meredith Lake. I am sure Johnathan has told you all about her".

"He has indeed, delighted to meet you Mrs Lake on this auspicious occasion," Bates replied.

"Meredith, I am deeply indebted to Bates, he is a man I would trust with everything I hold dear. He has taken the greatest care of Johnathan, and I mean the greatest of care, of him since he was three."

"It is a pleasure to meet you Mr Bates, especially on such a wonderful occasion as this. I must admit I am thrilled to be here," Meredith Lake confided in her soft spoken voice.

Bates then went on to say. "Please just call me Bates, and yes I am sure you would both agree with me if you forgive me for saying so. It is indeed not just a wonderful day, it is a momentous one".

"You are quite right Bates, I knew full well Johnathan would have no problems passing his exams. He is after all a Jefferson Stone. He comes from a long line of brilliant lawyers. His grandfather who I believe is regarded and probably was one of the very best. Bates as you have helped to mould him into the young man he is today, I know how very proud you are of him also".

"Indeed I am very proud of him, more than I can put into words. Bates replied then continued. "Now he and Lady Lucinda can at long last marry, what a year it is going to be for them".

"You are indeed quite right Bates my father agreed". "I hope everything turns out the way Johnathan, would like it to be".

"It will be my pleasure to continue to look after Johnathan, and let us hope the new Mrs Stone". Bates answered.

"Bates my father has booked the entire hotel, I insist you join everyone for dinner, I will not take no for answer it is after all a very special night for both you and me".

"Johnathan. I most definitely would not miss this wonderful occasion, you know how happy and proud I am of you."

"My father is enjoying rolling out the red carpet, he has even booked a band."

"Are your friends with their family's joining us?"

"They are indeed Bates, I know it will be an amazing evening, one I hope we will all remember."

"By the way Bates, I will not be home later. I have made other plans, which I am sure you understand. I have booked the finest suite in the hotel, having asked for it to be filled with roses and lilies. I want everything absolutely perfect when I make Lucinda mine".

"Johnathan, are you one hundred percent sure you are ready to commit to marriage?"

"Of course, I cannot wait to take my goddess in my arms, then make her mine. Bates you know that is what I want more than anything."

"Johnathan, you have still not answered my question. I asked you, are you sure you are ready to commit to marriage?"

"Yes Bates of course I am sure. Now please let us not go down that road again."

"Very well Johnathan, if that is how you feel. You know how much you mean to me, and all I want is your happiness."

"Thank you Bates. I knew you would understand. Lucinda does mean everything to me; I have waited four years to take her to my bed. Now she is a whisper away from becoming a woman! My woman."

"Well done my boy, I am very proud of you. I had every confidence you would succeed in fulfilling your dream in becoming a lawyer. Now the real work begins once you return home. I am looking forward to working with you, but be warned, Johnathan; I am a hard taskmaster".

"Thank you dad it will be a pleasure to learn from you."

My father then suggested we should re-join the ladies: "I am quite hungry this evening Johnathan, it has been a long pleasant day."

The main room looked romantic yet very stylish. The band, which had been invited to play had chosen their music well, playing softly as we ate. The food and wine both being superb, obviously my father having had a huge input in to what was served on the menu.

I sat for a few minutes trying to take in the scene before me, wanting to remember one of the most important nights of my life. Listening to the animated conversation of those close to me, wondering how all our lives will spread out in the years to come. In a couple of days' time, no longer as students, we will all return to California for the last time, knowing our future was now assured.

How strange so much had happened since I first flew to Boston. I had looked so forward to becoming a student at one of the finest university's in the world. Now I leave it for the last time with a heavy heart and even a degree of great sadness. The time has now come for me to take my place as head of a multibillion dollar organisation. Even after all these years, I am still unable to understand my father's decision of handing his empire over to me. Knowing I will now be the boss of those who share this room, and those who have shared the last four years with me in class is almost overwhelming.

Returning to the present, I must try to enjoy the next couple of hours if I am able to, before I finally fulfil my dream of taking Lucinda in my arms. Not just to kiss her lips this time, but to take procession of her. Tonight Lucinda did indeed look every inch a goddess, she had chosen her dress well. Being made of pure fine white silk allowing the drapes of her dress, which fell off one shoulder to fall perfectly over the curves of her beautiful body. It was the same exquisite classical design that had been worn by the ancient Greek goddesses themselves. It showed the outline of her figure to perfection. Her silver shoes resembling the kind worn by the goddesses as they played on Olympus. Aphrodite surely must have looked as Lucinda does this evening, and tonight she will be my goddess of love.

With dinner over, the speeches which complimented each of us at last completed, the toasts concluded allowing the dancing to start at last. As the room temperature grew warmer, the main terrace doors were opened.

Outside the weather had been ordered by the gods, it was a warm balmy evening, with a clear midnight blue sky. I took Lucinda's hand, kissing it first then tightly entwining her fingers into mine as we walked in the direction of the terrace. I had longed to take Lucinda in my arms enabling me to dance with her under the stars. Now there was nothing stopping me.

Tonight Lucinda could allow her emotions the freedom from the restrictive prison of promises, which she had kept entrapped all these years. The stars shone brightly, yet none were able to outshine Lucinda as she looked dazzling this evening. I opened my dinner jacket then drew her closer, closer than I had ever dared before. Through her thin dress I could feel her beautiful shaped breast next to my chest. Raining kisses down on her long exquisite neck, her shoulders, kissing her face until at last I found her tender lips. Her kisses tonight felt even more passionate than before.

My hands wandered up and down her back, until they reached her small bottom drawing her even closer to me. The sensations I began to feel were those of a man already possessed by Aphrodite herself. Sensations that made me feel like a teenager who had never made love to any woman, and desperately had the need to. Touching Lucinda for the first time the way I wanted to became more urgent, as she responded to each of my caresses. I murmured in a voice I did not recognise, hoarse with unprecedented lust. An emotion I had never experienced before, regardless of all the other women I had ever bedded. It seemed impossible to believe that a man of my experience could feel this way. Yet this beautiful untouched girl was now driving me insane, to the point that I wanted her now, this instant.

Instead common sense prevailed in telling me I must wait just a little while longer, until I am able to take her to my bed then make her mine. I kissed her delicate ears, then her mouth once again, as my hand wondered to caress her breast I softly said to her, "Lucinda I need you so badly, my body is aching for you". I then went on to say. "Every atom of my being is on fire, I have waited so long to make you mine. I have booked my darling the finest suite in the hotel and had it filled it with your favourite flowers. I hope their perfume will always allow you to remember how wonderful tonight will be. Lucinda I desire you more than I have ever wanted anything in my life. You are everything I could want or wish for in a woman. I want to kiss you all over, I want to teach you about love and how you should please me".

At that instant Lucinda pulled away.

"What did you just say?" she asked: "You want to teach me how I should please you. How dare you say that to me! Who do you think you are? More importantly who do you think I am, one of your whores? I have listened to you telling me how you ache for me, how you want me, how your body is on fire for me, how you even desire me, though I doubt you even know the meaning of the word. You even call me darling; you tell my friends that you love me. Which I now feel has been no more than just a front for your selfish needs? You have just told me I am everything you want in a woman, yet cleverly you did not say what kind of woman. Obviously from what you have just said, you must think you will turn me into one of your whores. While you have been very kind in the presents you have bought for me, which may I add; I thought you had bought with love, clearly not. As you have just shown you simply know nothing of love. Not once in the last two hours, never mind during the last number of years, have you ever told me yourself, having only heard it from my friends that you love me, or more importantly still, you want me with you forever. You have never even come close to saying, Lucinda I love you so much will you marry me, not even Lucinda will you eventually marry me. Jeff and Trudy are obviously quite right; I have been no more than a game to you. What is it Jeff said, a perverse game to fulfil your sexual needs? You are no more interested in how I really feel, as the whores you bed. Well allow me to suggest you go find yourself one, maybe two even, as that is the closest feelings of love it seems you are capable of. The type of degrading level, which you obviously prefer and are comfortable with. It will enable you to teach them how they can please you, the way you want them to. Real love is about teaching each other, not just the one sided way you want it to be. I never wish to speak with you again, quite frankly you disgust me. Good night Mr Stone".

As Lucinda turned to leave me, I lashed out at her by shouting, "Lucinda, you should try sex in the afternoon. It is terrific! You may find you like it".

Within seconds Lucinda had disappeared out of site. I stood there numb, shaking inwardly, unable to move or able to take in what had just happened. Why the bloody hell did I tell her sex was good in the afternoon! What possessed me to make such a statement? How in hell did I manage to frighten her away, what was it that I said that had caused her to take such damned offence?

Repeating to myself what I had said... that I would teach her to please me. What a bloody idiot I was, how could I have been so incredibly fucking stupid, as stupid as I had indeed been?

Now I have lost the greatest love of my life, due to my own inadequate ability, not recognising how to treat real love when I held it in my arms. Like a child I could have cried at the pain I was now experiencing. The loss of Lucinda, was now more than I could bear, this is how my father must have felt when my mother was killed in the car accident. Now I understand why he stayed alone in his office for so long. I walked to the bar and ordered a couple of bottles of whisky then asked for a taxi. There was a taxi already outside waiting. Telling the driver to drive me as far as two hundred dollars would take me, as that was all I had in cash. On opening the first bottle taking a mouthful, I asked the cab driver to drop me off at some motel, or other. I went on to say to him, "I have my whisky for company" which I continued to drink. "Better than a bloody woman, and I needed a bed for the night".

The cab driver looked at me in his rear view mirror then drove to a motel just the other side of town. After dropping me off I went to pay him. "We've have not come too far, you owe me twenty-five bucks".

"My voice full of anger I said, "I told you I wanted to get as far away as I fucking well could".

"Go sleep off whatever it is that is bothering you", he retorted. I was in no mood to argue with him, so checked into the motel.

"Here is to you Lucinda wherever it is you are," I toasted her as I drank myself into oblivion.

The following morning I opened and drank from the second bottle. I drank until I made myself sick. What was it Bates use to say... "There is always a way of sorting your problems out, without having to resort to drink".

Fucking bullshit Bates, I told myself taking another mouth full of whisky. Nothing is going to sort this problem out. I have been a complete bloody fucking fool, I have lost everything from the woman I love, to my heart and soul. Lucinda possesses it all, without her I am incomplete, I cannot function.

I remember very little after that for a further number of hours. It was the smell of coffee drifting around the room that eventually woke me up. I looked up to see Bates sitting there, waiting for me to come back to life.

"What the hell are you doing here?" I shouted at Bates.

"We have all been very worried about you Johnathan," Bates answered, his voice calm and gentle as always.

"Do not give me any fucking lectures, I do not want to hear a word. Do I make myself clear?"

"Yes Mr Stone, you make yourself very clear sir," Bates sarcastically replied: "May I suggest Mr Stone, you try to get some coffee down you as you are still pretty drunk".

"I do not want coffee, I want another bottle of bloody whisky."

"Well sir if you would prefer whisky to coffee, then I suggest you go buy it, as I have no intention of buying it for you," Bates told me in no uncertain terms.

"Go to hell then if you are not prepared to help me drown my sorrows."

Once again in his gentle voice Bates tried to explain: "Johnathan, all the whisky in the world is not going to solve your problem over Lady Lucinda".

Raising my voice, I told Bates, "I do not want to talk about her. In fact I do not ever wish to hear her name mentioned in front of me again. Do you understand what it is I am saying? I cannot bare to hear her name as it hurts too much."

"I understand exactly what you are feeling Johnathan, it was how I felt when I lost Beth."

"Why Bates, why has she run away from me? I love her so much, I truly do."

"When you feel more receptive to talking, perhaps we can come up with some answers. Until then let us try to get you a little more sober so we can go home. You can take a shower as I have brought you some clean clothes. First a mug of coffee would be a good idea."

"Thank you Bates, I have no idea what I would do without you. By the way does my father know where I am?"

"Of course Johnathan, he had you found very quickly. You should know by now how your father works. Never leaving, if I may say so, a stone unturned, particularly a young Mr Stone."

"Very funny Bates," his remark bringing a smile to my face which I badly needed.

We drove home in silence, which I was most thankful for. The house was now empty as both Jeff, and Ethan had returned to California with their families. My father had also returned to California with Mrs Lake in tow taking my plane to do so. He had told Bates he would of course send it back for me.

"The sooner Johnathan returns home, the better as far as I am concerned."

Bates knew that was an order, which had to be carried out sooner rather than later.

Going straight up to my bedroom I opened the door, which was directly opposite my bedside table on which stood a large photo of Lucinda set in a silver frame. She had bought the frame for me as a Christmas present a couple of years ago. Looking at her beautiful face, thinking to myself why Lucinda, why have you stopped loving me. I could not bear to look at her photo any longer, eventually putting it away in my draw. I knew Lucinda would always be an integral part of my life, no matter where I go, or what I may do. Unless I can retrieve my love, hold her in my arms once more, I was a lost man.

During the next couple of days I slipped into deep despair, helping Bates in doing what was needed ensuring everything was completed before leaving Boston. My father had decided we could rent the house out to people who were prepared to pay, a serious rent on a yearly basis?

"One day Johnathan," he said, "a child of your own may wish to come to Harvard and live there".

A child of my mine who now will never be born, Lucinda and I would have had beautiful children. A daughter as beautiful as her mother; a son who followed the men in my family for good looks and brains. Now there will be none, as I have no intentions now of ever marrying.

Lucinda was right of course, I should have asked her to marry me. Why could I never bring myself to utter those words? Now I will live to regret my folly all the days of my life. With a heavy heart I helped Bates pack the rest of my things, we spoke very little during this time, as I was not ready to talk to anyone.

A couple of days later, the house now cleared of everything that had to be sent back to California, Bates came into the little siting room now half covered in dust sheets, as sadly was the rest of the house, bringing with him a pot a coffee, quietly stating, "I thought you may like your coffee in here".

"Thank you," I replied. Was it instinct or just that I knew Bates so well, maybe a little of both.

"What is it you want to tell me?" I asked.

Bates looked at me then gently told me, "The plane was now ready to take you home.

"Home Bates, where is home? Home is a place you live with the person you love. I have no person to love, to share my life with. So I have no home, I have just a place to sleep nothing more."

Bates as always was wise enough not to argue or say anything to me. Instead he poured my coffee into a very large mug he had acquired on a shopping trip.

What should have been the happiest trip back to California, instead felt more like I was on my way to attend a funeral? Looking out of the plane window at the unbroken blue sky my mind started to drift, thinking what may have been between Lucinda and I. Some nights I would dream Lucinda was in my arms, kissing her tenderly, then making such passionate love to her. Waking up to reality was just another nightmare scenario that I had to face. Worse than the nightmare when my father informed me I now owned his empire.

The house I loved now came into view, Bates had warned the rest of the staff to keep their heads down and try to stay well away from me. The front door was opened by the housekeeper, who stood patiently waiting for our arrival.

"Good evening Mr Stone," she said quietly, I gave her a half smile then went directly to my bedroom.

I decided tomorrow I would ask my father if I could move into the penthouse. I had no wish, like him, to remain for the present in this house. This was a family house, without Lucinda being here with me. I never wanted to return to it again.

"Dad I need to talk to you personally, do you have some free time?"

"Yes of course Johnathan," he replied although he went on to say. "Unfortunately I am in court for the next couple of days, and after that I am free. By the way will you be coming into the office before then?"

"No definitely not!" Came my emphatic reply.

"Very well Johnathan, I will keep Thursday open for you. Ten thirty as usual."

"Ten thirty will be fine," I told him putting the phone down.

"Bates order me a taxi if you would, I need to buy a new car."

"Would you like me to accompany you?" Bates asked.

"No thank you, I am more than sure I can manage to buy a car myself," I snapped back at him.

"Very well if that is what you wish," Bates replied, as he left the room. I knew I was making the atmosphere in the house unpleasant, but I could not help the way I felt. My staff can either put up with it, or they can leave, I did not give a damn which.

I had decided I would buy another Lincoln, having loved the previous one. I wish now I had not sold it, as it held so many wonderful memories of being with Lucinda. After picking up the new one I drove to our favourite spot up in the hills, there within the privacy of my car, I sat and cried for my lost love.

* * *

"Good morning Mr Stone."

"Good morning Ben," I answered him, then without saying another word I took the lift directly up to the penthouse. Mrs Atkins greeted me, by asking if I would like a pot of coffee.

"Thank you, just bring it in when it is ready," I told her without a smile.

"Good morning Johnathan," my father said being polite as usual.

"There is nothing good about this morning, it is just another day as far as I am concerned."

My father gave me one of his ice-cold looks. For a moment I am sure he was thinking, I was being facetious, or downright rude. Then he must have realised this was never the way I would dream of talking to him. His voice now filled with a little warmth trying to be kind, he looked at me then said: "Johnathan, I am dreadfully sorry about Lady Lucinda and yourself, I truly am".

"There is nothing for you to be sorry about: I told him. "It is entirely my own fault, please may we change the subject."

"Johnathan, you do know Lucinda is working downstairs."

"It is of no consequence where she is working," I replied then said, "Lucinda has made her feelings very plain towards me, and that is that".

My father sounding very concerned then said: "All lovers have cross words from time to time, what makes you feel you are the exception to the rule?"

Answering him positively as I could, I told him: "Take it from me dad, there is no way back from this difference of opinion we have".

Changing the subject, going to divulge to my father the reason I came to see him. "I did not come here to discuss Lucinda, I came here sir to ask you if I may move into the penthouse, as I no longer wish to go back to the house for the present."

My father naturally being a very perceptive man, yet wise enough to hold his own council, reluctantly decided to be brutally honest by saying: "Johnathan it can become very lonely here at night, you know I am talking from experience, even for someone like myself having a huge circle of friends to talk to, or go out to dinner with most evenings".

"I know you love the house, which is why I gave it to you. Are you now telling me, you are thinking of selling it?"

"No Dad, I just cannot face going back there at present."

I knew it would be no good lying to my father, as he would see through me in seconds. Where my father is concerned, it is so much easier telling him the truth.

"Dad, having taken Lucinda back to the house everywhere I look I see her lovely face. I know you understand where it is I am coming from. I just need a place to heal from my loss. The cavernous space Lucinda has left in my life, will take a lifetime to get over. I have no wish to see or talk to anyone, not now, not in the near future. If I am here I can work for long hours, learning about our businesses without interruption."

"Very well Johnathan, if that is what you wish to do for the time being so be it, will you bring Bates to live here with you?"

"No sir. I just wish to be on my own. I will ask Bates to call to bring me clean clothes on a regular basis or if I have need of him for any other reason."

"Do you intend to do a lot of drinking while you are here?"

That was a question, I had not expected from my father of all people to ask me.

"No sir, I rather feel I have had my fill of whisky for a great length of time."

"I am very pleased at least to hear that," he replied with a smile on his face.

Then returning to his ice cool voice he said: "I have no intention Jonathan on giving you any lectures on drink. You know it can ruin your career before it even gets started, should you be caught for drink driving or have a bad accident".

"I know sir," I interrupted, "that was one of the reasons I took a taxi that night".

"Well done my boy for thinking it out, I am pleased to hear that. Even though you were in a great deal of emotional pain, at least you did the correct thing."

"When would you like to move in here?" My father asked.

"As soon as I may," I replied.

"Very well, today if you wish. You can phone Bates to bring you over some of your clothes, as that is important. Always ensure you remain fresh and clean, particularly when doing our job."

"Yes sir, I will, and thank you again. I am most grateful."

"Johnathan, I hope it will not be too long before you feel you can face the world again. You cannot hide up here forever."

My father had a way of practically being able to see into a person's mind. He never failed to amaze me with his natural ability to read people's thoughts.

"Johnathan before I forget, I am taking Meredith on a cruise in a couple of days' time. I will try to ensure that everything in regard to the business is in order. Mrs Atkins will help you in any way she can, if you need more serious help then you know exactly where to find it. In the meantime, with Meredith and I being away it will give you time to settle in. Perhaps allowing you to find a routine of sorts. You may find you even like being here, it will be interesting to find out when I return."

"Thanks dad," I replied. I went on to wish both Meredith and himself all the best, hoping they have a splendid holiday. "Dad I will be just fine, I simply need some time to sort my thoughts as well as my feeling out, as they are both raw for the present".

Bates brought over a great number of my clothes, plus of course the personal things a man needs.

"Bates why have you brought Lucinda's photo?"

"I thought you may like it with you," he said.

"Are you mad, of course I do not want her photo with me? I do not want her photo, or anything else that reminds me of her."

"Very well I will return it to the house," Bates answered.

"As far as I am concerned Bates you can throw it in the trash can."

"I will leave it on the desk and dispose of it on my way home," Bates replied.

"Mrs Atkins, please may we have a pot of coffee in here, and Mrs Atkins from now on I do not want any of the doors closed including the glass ones to my living quarters".

"Very good Mr Stone as you wish."

"Mrs Atkins you can just walk in should you wish to talk to me, you do not need to knock when bringing anything I may ask for."

Again Mrs Atkins replied, "Very good Mr Stone".

Bates ensured my clothes were carefully put away, then I asked him if he would like to join me for coffee.

"Thank you no Johnathan, maybe next time."

"Please Bates please have coffee with me."

"Very well if you insist," he agreed. We moved over to the big settees, which looked out onto the ocean. No wonder my father loved this particular spot, the view was indeed spectacular.

"Coming to live here for a while Bates, has nothing to do with you, you do understand that don't you? I just need somewhere to mourn my loss.

"I have no idea how I am going to find a way to live my life without Lucinda. Knowing she is so close to me, yet so far away is torture."

"Of course Johnathan I understand. Johnathan is there no way you can try to mend this situation between you?"

"No Bates, no way at all. Lucinda hates me, she has made her feelings very clear. I love her more than life itself. I would marry her instantly if she would allow me to."

"Then why do you not tell her so?" Bates asked.

I then opened my heart up telling my Bates my deepest feelings.

"Lucinda would simply regard it as another trick to get her into my bed. I have completely lost her trust, like the bloody fool I am."

"I am so sorry Johnathan I truly am," Bates replied.

"I know Bates you were very fond of her, as everyone else is. I cannot bear the thought that she will now grow to love another man, that thought alone is killing me. Worse still, the thought that she may have already given herself to someone else. Bates she is mine, I want her so badly, she has become such a vital part of my life, like breathing is to stay alive."

"Would you perhaps like your father, or I to have a word with her? We could try to explain how much you love her."

"No Bates. I know it would be useless, Lucinda simply would never believe either of you, she would regard it that I have put you both up to it."

"Very well Johnathan," Bates said kindly then continued: "If those are your wishes I will not interfere, time will heal a broken heart, it always does".

"It just depends on how quick you want your heart to heal. Lucinda holds my heart, as she holds my soul from the first time I kissed her.

"Please Bates, let us not talk of her anymore, at least not for the moment."

"Very well Johnathan, I will go and see how things are progressing back home. I will call again tomorrow with some further things for you. Before I go," Bates inquired, "may I ask what you intend to do about eating".

"I will go out for my meals when everyone has left. I dare say a few things for the fridge or freezer would be welcome if you do not mind."

"I do not mind at all," Bates replied. "I will see you then tomorrow, good night Johnathan".

"Good night Bates and thank you."

Bates left, leaving me in this sprawling, amazing penthouse, Mrs Atkins came to ask if there was anything further I needed.

"No thank you Mrs Atkins," I told her.

"Then I will say good night sir, and see you in the morning."

"Good night Mrs Atkins." As she was leaving the room I caught site of Lucinda's photo on the desk. I went over picked it up ready to throw it away in the trash can. I looked at her beautiful face, then carried the photo over with me to the settee. Oh Lucinda what a wonderful life we would have had together. I will love you my darling across time and space forever. No other woman will ever take your place, either in my love for you, or my life. I had fought against loving anyone, now I have lost my real love for all eternity.

I sat looking out of the window, watching the sun go down over the ocean. My lonely life was about to start in earnest, sitting up here alone in a glass tower watching the world below living, loving, being together.

Oh Lucinda who was loving you tonight, who dared to have their arms around you. Kissing you the way you loved to be kissed. With those thoughts tormenting me, how I wished I had a bottle of whisky to kill my pain. My father and Bates were quite right; drink would just make matters worse. I dare not go down that road.

How Jeff and Trudy must hate me, as I had proven them both correct, I wonder if they come to work for me, I will ask Mrs Atkins tomorrow. What of Ethan? He had never judged me. I must find out if he too had become part of the team. As for Poppy did she start at the hospital? I will ask him shortly, in fact I may even give Ethan a call later. No I will not call him, I will wait until tomorrow when I have spoken to Mrs Atkins.

I slept badly, which was to be expected, as always Lucinda was in my constant thoughts. After showering I would send out for something to eat though I was not particularly hungry.

"Good morning Mr Stone," came Mrs Atkins voice, "would you like some coffee sir?" She asked.

"Yes please, I would. When you bring the coffee in Mrs Atkins, I would like to ask you a couple of questions in relation to three of our employees."

"Very good sir," Mrs Atkins replied, "I will be about five minutes or so".

Mrs Atkins brought the coffee in carefully putting the tray down on the glass table. I then went on to ask her if she would enquire for me if, Jeff, Trudy and Ethan had started work at Stones.

"I will go and find out then let you know in a few minutes," Mrs Atkins informed me. It was indeed just a few minutes later when she returned to say: "Yes all three were working here, sir".

"Mrs Atkins, will you ask Mr Ethan Philips to come and see me now please."

"Yes sir certainly."

Ethan joined me within ten minutes: "Johnathan, I am so pleased to see you. Poppy and I are terribly sorry to hear that Lucinda and yourself have split up".

"Lucinda has split up with me, not the other way round. I will love her till the end of my days Ethan, I am lost without her. Do you know how she is managing?"

Ethan then quietly went on to say: "Lucinda appears to be doing reasonably well for the moment, she is renting a small flat and driving a two year old car".

"How does she look? Please tell me the truth Ethan."

"Sad," Ethan replied.

"I have been such a bloody fool Ethan. I think of Lucinda each and every day the nights are worse. I barely sleep wishing she was in my arms. I know she will never forgive me."

"Johnathan, let me stop you right there, no one knows what has happened between you two; Lucinda has never said a word."

"Tell me Ethan, what does Jeff and Trudy have to say?" Ethan replied.

"Whatever it is Lucinda has told them, they are keeping their opinions very much to themselves."

That is another thing I loved about Lucinda. Like me she could hold her own council, keeping her private thoughts to herself.

"Poppy started at the hospital?" I asked Ethan.

"Yes she has, thank you again Johnathan. It will make such a difference to our lives".

"You are more than welcome," I told him, "Ethan are you enjoying working here?"

"Yes Johnathan very much so, everyone is very kind to me."

"Excellent, Ethan, I would not have it any other way, if you ever need my help in regard to anything, you will come and ask me. Besides Jeff, you are my oldest friend and I treasure my friends."

"Thank you Johnathan, I am most grateful to you. By the way as you are now my boss, do I have to call you Mr Stone?"

"Not unless you wish to fall out with me."

We both laughed and then shook hands: "Ethan please give my love to Poppy. I will speak with you both again, perhaps you would allow me to take you to dinner."

"We would love that, thank you Johnathan."

Ethan left the office, leaving me feeling alone once again. The long hours that stretched out in front of me seemed daunting. The evenings were the hardest to live through, how I was growing to hate them, if only things had been different. My thoughts once again drifting to my lost love. Lucinda you will always be with me, in my thoughts, in my broken heart, but not in my arms where you should be.

Walking towards Mrs Atkins desk for papers that needed signing, her phone rang out, I could not help over hearing her short conversation to whoever was on the other end as she said. "No, no one. That will be fine. Of course. I will. I look forward to seeing you then."

Mrs Atkins did not come to inform me who it was; I guess it must have been personal. Even a conversation as Mrs Atkins was now concluding seemed welcome.

Each miserable monotonous day merging into the next, how can each day manage to be practically the same as the day before? Was this going to be the pattern of my life? Mrs Atkins disturbed my thoughts, when she came into ask: "Would you please sign these papers for me?"

I signed like a puppy dog, performing the next easy trick.

"Thank you Mr Stone. I will be leaving early this afternoon, is there anything I can get for you?"

"No thank you Mrs Atkins I am fine."

"Very well then I will see you tomorrow."

"Very good Mrs Atkins, thank you."

As she was about to walk out I stopped her asking: "Mrs Atkins".

"Yes sir," she turned looking waiting for me to ask her a question.

"Mrs Atkins can you smell, that smell?"

"What smell sir?" she asked.

"Are you telling me you cannot smell that indescribable smell?"

"No sir I am sorry I cannot smell anything." With that Mrs Atkins left the room, picked up her personal things and then entered the lift.

That intoxicating smell persisted, driving me out of my mind, the only time I have ever been in close contact to that smell was when taking Lucinda in my arms, as it is the perfume she used. I could smell it clearly, but Lucinda was nowhere to be seen.

Taking a newly purchased law book from the shelf, I made my way to the settee that faced the ocean. That wonderful smell seemingly permeating the room, instead of reading I gazed out onto the ocean, then noticed a reflection in the window, it was of a woman standing behind me. Was Zeus himself torturing me? He had gifted to me Aphrodite herself, and I had dishonoured her. Knowing she was now lost to me forever. This torture of being able to smell Lucinda's intoxicating perfume and now seeing what I thought was her reflection in the window. Was her reflection a punishment sent by the gods themselves, or was she indeed standing behind me?

I did not dare turn around, scared in case she was not there. Eventually I knew I must face the truth, was Lucinda truly here with me in the room? Or again was she just a vision from my hallucinating mind. My heart was pounding like the thunder of a thousand wild horses until I thought it would burst. I slowly turned around.

Zeus, had indeed taken pity on me, he had returned Aphrodite to my life.

Lucinda stood there looking ethereal, serene, every inch a sophisticated woman. Oh dear Lord had she already been given to someone else. Her beautiful blond tousled hair now coffered into a slick plait at the back. Her makeup a little heavier than she would normally allow herself to wear. The fine grey wool suit she was wearing, showed off her exquisite figure. The straight skirt and bolero jacket, must have been seriously expensive to buy. The type of cut and design that only a top couturier has the ability to create, under her jacket Lucinda was wearing a very fine silk, pale blue blouse, with tiny pearl buttons, which sat neatly in the hand-made button holes. The material being so fine like the gossamer of a web seen in the morning mist, allowing me to see the beautiful pale blue lace of the underwear she wore, her shoes and purse matched the colour of her suit. Drinking in every detail of her appearance, I was looking at a woman with not just perfect taste, she now appeared to be a woman of the world.

As we stood, each unable to draw our eyes away from the other, it was as if time itself had deemed to stand still, the magic of those moments will live with in me forever. Had Lucinda taken in how I was dressed, as I had taken notice of everything about her? For one moment clearly remembering how Lucinda had loved to see me clothed. Fawn slacks and white Sea Island cotton shirts.

"Johnathan," she would say, "with you being so tanned you look wonderful dressed that way, unless of course you needed to wear a suit and tie. Even then you still look every inch a handsome man."

Today I was dressed the way Lucinda loved to see me, would she notice I wondered. Of course she would notice, she noticed everything.

"The door was open," Lucinda said at last, her cultured beguiling voice breaking the spell.

"It is always left open for anyone to walk in," I replied. What I longed to say, was how much I have desperately wanted you to walk back into my life. Take you in my arms then beg you to forgive me to, plead with you to love me once more. Yet for the moment I knew I did not dare. Instead I stood there waiting until Lucinda continued to speak.

"This is quite some eye catching office you have here," she said, taking a long gaze around it.

"Would you like a drink?" I asked, "Sparkling water if I remember rightly?"

"Yes please, that would be perfect," thank you she replied.

I walked over to the drinks cabinet while talking about the office: "I think I told you that my father had the penthouse made after my mother had died".

"Yes you did," Lucinda answered as she continued to look around for a further few minutes. Lucinda then asked: "Is that a bedroom I can see just ahead?"

It was on view due to the doors being open.

"Yes," I replied, bringing the drinks over to where Lucinda still remained standing.

"Please sit down," I requested pointing to the settee, while handing Lucinda the drink she had requested. Lucinda placed her drink on the glass coffee table.

Looking at me steadily, she held my gaze as only she managed to do.

"Johnathan," she said: "Take me to bed now!"

I nearly choked on the mouthful of spring water I was in the middle of swallowing. Disbelieving what I had heard. I asked, "Lucinda, what did you just say?"

Lucinda replied: "I said take me to bed now! You said you like sex in the afternoon with a whore. Well I will be your whore for the afternoon."

I felt sick in my stomach, my brain numbed. All I could do was look at her. Had the love of my life really become a whore? I could not believe it. Gathering my wits about me, trying to engage my brain while playing for time, looking at her I then said: "Lucinda I will do you a deal."

"What kind of deal councillor," she asked her voice calm.

"A deal in two parts," I replied.

"Name the two parts of your deal, before I agree," Lucinda quite rightly told me.

"Part one, I am going to ask you a question and I want an honest answer."

"Agreed," Lucinda said: "And part two?".

"I want you to wear something I bought for you and nothing else."

"Intriguing, very well I will agree to that as well."

"Again I felt sick. I could not believe the fact she had agreed to wear nothing except what I was about to give her. I could feel my anger rising, but before I could say anything else, Lucinda interrupted.

"What is your question?"

My voice now slightly raised, I asked her: "Have you kissed another man since you last kissed me?"

Lucinda looked at me holding my gaze, then said: "None of your damn business Johnathan."

I could feel myself getting even angrier, saying in a voice that now sounded like my father: "Do not toy with me Lucinda, I want an honest answer".

"I gave you an honest answer," she replied calmly.

Of course she had, it was none of my damn business.

Very well if that is your answer councillor Osborn. I must accept it, I told her feeling mad as hell.

"Now the second part of your deal, what is it you want me to wear," Lucinda asked continuing in her calm voice, still continuing to hold that steady gaze; that no one else had the ability to do when challenging me.

I walked over to the built in wall safe, to withdraw the small box I had deposited into it when I first moved in. I walked back to where Lucinda was still standing. Gazing into her eyes, my heart pounding once again. I took her right hand in mine putting on the diamond ring I had bought her, then said.

"Whores as you know are well paid for their services Lucinda, and you are certainly going to be well paid for yours. This ring cost me a million dollars. I bought it with every intention of giving it to you the night you told me how much I disgusted you."

With that I pulled her into my arms, then cruelly kissed her lips.

"Stop it! I hate you, how dare you kiss me that way!"

Lucinda looked at me with fire in her eyes. I knew in that instant Lucinda was mine. Totally untouched by any man. I was not, going to let her get away for torturing. So played her game to the full.

"Men, Lucinda, do not give a damn how they treat whores, especially when they are paying them really well for their services. I am more than paying you for yours."

Again I took her in my arms kissing her passionately. This time taking total possession of her lips the way I had always wanted to kiss her, until she could barely breathe. Lucinda pulled away from me. Then so innocently said. "You can have your ring back. I no longer want to be your whore."

With that she withdrew the ring from her finger, thrusting it into my shirt pocket.

Lucinda went on to say, "I am going, this was a huge mistake."

"Where do you think you are going?" I asked her.

"I have no idea at the moment, somewhere, anywhere, well away from you, and Stones."

Lucinda made her way towards the doors, to find they were locked. Without her noticing, I had used the electronic lock to ensure I had the total privacy they provided for me, away from the world with Lucinda in my arms.

"Open this door immediately" she demanded, Lucinda's voice now full of anger.

I calmly walked over to her then said: "Lucinda, I will never allow you to go out of my life again." Taking her in my arms I continued: "I have been in torment, each day, each night you have been away from me. I cannot live the way I should without you, I love you beyond the stars. You are my life, my world, my very being. Darling you hold my heart and my soul in your beautiful delicate hands. I am begging you to please forgive me. Lucinda, please do me the honour of marrying me, please darling say you will as I am barely functioning without you. I will marry you every day for the rest of your life if you ask me to. I love you more than you will ever realise. More than life itself".

Lucinda looked at me for a moment or two, as if trying to make up her mind, then said: "Kiss me the way I loved to be kissed, then take me to bed, Johnathan Stone".

Looking lovingly into her beautiful eyes, holding her tight, I answered: "First say you will marry me, as that is what I want to hear".

"Oh Johnathan I love you, I have always loved you from the moment I first saw you. Of course my darling I will marry you."

With that I once again took possession of her sweet tender lips. Then I placed her ring on her engagement finger kissing her hands, then her lips.

Dear Lord, please let me get this right: ensure I do nothing, which is repugnant to her. I have waited four long years, lost her twice, now at long last I was about to make Lucinda mine. I must do nothing to frighten her, no matter how much I wanted this instant to take her and make her a woman. We kissed our way back to the settees that looked out towards the ocean. I kissed her hand, the ring on her delicate finger sparkled like fire, yet not as bright as my love for her or the fire that now consumed my body.

I turned Lucinda to face me then slowly I started to remove her jacket, gently brushing her breast as I did so. Her jacket was half way off when she stopped me, bringing her arms forward, Lucinda undid the buckle of my trouser belt, then she allowed me to remove her jacket completely. I released her magnificent head of blonde hair running my fingers through it, kissing her hair before lowering my lips to her neck. I kissed her ears, once more finding her mouth kissing it the way she loved, first tenderly then more passionately again and again.

Now being terribly careful not to upset her in anyway, I undid the tiny pearl buttons of her blouse. Opening her blouse and gently caressing her breast as I did so. I kissed her bra straps first one then the other, then slowly undid the fastening of her beautiful lace bra. Lucinda stopped me, this time she wanted to undo my shirt buttons. First opening one button, then pressing down with her finger on my chest to the next. Giving me sensations no other woman had ever done before, she continued in that manner until all the buttons of my shirt were undone. With my chest now completely exposed. Oh Lord, feeling her lips kissing my half naked body was beyond belief as she did it so delicately yet making me feel ecstatic. She took my hand, putting it on to her bra allowing me to remove it. Raising her arms Lucinda allowed me to caress her breasts then kiss them. Pulling her even closer towards me, her breasts soft and full next to my body felt like sheer heaven, all I had dreamed of.

Lucinda continued to undress me, first by slowly undoing the zip of my slacks, then pulling them over my hips.

"Step out of them, Johnathan," she whispered.

As Lucinda had never touched a man, I patiently stood waiting to see what she would do next, knowing I must not rush her in anyway. With her cool hand, which felt wonderful next to my skin, Lucinda gradually entered, then allowed her hand to travel down my shorts feeling every inch of my manhood. If kissing her breast was wonderful, what she was doing to me now was incredible. A minute or two later again slowly Lucinda's hand travelled round to feel my bottom then up my back. She kissed my chest again and again. Kissing me passionately she decided to remove my shirt, and again find my manhood.

Taking my time very carefully I unzipped her skirt, which fell to the ground. I lifted Lucinda into my arms I then carried her to the bedroom. We kissed and kissed more deeply more passionately if that was possible. I kissed her breasts I wanted to kiss her whole body but decided not at this time. Once I have made her mine then and only then, would I teach her a great deal more about love.

"Johnathan make me a woman, now!" she said.

I removed my shorts, praying I would get everything perfect. I slowly removed the last of Lucinda's beautiful underwear.

"At long last Aphrodite I hold you in my arms the way I have always wanted," I told her lovingly.

Lucinda looked at me then replied. "If I am Aphrodite, then you must be my demi god Nerites, my first lover".

"Your only lover Lucinda, as I will never allow another man near you. Today your first lover, tomorrow and forever your stallion in love, and your defender in life."

"Make me yours Johnathan this very moment."

"Are you sure darling this is what you want me to do? I will try to be as gentle as I can."

"Oh yes Johnathan I am sure", she said kissing me once again. I lifted my body gently on to my goddess, then carefully as I could made her mine.

"Oh Johnathan how can you invade my body like this, yet make it feel so wonderful". Lucinda whispered in my ear.

"I will take you to paradise my darling," I told her, which inevitably I did. The sheer ecstasy now filling both my mind and body was beyond anything I had experienced.

Making love to Lucinda was better than making love to a million women.

"Johnathan, oh Johnathan," Lucinda uttered into my chest, I knew then I had pleased her in every way that she should have been pleased.

"Johnathan, it was wonderful, it was beyond wonderful thank you darling," she softly conveyed to me.

Lucinda, there is something I want to tell you. "Making love to you was a first time for me as well."

"What are you talking about Johnathan?" Lucinda questioned looking at me disbelievingly.

"Lucinda I have never made love to a woman without using protection. You are the very first woman who I have made love to without using contraceptives."

"Oh darling that is so incredible, how wonderful of you."

"Johnathan, if we have a little boy may we call him Robin."

"Darling you may call our son whatever you wish. First I rather think we should marry as soon as possible, as that is my number one priority."

We kissed again and again until Lucinda asked: "Johnathan I would very much like to make love again, right now please! I took her in my arms, then across the skies, beyond the stars and planets once more to paradise.

As we lay holding each other, it suddenly struck me I had a need to know what it was that brought Lucinda back into my life. Looking down into Lucinda's beautiful eyes tenderly kissing her, I asked: "Darling in all sincerity, would you tell me why you returned to forgive me."

"Many reasons Johnathan. One, I have and will always love you; you may not realise, but from the moment I first saw you from under my hair I knew I wanted to belong to no one but you. Two, I would never have allowed another man to make me into a woman; even if I had to spend the rest of my life without love; it was you or no one. Again you may be surprised; Trudy and Jeff have been privy to this knowledge for a very long time. Three, I had no intentions of ending up in a hospital bed as I did last time pining for you; especially when you were just upstairs. Lastly and most importantly of all reasons besides loving you, I saw Ethan after he had spoken to you. I asked him how you were, he told me you were the same as I was. 'How am I Ethan?' He looked at me with a smile then replied by saying. 'Ask your heart Lucinda, there you will find the true answer you are looking for'.

"That is when I phoned, Mrs Atkins. I asked her to answer my questions, but not say to whom she was speaking to. I then proceeded to ask if you had any appointments. You heard Mrs Atkins say, 'no none'. Then I asked her if I could come up, again all you heard was Mrs Atkins saying. 'That will be fine'. I then went on to ask if it was possible she could get away. The reply you heard this time was, 'of course I will'. Lastly I asked, 'Before you leave Mrs Atkins, would you do me a great service, would you spray some of my perfume in the office?' Which of course I gave to her when I came up. The reply you heard was, 'I look forward to seeing you'."

"You minx! You adorable darling wonderful minx. No wonder I could smell your perfume. I thought I was going insane. Wait till I see Mrs Atkins, I will tell her off for lying to me then give her a big fat bonus.

"You will most certainly will not tell her off Johnathan Stone, instead you will kiss me now, the way I love you to kiss me."

The evening drew in, looking out across the panorama below, people were living and loving. Now having Lucinda with me, I had once again joined the human race.

"My darling enchanting wonderful Lucinda. I want to tell the world we are together, and that you have promised to marry me as quickly as possible. I want the universe to see we are lovers. Lucinda you have no idea how deliriously happy you have made me. I want to share that happiness with Bates, our friends everyone. But first I need to love you," taking Lucinda in my arms, kissing her once again I drew her into the shower.

"Promise you will be good?" Lucinda asked laughingly.

In a voice only a man hopelessly in love would sound like. I told her, "I will only be good at making love to you".

"Oh Johnathan," she replied kissing me once more.

Eventually we dressed, though by now it was quite late. I drove along the coast to find somewhere quiet to eat. I cannot believe I had fought off this love for so long, being in love with Lucinda was everything I did not think possibly existed. All I wanted to do was continually kiss her, make love to her then kiss her some more.

The emotion of driving back to my home for the first time since I went to live at the office, with Lucinda now agreeing to be my wife, gave me the feeling of sheer euphoria. Once again appearing at the end of the long drive, my home came into view. Now I knew once more it would be filled with love, the type of love that only Lucinda and no one else could bring to it.

As I opened the door the night staff greeted me.

"Welcome home Mr Stone so nice to see you."

"Thank you," I replied giving them the biggest smiled they had seen on my face for a very long time.

"Where is Bates?"

"In his room's sir," I was told.

Picking up the internal phone, Bates answered in seconds, "Bates come down now this instant, I have someone here you may wish to say hello to."

"Just give me a few minutes to dress," Bates asked.

"No put your dressing gown on, and come down now. I will meet you in the kitchen," I said, replacing the receiver.

Bates came down within a couple of minutes, "Johnathan, whatever is going, why"...

That was as far as Bates managed to enquire as he saw Lucinda standing before him.

"Lady Lucinda how wonderful to see you!"

"Bates," I interrupted: "Lucinda has agreed to become my wife, can you believe it? Zeus has returned Aphrodite to me, he has brought my love back to me, giving me once again a reason for living, no one could fill my life the way my darling does".

Lucinda's eyes outshone all the stars in the universe.

Bates with a huge smile on his face said, "I am so happy and delighted for both of you, many congratulations. It is indeed wonderful news. I will have my work doubly cut out in the most welcoming way I could think possible".

"Bates you are the first to know, I will phone my father in a few minutes, though heaven knows if he will answer his phone. Tomorrow everyone at work will be told, along with the rest of my empire. Bates I cannot put into words how incredibly happy I am".

"I think I know and understand Johnathan," Bates replied.

"Johnathan," Lucinda interrupted, may we just have a small family wedding, nothing to ostentatious?"

"Darling you may have any kind of wedding you wish for."

"Thank you Johnathan," Lucinda answered, utterly happy that I agreed to her wishes.

The wedding was perfect, the little church filled with family and friends, the air intoxicating from the perfume of the roses and lilies, which filled every conceivable spot. The service short but again perfect, and the love of my life looking as if she had just descended to earth from paradise.

"Lucinda my darling," my voice trying to express my love for her: "I have never seen any bride look as exquisite as you do. I will love you forever. Promise me Lucinda, you will never leave me again".

"I promise Johnathan, I promise," Lucinda replied.

Chapter 11

"Wow dad that is some story, I had no idea how much in love you can be when so young. Your love for mum is incredible, simply amazing".

"I rather suspect Robin I have told you a little more than I had intended to, in fact I would say I have told you a great deal more, than I had intended to. Not a word to your mother do you understand?"

"Yes sir, I most certainly do. At least now I understand what real love must be like."

"Robin it gets better and better, that I can and do promise you. Each time I make love to your mother, for me it is beyond perfection. It feels I am holding my goddess in my arms for the very first time".

"Robin I hope by telling you our story, you will take your time to seek out the most perfect of wives, in doing so you will eventually find that very special lady you are looking for. In the meantime Robin, I cannot emphasize, enough how important it is to make sure you wear protection at all times. It is beyond vital to your wellbeing, and your future happiness."

"After what you have told me Dad I will take on board all you have advised, that I promise."

"I am relieved to hear you say that, you will not regret it."

"Robin I was just wondering, would you like to use the house next year or do you have other plans?"

"I would love to live in our wonderful old house, I am sure it will make a brilliant base as you said, and will love it as much as you did".

"Delighted to hear you are pleased Robin. I will ensure the house is made ready for you and your friends."

"That is great dad thanks, I was not sure if you would allow me to have friends stay."

"Not have your friends stay, are you mad? Firstly it is great fun being with friends, especially those you have known most of your life, Robin you learn a great deal about people when you are constantly surrounded by them. They grow into the people you trust."

"Tell me would you like to fly to Boston on my jet, or have you boys made other arrangements?"

"Gosh dad that is really generous of you, we would love to fly out on your plane."

"So be it young man, but make sure you behave yourself. The coming years ahead of you at Harvard will be some of the very best of your life. I hope you will love them as much as your mother and I did."

"Thanks dad I know I will after all you have told me, I will try to take on board everything you have advised me as I am more than sure you are perfectly right."

"Hello my darling men," Lucinda said, as she came in from the garden: "What mischief have you both been up to?"

"No mischief as yet," my father said with a twinkle in his eye. My mother looked at my father, knowing perfectly well what he meant. So did I now.

* * *

"Well young man your plane is ready," Bates came into the room to inform Robin: "I will drive you just as I use to drive your father."

"Make sure you keep in touch my darling boy," Lucinda asked our son then told him: "You are so precious we need to know you are safe."

"Thanks mum, I will," with that Robin waved goodbye as Lucinda and I stood watching Bates drive him to the airport, as history repeated itself.

"Like some coffee darling," Lucinda asked.

"Yes please that would be perfect," I replied. "Where have the years gone my darling," I asked Lucinda.

"I have no complaints Johnathan, for me they have been filled with your love," my darling wife replied.

"Come here you gorgeous creature while I make love to you." I was just about to kiss Lucinda, when the phone rang out.

"Excuse me. Mr Stone. May I have a word with you," the housekeeper asked having discreetly knocked on the conservatory door. Her face ashen as she entered the room.

"Yes of course, how can I help you?"

"Mr Stone, Dr Penbrook is on the phone."

"Thank you for telling me I will take her call in the hall."

"Hello Poppy, its Johnathan, is there a problem how may I help you?"

"Johnathan, I am so sorry to have to tell you, your father has just been brought in. I am afraid Johnathan, he is not very well, may I suggest you come over to the hospital immediately."

I felt the blood drain from my face, "I will be with you as quick as I can, thank you Poppy for letting me know".

"Lucinda, come here now," I shouted.

Lucinda ran from the conservatory, "darling what is the matter, is Robin safe?" she asked, her first thoughts being of our son.

"Yes darling Robin is safe, it is my father, Poppy has just rung to say he has been taken into the hospital."

"Oh Johnathan no."

"Please get your coat Lucinda as we need to go now."

"Of course darling I will just be a few moments," she replied.

I gave orders Bates was to be informed, and to phone me the moment he returned.

"Very good Mr Stone, of course I will give Bates your message," the housekeeper replied.

"I will drive myself," I told our garage man.

Lucinda sat quietly, wise enough to not say a word. On entering the hospital, Poppy was waiting for us. In a grave voice, Poppy informed me as gently as she could.

"I am so sorry, Johnathan it does not look good."

"What has happened, where is my father?" I asked her?

"Johnathan, your father has had a pretty awful heart attack, if you will follow me I will take you to him." Poppy replied.

I hated hospitals now more than ever, seeing my father wired up made me feel physically sick.

"Johnathan there is little you, or anyone can do at present, perhaps Lucinda and yourself would like to wait in a private room? I will come and talk to you shortly, it would be best for both of you for the moment."

"Very well Poppy, any slight change I wish to be informed immediately."

"I promise Johnathan, I will come and tell you the moment there is any." Poppy escorted us to a room just a couple of doors away from the coronary unit.

After Poppy closed the door I looked at Lucinda: "Hold me Lucinda, hold me as tight as you can. I remembered the day when I was told my mother had died, all I had wanted then was to feel human contact".

Now I had the same despairing feeling once again. Just standing holding Lucinda in my arms not saying a word was so comforting. Eventually I disentangled myself from her loving arms and told her I needed a coffee.

"I will make you one darling," she said gently.

"Allow me to do that," Bates asked, as he walked through the door.

"Bates I am so glad you are here, Robin get off all right?"

"Yes Johnathan, he did indeed, he and his friends are now flying towards their future, I am sure he will love Harvard as much as Lucinda and yourself did," Bates confidently said, handing me a cup of coffee.

"Funny, Bates, I told him the same thing."

"Perfectly normal for you to have told him that Johnathan," Bates replied.

* * *

Poppy would come in every hour on the hour although there was no further news of my father's condition.

"Johnathan, if you would like me to stay with your father tonight, I am happy to do so, I will go home have a few hours' sleep then come back later."

"Would you Bates? That would be deeply appreciated, thank you."

"Lucinda would you like to go home with Bates?"

Lucinda looked at me then said in a very firm voice: "Absolutely not Johnathan, I will not leave your side for a moment until we can go home together".

"Very well darling if those are you wishes, you have no idea how much I treasure you," I told my wonderful wife, thanking her for her love and support.

"I will see you both later," Bates informed us as he was about to leave: "Is there anything I can offer or do for either of you?"

"No thank you Bates we are fine."

"Johnathan if there is any change, I would very much appreciate it if you would please let me know," Bates requested.

"I will phone you if there is and thank you again."

"Nothing to thank me for," Bates quietly told me, and with that he picked up his coat and left the room.

"Any news?" I asked Poppy, as she once again came into the room.

"I am so sorry Johnathan," she said: "There is still no change in your father's condition. Johnathan, may I suggest that Lucinda and yourself go home and try to get some sleep. I do understand it must be incredibly difficult for you both, sadly there is nothing any of us can do for the moment, it is very much a wait and see situation".

"Thank you Poppy, we will just wait until Bates arrives, he has kindly agreed to stay at my father's bedside for the night."

"Is there anything I can get for you before I go off duty?" Poppy asked.

"No thank you Poppy, thank you for your kindness and help. My family are indebted to you and to the rest of the staff, I know you are all doing your level best for him. Would you please ask your boss to come and see me when he has a moment?"

"Of course I will Johnathan."

"Please give my best to Ethan," I requested of her. Poppy gave Lucinda and I a kiss before she wished us good night.

Looking across at Lucinda, "darling are you tired?" I asked.

"A little Johnathan," she replied.

"Bates should be here shortly. I rather wish you had gone home with him, I do not want you to get stressed."

"Johnathan, I have told you I will not leave your side for one moment, you should know better than to ask," Lucinda replied in her firm voice which at times like this I found very comforting.

At that moment Bates walked in.

Bates I am so pleased you have arrived."

"No change Johnathan?"

"No change Bates, are you sure you will be fine for a few hours?"

"Absolutely Johnathan, I will say good night to both of you, if you feel you need me I will be at your father's bedside."

"Good night Bates, and thank you again."

Chapter 12

Leon Bates

"Bates is that you?"

"Yes Mr Stone, please do not say another word, I will call the doctor."

"No Leon, you will not call the doctor, I have things I need to talk to you about."

James Stone, had never called me by my first name in all the years I had worked for him. To hear him now call me by my Christian name came as a bit of a shock. "Mr Stone, please do not talk, I beg of you. Please sir let me call a doctor."

"Leon do not argue with me, I need you to listen very carefully to what I have to say. I am no fool Leon, I know I do not have long to live therefore it is imperative you listen to me."

"Very well sir, if that is what you wish."

Trying to make James Stone relax had never been an easy task, I thought humouring him would probably be the best course of action under the circumstances.

"Leon how long have you been looking after Johnathan; since he was thee if I remember rightly"?

"Yes Mr Stone, you do remember quite rightly."

"Do you remember Leon when you first came to the house? The fact I took a liking to you right away, you were so very much like myself, not just in looks or character, but in personality? Naturally I knew why you had all of my traits, and why I trusted you, but sadly I could never tell you as to why even though I always found it easy to talk to you. Most importantly of all, why I trusted you with Johnathan's wellbeing, do you remember on rare occasions, I would tell you things I would never tell another living soul? There were many good reasons as to why I confided in you the way I did; which I must now divulge to you."

"Mr Stone, please I am begging of you allow me to call the doctor."

"No Leon that is an emphatic, no! Do I make myself clear?"

Yes Mr Stone you do," I could hear Johnathan's authoritative voice in him. I should have known better than to argue. "As you wish sir, I do not want to upset you," I replied.

"Leon do you remember me telling you about how much I loved Johnathan's mother? How I would have travelled the world until she married me?"

"Yes sir, I remember you telling me all that."

"I did love her. I loved her more than I have loved anyone in my entire life except for Johnathan. Even after all these years Leon I still miss her, it broke my heart to have her killed."

"You never had her killed sir, she died in a car accident."

"Leon of course she died in a car accident, the car accident that I had arranged."

"Mr Stone, I think you are having a bad reaction to the drugs you have been given."

Leon will you listen to me instead of interrupting all the time."

"I am sorry sir, I did not mean to be rude."

"Leon I need to tell you the truth about my marriage, it was a bloody sham from the beginning to the end. When I met Marina, on what I now regard as that fateful flight to France I had no idea back then that she already belonged to another man. Leon she was indeed such a good actress the way she pretended to fall in love with me, what fools men are. Certainly men like myself who become besotted with a woman who was as beautiful and beguiling as Marina. You believe everything you want to believe in a pair of beautiful eyes or a flashing smile that promises you the world. Having loved your own wife you know full well what I am talking about.

"I did not expect her to be like Lucinda, very few women are in her category, I did though expect Marina to be in love with me the way I loved her when I asked her to marry me. How happy she appeared to be in taking my name, and all it would provide her with.

"The truth is Leon, she had already given herself to a student she met at her high school. Marina it seems had fallen head over heels, and was madly in love with him. Can you imagine my devastation when I found out she saw him as often as she could, refusing to give him up even after we were married?

"Marina as you know had been brought up in Aspen and with her family living out there, naturally she would go as frequently as she wished to visit them. In doing so it gave her the perfect cover to meet up with her lifelong lover, her family it seems knew nothing of the relationship after she married me, though they knew about her relationship with him when she attended school. In fact Leon they knew perfectly well about Marinas dirty little affair. They continued to hold their daughter's dirty, vile, rotten secret for as long as they could, pretending all was well. I hated them and their scheming rotten pack of lies until the day they died.

"The man she had given her heart to is called Blain Cord. He was a handsome athletic devil, I must say though not quite as handsome as me, or as wealthy, one assumes he must have been good in bed, as she loved the constant sex we had together. Blain Cord had a good business of sorts, but nothing anywhere near the type of business; the Jefferson Stone Empire holds.

"Marina and I had been married a number of months, when she asked could she go with her family on holiday. Her family owned a fairly substantial house in the south of France and I saw no reason why she should not have gone. What better chaperones to keep my wife safe than her parents and her sister. Marina had planned to go for a month, to six weeks, I told her if I could, I would join her later. Every few days Marina would phone to ask how I was, then went on to tell me all that she did, and how much she missed me. Leon I believed every single word the lying bitch had to say, every single rotten sticking lying word.

"Six weeks came and went then a further number of weeks, by then I told Marina I would be flying over.

"'Darling James', she cleverly told me: 'My sister and I, have decided to do some traveling around Europe. There is so much to see, and with you not here darling it seems a perfect opportunity.' 'Very well I agree, as long as you keep in touch, I will be quite happy for you to extend your holiday'. 'Thank you James, I knew you would not mind'.

"Marina and her sister did indeed travel all over Europe. They travelled for a further three months.

I knew of course where they were, as I checked the financial paper trail they left behind which, stupidly I was more than happy to pick up. Marina was of course not stupid; she kept in regular contact with me, phoning from this country or that.

"'I have so much to tell you darling as well as photos to show you,' she would say.

"When I did eventually come to see the photos. There were very few of her in them after the first month or so. Then none after that. Marina photographed buildings, ruins, everything, but none of Marina herself.

"By this time her parents had returned to Aspen. Summer was drawing to a close and the skiing season would shorty commence. Marina flew back to America, though under the circumstances did not inform me. Instead of flying home to California, she flew directly to Aspen. A few days later she gave birth to a daughter, who she called Lucienne. Lucienne was Marina's second name. The father of the child as it turned out was none other than Blain Cord".

"I had no knowledge that my wife had given birth to child, a child which had been very cleverly concealed from me. What I hated most about the whole ugly episode was that her family knew, they knew the whole time of the sordid continuing affair she was having with Blain Cord. They knew of the birth of her baby, helping her to conceal her pregnancy.

"Now you understand Leon, the reason why I have never allowed Johnathan to see or stay with them. What I found so difficult to understand was that not one member of her family were prepared, to ask her to put an end to the affair once she had married? The intensity of my hatred for the child and Marina grew each day until she died. When the child was born, Blain Cord took his daughter to live with him, as that is what they both wanted.

"Marina knew she would have to let me know sooner or later she had returned to America. It appears a couple of weeks after she returned she had the child, she then phoned from Aspen. 'Happy surprise,' she said, 'I am home James. I brought my sister home first darling, so will be flying back to California at the beginning of next week'.

"This gave her a little more time to try to get her figure back into some shape. What could be more natural Leon, when you have been on such a long holiday? You automatically eat all the wrong foods, then gain weight. The thought of holding Marina once again in my arms, making love to her made me feel so thrilled, I could not have given a hoot, how much weight she had put on.

"I decided to buy her a pair of diamond earrings, I loved buying her presents. Remember Leon, remember how much I enjoyed buying her wonderful pieces of jewellery?"

"Yes Mr Stone I remember very well."

"Please Leon, stop calling me Mr Stone, or sir. Please call me James."

I could hear Johnathan's voice, just as he had said the same thing to me all those years ago.

"Very well James, if that is what you wish." It felt so strange hearing this powerful man who was my boss, now requesting me to call him by his first name after all these years.

He went on to say: "I bought the most expensive earrings I could lay my hands on at such short notice. I wanted to surprise Marina with them the moment she returned. The knowledge she would soon be home after such a long absence, could not come quick enough. I would take her in my arms, make love to her all night, and she would be wearing nothing except those earrings".

"How wrong I was. The night she arrived home, I can remember how terribly tired she looked. I could tell she had been crying, as her eyes were quite red. "Darling," I asked her, "whatever is the matter'. 'Oh I am just missing my family,' she lied. It was her child and Blain Cord she was missing, not her family.

"We never made love that night, neither did we make love for many more nights to come, in fact we never made love again, we just had sex. After a few days not knowing about her child, I decided to try to cheer her up by giving her a surprise. I went to her bedroom to put the earrings in one of her bedroom drawers, as I opened one of the drawers, carefully making a space to place the little the box in, I spotted another fairly small size black box towards the back of it. The box was not one I recognise. On lifting the box out then gently opening the lid, inside I found a small gold locket.

"You know me Leon, my curiosity got the better of me. I opened the locket, then came face to face with a photo of a baby. I lifted the photo out, behind the photo there lay a tiny note which had been written in Marinas hand writing. It read. I will love you always my darling daughter. The photo was new which told me this baby was not that old. I put the photo back in the locket but kept the note. Then replaced the box back in the drawer. The earrings I took with me back to the office placing them and the note in the safe.

"I sat there for many hours unable to think straight, sick with anger! Not an emotion I have ever experienced until then. I kept asking myself, how in hell had the woman I loved. Managed to hide her nine-month pregnancy from me? To then give birth to a child that was not mine. Marina must have been at least two, or three months pregnant, before she set off for on her grand tour, no wonder she remained in Europe all those months. Cleverly travelling around, ensuring I was unable to catch up, had I done so I would have observed her stomach growing? The low life bitch how well she had planned everything. Including her returning to Aspen to have her child. How cleaver indeed she had been, she had organised the whole circus from beginning to end incredibly well.

"I had offered her everything, and she had taken everything, including my love. Her life style was that of a queen, the finest clothes and jewels money could buy, a private plane on constant stand by to take her all over the world, if that was what she wanted, a fabulous home with twenty-four hour staff. All the money she could spend as and when she wished to, most importantly of all, a husband who loved every bone in her beautiful body. At that moment in time, I could cheerfully have broken every one of them, not only had Marina broken my heart, worse still she had betrayed my trust. No worse than that, she did not give me the child I longed for.

"Having a child of my own meant everything to me for so many different reasons. After barely sleeping having stayed in the office that night. I decided to investigate who the baby's father was as discreetly as I could, I would leave nothing to chance, I did not give a damn what the cost may have been. I wanted every tiny sordid detail of her affair documented. Not just the affair,

I wanted to know everything there was to know about Marina's life before I met her, after I met her.

"When I found out about Blain Cord. I wanted to know all there was to know about his life as well as his business. On top of that I wanted to know all there was to know about Marina's parents and her father's business, every detail was brought to light and up to date, until I was ready to go to court. I had every intention of shaming them; no destroying them if I could would be more honest. When I had all the information I felt I needed, I would then start divorce proceedings. You know full well Leon about the men in our family. We are damn good in bed, and we do not damn well divorce. We also go in for the kill in court.

"In this case there would be no other option. I knew her family would not want a scandal, so may advise Marina to settle for whatever financial decision I decided on, I swore there and then I would never again have unprotected sex with her. I had to keep up the appearance of a normal happy life. Until I had all the information I needed, then I would go for the jugular! As is my way.

"I let it be known to my people I did not give a damn how long it took, every miniscule detail must be exact, this was a special case they were working on. No expense would be spared but, if you fail me, you can forget ever working for any company I owned.

"Marina hated having sex with me using protection, I lied by telling her I did not want children just yet. 'As you are not on the pill this is the best way forward'. Marina did not argue the fact, I dare say, as she was still getting over the birth of her daughter. I suspect in some ways she may well have been quite relieved, giving her body time to heal.

"My people worked diligently, slowly gathering the information I wanted, after a few months I had gathered all the facts I needed to take my case to court. I told my people this case must be water tight, not a thing left to chance. As a man I had my needs, having my own built in whore I used her, ensuring I was always wearing the protection she hated, thankfully she had no suspicion of what I was planning.

"During those few months I sometimes had to fly to different states on business. I had decided, as I did not trust my unfaithful wife for one moment, on those trips away I would have her followed. Not a thing must be left to chance; in the end I employed a team of private detectives constantly. No matter whether she went on a simple errand like to her hairdressers or a shopping trip, if she needed to visit her dentist, even if she was meeting up with her friends for coffee. Whenever she stepped outside of my home I ensured the detectives followed her. Every detail of what she did I needed to know about. The case against her now was practically completed the way I wanted it.

"I started to think about the financial side of things, so went to see our top man up in San Francisco, to discuss the sort of money I may be looking at as a settlement. While flying up there I remembered like a fool there was no pre-nuptial agreement in place, how the hell did I come to miss ensuring one had been drawn up? Easy? It meant at the time I was thinking with my penis, instead of my brain when I married. On reaching our office I was now inordinately troubled, what kind of blasted deal may I have to make, to get my vile wife out of my life.

"'Good morning James nice to see you again', Toby Wilson greeted me. 'Good morning Toby, how are your family?' I asked to his greeting. Toby was the very best divorce lawyer we employed. If he could not get me a good deal, then no one could. After pleasantries had been exchanged. I went on to tell him about my so-called client, who unfortunately needed some very good advice. Not just good advice, brilliant advice would be nearer the mark. I knew eventually I would have to take Toby into my confidence, but until then I would be guided by what he had to say.

"'James, if your client is as seriously wealthy, as you are telling me, you should know, it will cost him millions, regardless of all the dirt your client may have on his wife. Naturally your client will not be responsible for the child, but the wife James. Even though they have been married such a short length of time, unfortunately she will be entitled to a vast one off payment. It will cost him a serious fortune, no matter what he may think". 'What sort of fortune are we looking at?' I asked. 'Like I said', Toby replied, 'millions'.

"We talked about other things then shook hands. 'Thank you for explaining the position to me Toby. I doubt my client will be pleased'. 'I look forward to seeing you again James'. Did he guess it was me who needed his advice, I hoped not.

"As I flew back I digested and hated every word that Toby had discussed me, that bastard Blain Cord He had bedded my wife, had a child by her, now he would be in the position of spending a vast fortune from my personal and business finances. Surely there had to be some other way out of this sickening situation, but what other way was there left open to me?

"I hated the site of the whore dirtying my home with her presence. The thought that both she and her lover had produced a child, and now wanted to live in luxury on the proceeds of my family's hard work. Bastards the pair of them. I would dearly have loved a child of my own, a boy in particular. I needed a child to inherit my business empire as Johnathan calls it, as I had inherited from my father, and his father before him.

"Marina would have given me a handsome son, or a beautiful daughter. Or so I thought, now I would have to start looking for someone I could trust. That will never happen, I knew from that moment. I could never bring myself to trust any woman again.

"Maybe if I had met someone who was less pretty, more motherly, things may have been different, history will now tell a different story. In the meantime how was I going to get rid of the slut that called herself my wife, without being financially crippled by the bitch? By the time I arrived back home, I still had no ideas, all I could now focus on was how could I get rid of Marina. I felt both dirty and tired, so firstly went to take a shower then change.

"I went downstairs into the office, the housekeeper we had at the time knocked as normal, then waited for me to ask her to come in. On entering she quietly asked. 'Mr Stone, would you like something to eat and drink?' 'Thank you that would be welcome'. I told her.

"Why was it not my wife who came to ask if I was hungry instead of it being our housekeeper? Anyway where was the bitch? Why was she not at home at this time of night? After I have eaten I decided I would phone one of the men who were supposed to be trailing her.

"'Good evening Mr Stone'. 'Were are you?' I asked the detective. 'Sitting just inside a bar sir, with your wife at the bar drinking'. 'Anyone with her?' I asked. 'No sir, not at present,' the detective answered. 'Has she been drinking long?' 'A couple of hours?' He answered. 'Is she driving?' 'Yes sir she is,' he replied. "Very well just keep me informed'. 'Very good sir, good night'. With that I put the phone down.

"My brain was working overtime, thoughts entering my mind were now becoming prominent. Thoughts Leon I would never have guessed I could be capable of, especially in regard to someone I had at one time loved so much. The solution was staring me in the face. What if she got herself killed while intoxicated driving her car? Killing herself that would indeed be a perfect alibi. It would certainly solve all of my problems. I could not imagine a more perfect thought.

"From now on, I will encourage her to go out every night, it is all the drunken slut deserves. If she does not get herself killed, it would at least give me further evidence to prove what a low life drunken slut she had become, who quite frankly is not even fit to look after her daughter. No I cannot settle for her being just a drunken slut. The bitch must destroy herself, it would then save my company millions, the sooner the better."

"Leon you are still here?'

"Yes James I am still here," I replied.

James then went on with his story.

"Marina continued to go out drinking and driving. Always angry as she hated so much, that I would not have sex with her, without the protection I wore. On rare occasions during those months, I will be honest with you Leon. I would have loved nothing more than to have made love to my wife, without wearing any-thing. Then the thought of her enjoying sex, with Blain

Cord, made me feel physically sick, bringing me back once again to face the of reality of my marriage.

"Her drinking was becoming a nightly occurrence, as she wanted to be loved the way we use to make love. I can remember the night we had had a pretty awful row, she was hitting the bottle hard. The next thing I saw was Marinas black sedan speeding down the drive. I should really have stopped her, but I didn't. The detective followed always keeping at a respectable distance. Marina headed out towards a small town where she pulled in for gas, and bought a bottle of whisky at the small local garage.

"Leaving the garage she apparently opened up the whisky bottle, drinking heavily from it. I was told she became pretty drunk that night. Driving back she saw a guy on the sidewalk who also had been heavily drinking. Marina pulled over and asked the guy to get in, which he did. Then she had sex with him, he must have been pretty good as he was in her car for over fifteen minutes regardless that they were both drunk. When the guy got out she threw him a big fat wad of notes. A thousand dollars actually.

"Do you remember that Leon?"

The blood drained from my face.

"Dear Lord, James, are you telling me it was your wife who I had sex with that night? I had no idea. I am so very sorry James I truly am".

"Of course you had no idea, why should you? You needed a woman that night, Marina wanted sex with a guy who was not wearing protection, you both achieved what it was you wanted. End of story.

"Unfortunately it is not the end of the story. When the detective told me the following day, you had not picked up the bundle of notes, which incidentally he did return to me. I was most intrigued to know what sort of guy though drunk himself, can pick up a drunken slut, make out with her then walk away, and yet leave a thousand dollars in the cutter. In my entire lifetime I had never met any man, who would ever have behaved in that manner. Once I was told about what you did, I had to find out what type of man you were.

"You know me Leon, I leave no stone unturned until I find out what it is I want to know. And you my dear Leon, I wanted to know every damn thing there was to know about you, I regarded you as the biggest bloody fool out, or one of the most remarkable men that would ever come into my life. You have certainly proved you are not just a remarkable man, you are a great deal more, which I will now tell you.

"Naturally I found out you had lost your wife and baby son, that would make any man want to drink himself into oblivion. I am deeply, deeply sorry that happened to you, as you would have made a wonderful husband and father. You have not failed in that I can assure you. I will come back to that information presently.

"A few days later Marina walked into my office then said, 'Well James so much for you wearing protection I am pregnant, I should have had my period a few days ago. I just thought I would tell you, as you did say you did not want children just yet'. Marina then went on to say. 'James, I have no intentions of getting rid of this child, do you understand. Perhaps next time you should buy better quality little packets'. I was not just shocked at that statement, I was totally shaken by it.

"Knowing it was not Blain Cords child, could Marina possibly be right? Was one of the condoms faulty? All the plans I had in place for months, the organised teams of detectives, the mountain of paper work that had been collected. The information now at my fingertips, all was now non-applicable; inconsequential. Marina had openly admitted she was now pregnant, could this child she was now carrying, be the son I had longed for? If it is then I would be prepared to forgive her a great deal, I would though never allow her to take my son ever to Aspen or see his other grandparents. I would never allow her to take him anywhere, without either myself being there, or the constant bodyguards I would now employ to protect him".

"'Are you sure Marina that you are expecting? I asked'. 'Of course I am sure James,' she replied. 'Then I would appreciate it if you would stop drinking. I will buy you the world, anything you want if you promise to keep yourself, and this baby safe'. 'Will you grow to love me again?' She asked. 'Yes I lied, but first you must prove to me how much you will take care of yourself, and my unborn child'.

"I knew I would never love Marina again, I hated her treachery, her lies, and the child she had with Blain Cord. All I could now focus on was my unborn son, or daughter. I would ensure she went to Harvard, to become a lawyer like the rest of the Jefferson Stones, whether she liked it or not she would be treated like a royal princess, with twenty-four hour protection, after all she was a girl. If Marina had my longed for son, how handsome and talented he would be, I was ecstatic at the though.

"'James can we go baby shopping?' Marina asked. 'Of course we can. You can buy anything you want', I told her. 'James can we have a new nursery created'

'We will have the very best nursery money can buy for our baby'. I promised her.

"For a few months we both seemed content with all the activity that was being created around this baby. 'When our son is born James. I would like you to name our new child'. As we had now found out we were to have a most welcome son.

"I was over the moon that she had allowed me to name him without argument. I decided to call him Johnathan Robin. The names had been in our family generation after generation as well you know. It was when Johnathan was born that my world came crashing in around me. I had asked for a DNA test to be done, it was then that I found out I was not Johnathan's real father. How the hell did Marina expect to get away with it? Did she think I would not have asked for a test to be done? I guess she thought she could bluff her way out it by trying to say the hospital had made a mistake.

"Who the hell was this baby's father? The son I had longed for and desperately wanted. Facing the fact he was no longer my mine. The inevitable question was, so whose son was he, damn it? Instead of my blood running through his veins, he had a faceless nameless person's blood in them. How can I bring a child up, to inherit such vast wealth when he does not have a drop of my families blood in his body?

"I had no one to talk to for advice, the great joy I should have felt had now turned to utter devastation. Why had I believed Marina, my own common sense should have forewarned me, now I was faced with bringing up a child, I had no input in creating. Now you know why the nursery basically become Johnathan's prison, as that is where he spent his first years.

"I saw as little of him as possible, it hurt terribly looking at his handsome little face, knowing he was not mine, as for Marina I did not give a damn after that where she went, or for how long. I knew having given up on one child, she would never give up her son, if she wished to continue being part of Johnathan's life, then she had to conform to being my wife; for the sake of outside appearances. I never went to her bed again, paying an honest whore was so much more preferred.

"In the meantime Leon I found out everything there was to know about you. You were a man I wanted to get to know a great deal better, I was delighted when you took the offer up of coming to work for me. Knowing all there was to know, having first done a great deal of research on you, I knew then I could trust you from day one and I am sure you would not have expected anything less of me."

"James that was precisely what I would have expected of you. You would not be one of the finest lawyers in the country, if you did not do your homework."

"Sometimes Leon on rare occasions, I wish I was not as good as I am. Sometimes things come to light, that you wish could stay in the dark places. The darkest place that can be found, where some secrets should always belong.

"I found I had choices to make Leon where you were concerned, a number of serious choices. I either let sleeping dogs lay, or do I stir up a hornets nest? I tried to make the correct decisions, those decisions were the hardest of my life. Not for my sake or yours but for Johnathan's. While he was growing up I knew he needed a father figure, nobody fitted the bill better than you, something I could never be to him.

"When doing my research on you, I found that your mother had never married your father."

"Yes James I do know that."

"Please let me finish Leon. You never knew who your father was did you?"

"No James my mother never told me, my mother did tell me she loved my father very dearly, but knew and accepted he would never leave his wife. He was apparently a very wealthy man, who did not believe in divorce, he also had a son that he loved, and who one day would inherit his business".

"He was a very generous man to my mother and I. What little time I did spend with him he treated me well, always being exceedingly pleasant and kind to me. I simply knew him as Uncle Robin. Sadly he died before I could finish law school, my mother could not afford to continue paying the fees, plus Beth had then come into my life at that time."

"Did you never want to know who your father was?"

"Yes James? Sometimes I would dearly have liked to have known who he was, unfortunately my mother had sworn she would never tell a soul. Not even me."

"Would you like me to tell you, Leon Who your father was?"

"James are you saying you found out and really know the truth?"

"Yes I do. Would you like me to tell you? Yes or No?"

"Yes James I would indeed like to know."

"Your real name is Leon Robin Stone. Your mother's surname name is Bates."

"Are you bullshitting me James?"

"No not at all, you are my half-brother.

"I am afraid I have further secrets to reveal to you, I had you watched as I said, I would have liked and yes wanted you to come earlier into my life. I knew you were hurting terribly at the loss of your wife and baby son, so I left you to grieve in peace. Once I felt you were ready to pick up the strings in trying to put your life back in order. It was then you were guided to join my home. You are in fact Leon not just my brother. You are my younger brother.

"Knowing these facts, I felt I needed to take care of you, I decided to give you a home and security without causing a scandal. Not once have I ever come to regret that you are part of my life. Now I have many more important secrets to divulge to you."

"How the hell can there be more James, it seems impossible."

"There are my dear Leon, quite a few more facts I must tell you."

"After many months watching how both Johnathan and yourself interacted with each other. It dawned on me how Johnathan was growing to look very much like both of us. Knowing he was not mine, yet Johnathan looked incredibly like me. I waited until one day you went downstairs. I got a sample of your hair, and a swab from your bathroom. The DNA proved that you were indeed Johnathan's father."

"What the bloody hell are you talking about James, are you telling me Johnathan is my son?"

"Yes Leon; Johnathan is indeed your son, making me his uncle."

"Why the fucking hell did you never tell me? I have always loved Johnathan, you know that."

"Simple Leon, Johnathan has an empire to run, had anyone found out that he was not my son shares would have crashed, the business would have lost millions, the fact Johnathan does have my blood in his veins through you, means he will inherit everything. Not telling you meant I was protecting Johnathan."

"Protecting him from what James?"

"Protecting him from that bastard who would love to destroy him; Marina continued her affair with Blain Cord, she had decided once Johnathan left to go to Harvard, that would be the right time to leave me, then ask for a divorce. Leon she would have been entitled, to untold millions. It would have affected the business; I could not allow that to happen. Johnathan must keep his empire, just as one day your grandson will inherit it.

"Sometimes in my line of work you come across certain people; people Leon, you would never wish to know. If you are as damn good lawyer as I am, on rare occasions you can call in favours, the kind of favours you never talk about, and the repayment can become very expensive. Johnathan is more than worth any price I had to pay, would you not agree?

"Johnathan is my world James. From the first day of meeting him, even not knowing he was my son, I have always loved him. James he is everything to me. But murder that is a whole new bloody ball game. "

"Leon you forget, the moment you had sex with my wife, you created Johnathan Robin Jefferson Stone. He is a Jefferson Stone, with Jefferson Stone blood running through his veins. I ensured he became the head of the Jefferson Stone multibillion dollar empire, built by generations of his family, your family as we both have the same father, and grandfather. That Leon is all that matters.

"Johnathan knows nothing of what I am telling you, ensure you behave like his father, protecting him at all cost as I have done by keeping my silence, and now yours. If you feel you are unable to do so, walk out of his life this instant, as that is the only choice you have. Now if you will allow me to continue without further interruption, I will tell you all you need to know."

"I suppose James I have no bloody choices as you said. Very well damn you, I will listen to the rest of what I must do, to protect my son."

"Good I will not elaborate on exact details Leon, unfortunately the first time an attempt was made on Marina's car. The wrong car was hit killing its passengers, the man unfortunately worked for Stones".

"Stop right there James, are telling me it was Lucinda's parent's car that they hit?"

"Yes Leon, sadly it was. Why do you think I have tried to protect her ever since."

"You fucking bastard James, you had two innocent decent people killed, for the sake of money."

"I have always regretted it was Lucinda's parents that were taken out by mistake, it was an unforeseeable tragic mistake, one that I could do nothing about. I liked Major Osborn he was a good man, but I was not going to let Marina destroy my son; your son.

"That is what would have happened. The vile bitch would have been entitled to half of my personal fortune, she would also have been given a massive pay out from the business. Worse than the money, she would have taken my son with her, I doubt Leon you would have seen Johnathan for a very long time. The amount of money she would have been awarded, would have run into untold millions, causing irreparable damage to the business.

"Johnathan would have been badly hurt, not that she gave a damn, all she wanted was to marry Blain Cord and play happy families. Never in a million years would I allow that to happen. The second attempt was successful as you know, I deeply appreciate Johnathan misses his mother, sadly he is far better off without the drunken bitch, eventually she could well have killed herself or someone else. Her drinking became so bad I did not want Johnathan; to see his mother drink herself to death. He would have hated to watch his mother degrade herself by becoming a disgusting drunk. It is much better for him to remember her the way he does. Now I need to tell you other things."

Chapter 13

"Leon, the necklace I brought back with me from San Francisco do you remember it?"

"Yes James I remember it perfectly well."

"That necklace Leon, helped to give me a perfect alibi? I am sure you knew I had purchased the earrings many months before buying the necklace, they were a perfect match making a wonderful set. I made sure it was purchased from one of the finest jewellers in San Francisco, knowing I would shortly be sending the damn thing back to them; let's face it no man spends a small fortune on a necklace, unless to the outside world he loves his wife.

"When we were first married I loved buying Marina jewellery. When she became pregnant with Johnathan I allowed her to buy what the hell she wanted. Back then the bitch cost me a small fortune. The fact was Marina was taken out with me still in the air, ready to present her with a seriously expensive present sitting in my briefcase once I returned home. It was so simple, so perfect, in fact far too easy. A good lawyer can indeed find an outlet to get away with murder.

"After the funeral the necklace was returned to the jewellers, it was something I never wanted Johnathan to set eyes on. I thought I had removed all sources of annoyance from Johnathan's life; I did not for one moment give any thought to Marina's daughter.

"On returning home after the many months I had been away, Marina's daughter Lucienne called me at the office. It was quite eerie to hear her voice on the phone, sounding so similar to that of her mother. Lucienne informed me that she had decided she should be entitled to all her mother's jewellery. Not just content to be given her mother's jewellery, she also wanted half of Marina's estate.

"Lucienne went on to demand an appointment enabling her to discuss all this, and more. Unfortunately for her, she made it abundantly clear that if I did not comply with her wishes, then she would resort to black-mail! Blackmail to me Leon, is the dirtiest business in the book, I regard it worse than murder. It becomes a living death for those who find themselves in that position.

"Can you imagine the untold amount of money she would eventually have bled out of me, had I been fool enough to capitulate in trying to buy her silence? Not just from me over a long period of years, but from Johnathan as well, he would have been crucified by her, probably for his entire life.

"You and I both know, Lucienne would never have been satisfied with a one off payment, no matter how generous it may have been. On top of having taken full possession of her mother's jewellery, which I had of course already given to Johnathan. The fact she was prepared to allow the world to know that she was not only my stepdaughter, which to me was sickening, having resented her existence from the day she was born. The fact that Johnathan would then have found out he had a half-sister, a half-sister he had no knowl-edge of in his entire life up until then. A sister who was nothing more than a nasty greedy grasping bitch like her mother, a bitch who was prepared to blackmail him, maybe even try to destroy him.

"Never would I allow that to happen, not under any circumstances no matter what it may cost, even my life this time if it had been necessary, So once again I had to place myself in a dangerous position! Of going to the people I had to play games with, yes they are the best, even though they made a terrible mistake over Lucinda's parent's car.

"You are no fool Leon. You can imagine the unprecedented scandal, which would have eventually broken. Not for me to face, but for Johnathan. It would have broken his heart, that his mother who he thought was so perfect had given birth to a child before he was born, then had deprived him of any knowledge about her. This half so called sister, who was now more than happy to bleed him dry for money; for the rest of his entire life

"Like mother like daughter, once again there was only one option left open to me, Lucienne had to be disposed of. Only this time completely, no body under any circumstances must be found, no connection with the firm that we had any dealings with her, no slip-ups of any sorts this time would be acceptable. The fee was high but the stakes higher; Johnathan's future.

"All arrangements were put in place that if Lucienne chose to come into town, she booked herself into a hotel of my choosing, as my guest of course, that hotel naturally belonging to, should we say the disposal firm. I asked her to phone a certain number when she felt she wished to meet me and I would arrange for a chauffeur driven car to pick her up, then bring her to my office. Lucienne was happy so far to go along with that offer, after all she was being given five star treatment.

"The driver who eventually picked her up, explained that instead of going directly to the office as it was such a lovely day I had arrange for her to come on board my yacht. Not owning a yacht of my own the disposal firm ensured one was made available. Lucienne was told it would enable us to talk in comparative privacy, without being disturbed.

"Once again the blackmailing witch went happily along with that plan also. What young girl would not enjoy being wined and dined in luxury? Taken out for a sail on board a beautiful private yacht, believing she would very shortly enjoy the benefits of receiving a vast sum of money, not just money, she would also be given a King's ransom in jewels.

"It must have all seemed perfectly natural to her as her own family were not without money, and I am sure had related how wealthy I was. Lucienne was obviously under the impression this was my normal lifestyle. Every courtesy was extended to her from the moment she stepped on board by a very handsome crew, how could a young woman say no to a handsome man? One of them directed her into the main cabin, where another asked if she would care for a drink, which she accepted. Then another handsome crewmember came into tell her, I would be with her directly, until then please feel free to make yourself comfortable.

"By this time the drink she had requested had been produced, which incidentally was poisoned! Lucienne died practically instantaneously. The crew set sail out onto the Pacific, where her body I believe made a delightful meal for the sharks... The crew first ensuring her throat was cut draw them in.

"I on the other hand, had of course called a full board meeting that day with all our top lawyers, which gave me a perfect alibi once again. Leon I am delighted to say no trace was ever found of the blackmailing bitch, the sharks and the firm this time did their job very well.

"Her trail went cold instantly from the moment she stepped out of the hotel into the chauffer driven limo. Unfortunately for Blain Cord, it seems she never told him or anyone where she was originally going. Apparently not telling her father, leaves me to believe maybe he did not condone blackmail. Strange really as he was happy to take what he could from me, through Marina".

"He had hoped for years to enhance his lifestyle, on top of giving him the ability to destroy me. Annoyingly he will never know what a very nasty greedy girl his daughter became. More importantly he will never know what a pleasure it is to me, in knowing that I have been instrumental in destroying his evil daughter who he loved, and who I have always hated. On top of knowing I had taken from him the woman he stole from me.

"Tell me something Leon, would you tell someone you had decided to blackmail them, when you knew they were a lawyer, not just any lawyer but one of our countries top lawyers? I would have thought that was a dangerous course of action, which of course proved to be the case as far as Miss Lucienne Cord was concerned.

"I have laid my life on the line for the son I have loved so dearly, regardless that Johnathan was never really mine. Transferring the business into Johnathan's name was vital, even though he was still so young and at Harvard. Had the authorities found out about Marina, or Lucinda's parents I would have been in no position to save the company for Johnathan, by gifting him the whole Empire as he calls it, I knew he was protected.

"I would never have stood trial you know that, with the business in Johnathan's name, that bastard Blane Cord could not get his hands on a single dollar. Though Johnathan was only eighteen he already had the makings of a young man who knew his own mind. With you to guide him I knew you would ensure he grew to be the man he is today. He has made a brilliant job of running the business, I have such pride in him, as I now know you have.

"Leon one of my biggest regrets is that I was unable to send you back to law school. I have few regrets in my life, but that Leon is sincerely one of them. I am deeply sorry as I am more than convinced you would have also made a brilliant lawyer, just as your son has.

"Now listen to me very carefully what I am about to tell you, as it is vital Leon. There is a dossier in my office, which I need you to retrieve before Johnathan finds it. It is nothing whatsoever to do with the disposal of Marina or her daughter. It is the full documentation of the DNA test, proving you are Johnathan's father".

"What is it you are asking of me, James? Are you saying you wish me to dispose of any evidence, that I am Johnathan's father? What if I do not want to, have I no rights to be able to tell him that he is my blood. What of my grandson, does he also have no rights to now know I am his real grandfather?"

"Do not be a bloody fool Leon, I have already told you if any scandal gets out, it will cost Johnathan dearly. You must allow in this instant, sleeping dogs to lie".

"Damn you James, damn you to hell! I hate to admit it, but as always you are of course right".

"Thank you Leon for that, at least I can die knowing you will do the right thing by a boy we both love so dearly. You will find the dossier in the bottom drawer of my desk. There is a catch behind the middle drawer, which will release that particular section. Johnathan will go through everything, you know full well he is like me in that respect, he will not leave anything without first investigating, certainly not my personal desk.

"It is imperative Leon, the second you leave here you go directly to the office. Promise me Leon you will do this, Johnathan's life and happiness is at stake. Both must be fulfilled the way they should without scandal, that allies also to his inheritance."

"James of course I promise you, I have already said I would. James I will do everything in my power that I can to protect my son, our son, you know that."

"Thank you for that Leon."

"Now please James, will you allow me to call the doctor?"

"No Leon I rather you just sat here for a moment of two with me. Having my brother with me at the end, leaves me with a good feeling"

"James please try and get some sleep, we can talk again tomorrow."

"Please Leon, I am begging of you to go to the office first thing in the morning, and destroy that damn dossier."

"I promise I will James, now do try to get some sleep."

Those were my last words to my brother, James Stone passed away peacefully in his sleep just a few minutes later.

"Johnathan, it is Bates. I am deeply sorry to be the one to phone you with such sad news."

I could barely relate to him that the father he had always known had passed away.

"Johnathan is there anything you would like me to do before I come home?"

"No Bates I will come to the hospital immediately."

"Very well I will see you there shortly."

So many thoughts now crossed my mind to protect my son. James was of course right; the anger I felt towards him would very soon diminish. Damn you James, how the hell am I going to get into your office? Why did you keep the damned dossier in the first place? It is a good job Johnathan always keeps the doors open. How the hell am I now going to get there in time, it will be difficult getting away from him under the circumstances?

How I wish I had known all those years ago, Johnathan should have known the truth, I should have known the truth. Now Johnathan, Robin and I, will have to live with nothing more than a miserable pack of lies. Blast you James, you made a bad call. A stupid lousy bad decision, probably for the first time in your life, now I have to clean up your bloody mess.

* * *

The following morning I decided to try and make my way to the office very early.

"Good morning Bates," Lucinda greeted me, she was up and dressed unusually early.

"Good morning Lucinda, do you know where Johnathan is?"

"As far as I know Bates he has gone to see the funeral director." Lucinda answered then ventured to comment.

"I suspect my father in laws funeral will be a rather large affair".

"I am sure you are quite right my dear," I agreed".

"Lucinda, please forgive me but I have to go into town for a few messages, I am not sure just how long I will be. Please will you excuse me for at least a couple of hours or so?"

"Of course, Bates, you must do whatever you feel is necessary," Lucinda kindly replied.

I went on to ask her: "Are there any errands I can accomplish for you while I am out?"

"No thank you," Lucinda politely replied her manners charming as always

"Very well my dear I will see you all later."

I drove to the Jefferson Stone Head Office, fearful in case I would not be able to keep my promise to my brother. Stepping out of the lift to be greeted my Mrs Atkins as I entered the hallway.

"Good morning Bates how are you?" She inquired. Mrs Atkins continued to say: "Sadly not a good morning really is it".

"No Mrs Atkins it most certainly is not a good morning," I replied, then went on to say. "Mrs Atkins I have come on behalf of Mr Stone. Mr Stone sadly gave me instructions last night just before he passed away. He wished me to find some personal papers, which he felt, I should take a look at. I rather wish my dear he had given them to me while he was still alive. Annoyingly you know what Mr Stone was like occasionally".

"I do understand Bates exactly what it is you are saying, Mrs Atkins stated. My boss was a law unto himself. I must be honest though not everyone would agree with me, to me he was a brilliant boss".

I looked at Mrs Atkins for a few moments then replied: "You have never said a truer word my dear, Mr Stone was indeed a law unto himself. More than you may ever realise".

"At least now the company has a wonderful new boss, though Johnathan has been my boss, since he was a little boy".

This statement brought a smile to Mrs Atkins face.

"If you will excuse me for a few minutes Mrs Atkins. I will go and see if I can find the papers Mr Stone asked me to look over. I will speak to you shortly: I told her as I left the hallway.

Going over to James desk, then following his instructions. I found the catch within the middle drawer, which in turn did indeed release the bottom drawer. The damn dossier that was supposed to have been enclosed in it was no longer there. I felt sick, maybe I had misheard or misunderstood James instructions. Then I heard Johnathan's voice as he stepped into the room from his bedroom.

"Is this what you are looking for?" he asked, in the ice-cold voice normally used by his father?

Looking at me with the same ice-cold stare the way James would look when questioning one of his victims.

"How long have you known?" Johnathan asked.

"I only found out just before your father died? I answered looking directly back at him.

"How long have you known Johnathan?"

"Last night after I left the hospital I came here," Johnathan replied. Changing his tone of voice completely, he went on to say. "I loved Uncle James, but I love my real father so much more".

Lightning Source UK Ltd.
Milton Keynes UK
UKOW01f2037050318
318927UK00001B/8/P